TO WIN HER HAND
REGENCY OUTSIDERS

MELISSA ADDEY

To Win Her Hand

Copyright © 2025 by Melissa Addey. All rights reserved.

First Paperback Print Edition: 2025 in the United Kingdom

Published by Letterpress Publishing

The moral right of the author has been asserted.

Cover photograph by Servian Stock Images

Cover design by 100Covers

House illustration iStock from a vintage engraving

eBook: 978-1-910940-49-5

Paperback: 978-1-910940-43-3

No part of this book may be reproduced, scanned, or distributed in any printed or electronic form without permission. Please do not participate in or encourage piracy of copyrighted materials in violation of the author's rights. Thank you for respecting the hard work of this author.

DEDICATION

For Christina,
Celebrating almost forty years of books and bonnets together!

VISIT MY WEBSITE

Pick up a free novella from my website www.MelissaAddey.com and join my Readers' Club to be notified about new releases.

COMERFORD HOUSE, LONDON

England, November 1813

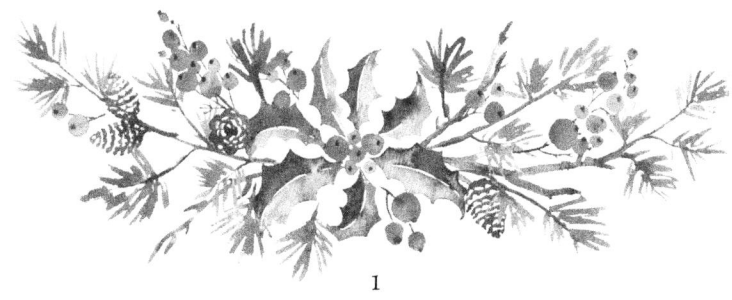

1
AN ENGAGEMENT OF A PECULIAR KIND

Alexander walked across the vast ballroom and heard his footsteps echo. The last time he had been here the building works were still in progress and his older brother, the Earl of Comerford, had shown him through the rooms, heedless of the dust and noise around them.

"It will be magnificent," he had half-shouted above the scraping and hammering, beaming with pride. "The columns in this room are to be decorated in green and gold at the tops, as though they were palm trees. Through there, in the centre, will be the great room, or ballroom, for dancing. The dining room is on the other side. It can seat fifty at a pinch, twenty-four in the usual way of things."

"You intend to hold a great many parties, by the looks of it," Alexander had commented when they had reached a quieter room overlooking Green Park. "The great room is larger than some assembly rooms."

"We do," agreed his brother, well pleased with the comparison. "For Charlotte loves to dance and I intend to educate myself on many matters of interest – politics and social economy, scientific discovery and suchlike, there are so many interesting men in London with whom one may converse these days. We intend to give very many dinners and balls."

Alexander had listened to all his brother's plans with interest, bowed goodbye to his new sister-in-law and returned to his ship, the *Vela*, of which he was now captain. As the younger son, he had been given his choice of going into the church or the navy as many young men of good families did, for if one were not the heir, then one must find one's way in the world. Being an active boy, not much given to studying, he had chosen the navy, which had seemed to him to be full of the possibility of adventure. He had gone aboard his first posting when he was but fifteen. The life there suited him and although he admired both the palatial plans for Comerford House and the pretty new wife his brother had married, he had been happy enough in his chosen career and had not felt envy for his brother, rather a kind of relieved gratitude that the title and its burdens had fallen to another, even if the title also came with many privileges and much wealth. He was on good terms with his brother and was well enough provided for. He also knew that within a year or two his bride-to-be, Lady Celia Follett, would add to his wealth and – he hoped – happiness. He had never been one for balls and dinner parties, for entertaining important men of the day or fussing over his jackets and cravats. Through his brother he would still enjoy visits to Comerford Castle, the family's estate and his childhood home, and that was good enough for him.

The letter which had reached him one year later had been bordered in black and its sombre aspect had already forewarned him that there had been a death in the family, but when he opened it, his whole world changed line by line as he read its contents. His brother John had been caught up in an outbreak of cholera in London and while his wife Charlotte had escaped the illness, having been in Comerford Castle at the time, John had succumbed and Alexander suddenly found himself no longer Captain Comerford but Lord Comerford, the title of earl descending on him since Charlotte had not fallen with child in her brief marriage.

Leaving his ship had been a strange moment. His men were sorry to see him go, for he had been a fair captain and a good man to serve. He had been part of the navy for fourteen years and expected to spend most of his life at sea, but now he would never set sail again as captain, only, perhaps as a passenger one day, should he wish to travel. It took several weeks before his legs lost the rise and fall of the sea and still his eyes sought the far horizons for the endless blue he had been accustomed to, but now they met only the green rolling fields of Castle Comerford's large estate or the uninterrupted buildings of London.

HE SPENT HIS FIRST FEW MONTHS ON LAND AT CASTLE Comerford, which had the advantage of being familiar to him from his childhood. The rooms, the servants, the grounds, all were known to him. He had disbursed all matters relating to his brother's will, including caring for Charlotte.

"I am always at your service," he had assured her, before she drove away in weeping black, back to her family's home. She had been well provided for by John's will and Alexander honoured all his brother's wishes with a generous hand, but finally the time had come when everything seemed in good order and his steward had hinted that it was time for him to visit London and take ownership of Comerford House.

"Your lordship will wish to visit your tailor while you are there, since you have been accustomed to wearing uniform. You will be much in society," he had delicately suggested, hinting that Alexander's habit thus far of wearing his father's cast-offs, both worn and sadly out of fashion, would no longer do.

Dutifully, he had visited his brother's tailor to order an entirely new wardrobe just to be certain of being adequately turned out, noting as he did so the change in the level of obsequious attention bestowed on him now that he bore the title of earl rather than being the second son of one. Boxes containing coats, jackets and breeches, along with others from cobblers, hatters and more, containing everything from boots and shoes to hats, cravats and stockings, had been delivered in absurd quantities and his newly appointed valet had been helpful in ensuring he looked his best, though Alexander was still distinctly uncomfortable in his stiffly new clothes and boots, none of them worn in to sit comfortably on his body and feet, so that he felt always aware of them and how different he looked as the Earl instead of the captain he had used to be. As a navy man he had relished the change from the stifling manners of his youth, but now he was brought back to a world of fine manners and dainty dancing steps, to a world where how one tied one's cravat seemed to matter more than whether you were a man of your word. It was a world he had thought to have left behind and to be forced back to it was proving neither easy nor pleasurable.

He had sent word ahead before arriving that any personal items belonging to Charlotte should be packed up and sent to her, that his brother's personal effects should be put away or repurposed. The result was that when he arrived at the house the rooms seemed empty. Each one was beautifully finished, in jewel tones of reds and blues, greens and pinks, with everywhere a lavishness of gold finishes and fine furniture. The servants, forewarned of his coming, had ensured that all was spotless and ready for use, there were warm fires and fresh flowers everywhere, but every room seemed desolate, full of reminders of the lives that ought to have been lived here – the portraits of John and Charlotte in the library, the beautifully appointed suite of rooms for each of them, now stripped of the personal belongings that would have made them feel homely.

For the first few weeks he had put off seeing anyone excepting his man of business and the house staff, but now he was faced with his obligations and all too aware that there was no way out of them. He was the Earl of Comerford now, dressed as befitted such a position and with both Comerford Castle and Comerford House under his command. Before him lay only one more action which he must shortly take.

A clockface in the library reminded him of his current plan and he retraced his steps, returning to the front door of the house. A bitter November wind blew through London, but he did not shiver or look about him, only kept his eyes fixed on the approaching groom and steed, giving a brusque nod when they reached him.

"Sorry to have kept you waiting, Sir."

"You didn't. I was early."

He swung into the saddle with ease and nodded to the groom, then set off at a smart trot through Green Park, which bordered the garden of Comerford House. Hyde Park was the more elegant place to see and be seen at this time of day, but that was precisely why he was avoiding it. It would be no respite at all to have to raise one's hat every thirty paces or find oneself obliged to ride alongside an acquaintance when one desired to be alone.

He chastised himself. He was ungrateful. Fate had unexpectedly bestowed on him a far more elevated life than he could ever have expected. It was his duty now to do his best in his new position, to care for the estates and houses of which he was now master. And above all, given the fate that had befallen his unfortunate brother and sister-in-law, to marry and sire an heir. Failure to do so would leave the title and estate at risk of being passed to a distant cousin, should he himself die.

He urged the horse to a gallop, keen for release from the constant feeling of being cooped up inside the echoing rooms of Comerford House. It did not feel like a home to him, he would have preferred to have been at Comerford Castle where he had grown up, and where at least there were great open spaces to ride or walk, fresh air and above all things to do, an estate to manage and farms to be supervised. He was fond of the people on the estate, from his steward with whom he could have meaningful conversations, to the gardeners, farmers, even those women and children to whom he could wish a good day.

But London. London was nothing but clothes and gossip, as far as he could make out. The heaped cards on a silver tray from people calling weighed heavily on his mind, for all of them would have to be called upon in return if he was not to be considered rude. And he could not ignore all such nonsense and close up Comerford House, he must perforce stay here for some months and attend balls and other parties, for he was engaged to be married, and must shortly meet his wife.

of the grooms, the family motto, *Strength Through Love*, emblazoned on their coat of arms – black with a golden spring of mistletoe, the whole emblem making him think of some lovelorn medieval knight far back in his ancestry who must have chosen the symbols and words by which his family would be thereafter known. An overly romantic choice, in his opinion, but no doubt well-meaning. A motto and emblem which his brother had taken to heart when designing his future home. Comerford House was full of references to love and the joys of marriage, from the paintings to the colours and symbols chosen throughout. But the happy marriage which had prompted such devotion was now broken, his brother harshly taken after less than two years of wedded bliss.

He swung out of the saddle and down to the ground, patted the horse's neck and nodded to the grooms, his heart still heavy. The ride had done nothing to lift his spirits after all, had only reminded him once more, as though it were needed, of the weight of duty now bearing down on him from all sides and the challenge still lying ahead of him: to make what he could of what amounted to an arranged marriage, one in which he had had no say in arranging.

He handed the reins of the horse to the waiting groom and walked through the door being held open by a footman. A second footman took his coat and hat, a third opened the door into the drawing room. He hesitated, for he had intended to go upstairs, but he walked through the open door, to find a welcome fire with hot coffee and freshly baked cake on the table waiting for him. Sometimes it seemed easier to do whatever the servants thought he was about to do. A vast house and huge staff, with only one man – himself – to look after. It made everything feel overly fussy and lonely, the huge rooms echoing about him every time he walked from room to room. He had been away from 'civilisation' as his mother liked to call it, for too long. As captain, naturally there had been servants and deference shown to him. But not on this scale. There had been the need to muck in with his men at times, to accept rough lodgings and food, to roll up his shirtsleeves and join the men during tempests or war with no expectation of being treated like a china doll. He supposed he would have to get used to all this endless fussing as well as the balls and polite dinners to which he would now continually be invited.

His thoughts wandered again. His deceased brother and the wife he had so loved. Perhaps the two of them had been able to fill this house, for by all accounts they had held constant parties, dinners, balls and receptions of one kind and another, just as they had planned. John had been interested in politics; Charlotte had soon built a reputation as one of the *ton*'s best young hostesses. The empty ballroom, dining room and the size of her private parlour for smaller gatherings of her female friends spoke to how popular they had been, how socially minded. Whereas he... Alexander was not a recluse by any means, but his company had been his men for the past five years and the years before that had been those of whichever ship he had been posted to. There had been infrequent visits home, and although his mentor Captain Rose had always reminded him that a navy man of any ambition must also be able to dance and hold polite conversation in society, there had been few opportunities to display such social niceties. Now that he was surrounded by those who demanded them he was finding such society both overly fussy and sometimes downright tedious. His idea of society was to be surrounded by friends and family, where good manners did not get in the way of merriment and good cheer. He recollected with fondness occasions such as

Christmas or Twelfth Night as a little boy, when neighbours and family would fill the house for jolly games and good food. Now, returned as a man, it seemed society was full of nothing but rigid adherence to excessively particular standards of behaviour, most of it gone well beyond good manners and common sense. It was wearying. Still, there was nothing for it. In one week, he would meet his bride at a ball and from then on, he would be obliged to attend a great many balls and parties as he escorted her through her season.

Lady Celia Follett. Daughter of the Duke and Duchess of Winchester.

He tried to recall her face, her figure – not that there would have been much of a figure, for she had been only twelve when last he had seen her. He had a dim recollection of a noisy girl, with bouncing black curls and rumpled skirts. He had ignored her for the most part, despite the adults making little jests and giving knowing looks towards the two of them. He had been twenty and certain that he was a grown man, while she had obviously been nothing but a child, and he had found it laughable that he was betrothed to her. Surely it would never really happen... but here they were, and it was all in place. He was to marry a woman he was barely acquainted with in just a few months' time. It had been decided long ago, and no-one had ever really questioned it. He could not consider himself an honourable man if he withdrew now and therefore it was his duty to go through with it.

IN THE PREMISES OF MRS GILL, ONE OF LONDON'S BEST modistes, surrounded by bolts of fine silks and muslins, soft wools and every possible kind of trimming, the Duchess of Winchester made a face at her daughter's fourth choice of gown for the coming season.

"They can't *all* be red, Celia dearest."

"Why ever not? It is a jolly colour."

"It is..." the Duchess hesitated. She wanted to say that it made her daughter look too bold, too much a woman of the world, or indeed worse than that, a woman of... of... well, anyway, not a debutante about to have her first season. With her black curls, merry smile and too many opinions, Lady Celia Follett was already forward enough, in her mother's opinion. "Perhaps the pink?" she suggested, hopefully. "Or the yellow?"

But Lady Celia shook her head. "No. I don't care for any of those pale colours, they are all far too insipid. If it's to be my only season, then I want to be *seen*."

The Duchess sighed. Once again, she doubted the wisdom of only having given her daughter a proper London season now, with her wedding planned for June. She was not strictly a debutante, she had been allowed to attend local balls and parties for over two years, but as she had not yet been granted a real season in London, she had been promised she might have one before she married. Since the engagement had been in place so long, there had not seemed much need to enter the marriage mart, but perhaps, the Duchess now reflected, it had made Celia focus too much on this season, a desire to see and be seen before marriage which most young ladies, however charming, might well enjoy over a couple of seasons before they were wed.

The modiste was not helping. Usually obedient to the Duchess' desires, she would know all too well that Lady Celia would soon be a very wealthy married woman and free to choose her own modiste. She would remember whether Mrs Gill had allowed her free rein or had made her comply with her mother's demands. It was an important opportunity to secure the future Countess of Comerford as a new client, and Mrs Gill seized it with both hands.

"You need not trouble yourself, Your Grace. Please, take a seat and my girl will bring you some refreshments. I shall take care of everything for Lady Celia. We have a wide range of colours which may suit. Ruby, Ponceau, Morone, Puce, Claret, Amaranthine, Coquelicot…"

The Duchess allowed herself to be gently steered some yards away to an armchair which was twisted at an angle that made viewing her daughter difficult, while a maid brought tea and biscuits. She tried to make herself comfortable, while struggling to put aside the worrying feeling that every colour Mrs Gill had just listed was, in fact, red.

Now set free, Celia ordered a wardrobe which made full use of all the colours Mrs Gill had enumerated, adding Pomegranate and Crimson to the list as well. In the next hour she bespoke a magnificent crimson opera cloak as well as three pelisses in shades of red, one embroidered with roses, one trimmed with white swansdown and the third embellished with glittering beading. Her dresses for the coming season now ranged from a shining red silk to a white dress overlaid with a scarlet gauze, a warm cherry red wool to a deep ruby rose and everything in-between.

"Do you have everything you need, Your Grace?" enquired Mrs Gill in passing.

"Yes," fretted the Duchess. "Only I do not want dear Celia to appear too… forward. She will be meeting Lord Comerford at a ball next week and I would like him to be… pleased with her. He has not seen her for so long."

"How long have they been apart?"

"Oh, since she was twelve, I think."

Mrs Gill's eyebrows went up. She was accustomed to the odd ways of the *ton*, but this did sound more unusual than most.

"The engagement is of a peculiar kind," explained the Duchess, noticing the eyebrows. "It was planned while they were both in their infancy. And all parties have continued to respect the plans. When Lord Comerford recently and unexpectedly acceded to the title, His Grace my husband saw fit to enquire of him whether he still wished to proceed with the marriage, and he, citing loyalty and duty, agreed that it should go ahead. So all is well, but he has not seen her since she was a child, so I would like him to be favourably impressed on seeing her again."

Mrs Gill nodded. "Your Grace need not worry. When Lady Celia's wardrobe arrives, I promise you will be delighted with how she appears."

The Duchess nodded, reassured, and sipped more tea while her daughter continued to claim Mrs Gill's attentions. Having left the modiste's and spent a further happy hour in a milliner's establishment, Celia was able to assure her mother that she had ordered bonnets of every imaginable colour, including blue, green and even white. The Duchess was relieved, but changed her mind when she saw the final items arrive at Follett House.

"You can hardly call it a *blue* bonnet," she remonstrated weakly. "It is lined in red silk and covered in red berries, red roses and red silk ribbons!"

Celia could not help giggling. "But the bonnet *itself* is blue wool," she said, embracing the Duchess. "Do not fret Mama, you need hardly worry about whether or not the young men of the *ton* will find me attractive, when I am already engaged."

The Duchess allowed her shoulders to drop. It was true. The engagement had been in place these last twenty years and the Earl was due to meet them at the Berrington ball next week. This was a comfort. But one thought still weighed on her mind. "I have ordered you a dozen new pairs of gloves," she said. "I hope they will all arrive by the end of the week."

Celia's shoulders drooped at the reminder. "Yes, Mama," she said quietly, and turned back to the novel she was reading. All her life she had been indulged in the matter of clothes, for the Duchess was fond of fashionable choices and the Duke her father was an amiable sort of man who was generous in his clothing allowance for both women. And so Celia had been able to order all sorts of gowns and cloaks, every kind of pelisse and spencer, bonnets and dancing slippers – but there had never been any choice regarding her gloves. These were always mandatory, both in and out of the house, and their choice rested solely with the Duchess.

Celia flexed her right hand inside its glove and looked down at her hand as the little finger and thumb moved accordingly, while her three middle fingers made an odd movement, a sort of waggling without any grace or fluidity. Inside the glove, hidden from view, the three central fingers were padded with wool and sewn shut, for there were no fingers to occupy the space. She had been born with an oddly deformed right hand, with a fully formed thumb and little finger and between those two digits, three small stubs, half the height of a knuckle. They were made of flesh, but contained no bone within, more like three tiny earlobes than anything else, incapable of movement by themselves. The hand had come as something of a shock to the family, who had never seen such a thing in their circle before, and from the day of her birth onwards, Celia had worn gloves on both hands, the first pair of mittens hastily knitted by a startled aunt. Later an accomplished glove-maker had been taken into the family's confidence and had supplied the altered stuffed gloves ever since, in every fabric from lace to wool and leather. Few people had in fact seen Celia's right hand, only her family members, her lady's maid Aveline and a few other servants about the house. Celia herself did not mind her odd hand, she was grateful to be able to make a pincer-like grip using her thumb and little finger, and had grown dextrous with them, so that skills such as painting, embroidery and knitting were all well within her abilities. She disliked, however, the way the stuffed fingers moved, for it made it all too clear to any observer that there was something different about her hand and for herself, she would have preferred to have been open about her hand and worn gloves only for warmth or fashion, not to hide what lay beneath. But the Duchess was adamant, and Celia had given in long ago. She wondered what her betrothed, the Earl, would make of her hand, especially since he had never seen it. He would have to see it one day, perhaps on their wedding night? The idea seemed uncomfortable to her – that at an already awkward moment he might be distracted by her hand, or even repulsed by it? And then it would be too late, for the marriage would have been celebrated. A small part of her which she tried to keep locked away hoped that she would not have to suffer a look of disgust followed by a lifetime of continuing to hide her hand from her husband. She tried not to think about that moment, but it was there, lurking in the back of her mind. Perhaps she should show it to him as soon as possible, so that she might judge his reaction there and then and know the worst at once. It might even give her what she hoped for – a way out of the marriage.

For she did not want to marry him. That was the truth of it. It was absurd to have been betrothed without her consent to a boy eight years older than her when she was but a baby. Two friendly families joined together: a happy thing, to their minds.

Not to Celia's.

No.

She had determined that she would give the Earl a fair chance to impress her as a suitable husband, and by that she meant a husband whom she herself would have chosen. And if he did not impress her – if he was a clumsy oaf, a man without a romantic bone in his body, who could not dance or hold an intelligent conversation, if in short she did not feel any romantic feelings towards him – why, then, she would find another suitor. She would find a man who met her requirements, and she would break off the engagement to the Earl and marry the other man instead. It could not be so hard. She was the daughter of a duke, with a generous marriage portion. She was a pretty girl (she did not claim great beauty, but she did believe she was possessed of a pretty enough face to hold her own amongst the young women and girls of her acquaintance), she could do all that was expected of her in the way of riding, sewing, drawing, dancing and so on. She was modishly dressed.

There was her hand of course. That would put some men off, there was no denying it. But that was all to the good. If it frightened off a man, then he was not worth having. Her chin lifted. Yes. The Earl would be given a fair chance, since she could barely remember him. But if he failed to match her expectations, she would not hesitate to find a better husband and find him fast. There was one singular disadvantage to her plan – all the *ton* knew that she was already betrothed – but that could be overcome. Should she find a man who pleased her, she would give him to understand that the betrothal was not, after all, as binding as it seemed, and should a better offer be made, it would be met with a willing ear. It was November, she had until May if the wedding was to be in June. Enough time, surely, there were marriages made at greater speed every year. She need only assess the Earl first, then proceed with her plan.

THE BERRINGTON BALL WAS WELL UNDERWAY. THE room dazzled with hundreds of candles reflected in the glittering chandeliers, the floral arrangements of red camellias set against dark laurel leaves had been deemed beautifully dramatic and the *ton* was well represented, with a few dozen debutantes eager to start their season early by partaking in the little season before Christmas, all of them showing off the very latest fashions and hoping in their little hearts that they might secure a husband at once, so that they might spend the rest of the year in the glorious position of being much desired but also fully spoken for, with no risk whatsoever of ending up unclaimed by the summer. The musicians were preparing to play the third dance of the evening and Celia was looking about her, nerves rising. At any moment her husband-to-be would enter the room, but so far, she had not spotted him and therefore her dancing, usually graceful, had been stiff, head constantly turning to make sure she did not miss Lord Comerford's entrance.

"Lady Celia." A tall man with fair hair and an open, easy smile was standing by her side.

She dropped a curtsey. "Lord Hyatt." Robert

Worthington, the Earl of Hyatt, was a familiar and friendly face. A pleasant dancing partner with a charming manner to all, he was reckoned quite the catch by those mamas who had daughters to marry off. His estate was not only pretty – with a charming folly of a tower in the grounds from which one could view half the county, most of which belonged to him – but also well maintained, giving him an ample income. He had come into his title four years back and his mother had then remarried two years later, which meant his future wife would not find herself living with a meddling mother-in-law, always a fine thing for a new bride. He had siblings, but they were all married off or about to be so. All in all, he would make an excellent alternative suitor, and he was already high on Celia's list of possible future husbands. "I am glad to see you here already; not all of the *ton* has yet arrived in London."

He looked at her dance card and added his name to it. "I had business to attend to and besides, it is always a pleasure to see one's acquaintances after a summer away. This is your first proper season, is it not?"

"It is," she smiled.

"Then I hope it will be an enjoyable one and that I shall have the pleasure of seeing you at several events."

She broadened her smile. This was already going well. "That would be delightful."

He tilted his head. "I believe you will be escorted by the Earl of Comerford tonight?"

"He will be attending, though he does not seem to have arrived yet. And as you also no doubt know, we have not seen one another for many years now, he has been in the navy. We are all but strangers."

He gave a small smile. "Of course. An unknown bridegroom then, that sounds as though you will have an interesting evening."

"I hope so," she said.

He nodded, as though to indicate that he had caught her tone and inference and understood her position. "The dance is about to begin. May I accompany you to the floor?"

She nodded and followed him. It was going well. She could not make it much plainer than she had. She need only find a few such men to ensure that she had a plan to save herself from the Comerford marriage, should she decide to break off the engagement. It was not an impossible task for a girl with any common sense. She could only hope that the Earl of Comerford would be dashing and handsome and none of her plans would be required. Although he had been in the navy for many years amongst rough sailors and the like, so she hoped his manners had not grown accordingly coarse. Her father regularly pontificated about men coming to too great a fortune or status from their time in the navy when they were not even well born. Although to be fair such an accusation could hardly be levelled at Lord Comerford, who had fought at Trafalgar and commanded his own ship but was also from a titled family.

ALEXANDER STOOD AT THE EDGE OF THE BALLROOM, bracing himself for the meeting to come. He had been announced by the footman and had bowed over his hostess' hand; it could only be a moment or two till his future mother-in-law spotted him.

"Ah, Alexander, it is so good to see you after all this time." The Duchess of Winchester, in rustling deep green silk and a diamond tiara, was closing in on him. "You do not mind if I call you Alexander? You are very nearly family already, I have always thought of you so, your dear mama and I being such close friends."

He bowed. "Duchess."

"Have you just now arrived?"

"Yes."

She nodded to a watchful footman who hastened to her side. "Champagne for Lord Comerford."

"Yes, Your Grace."

"There is no need –" began Alexander, but she ignored him.

"We were so sorry about John, God rest his soul. He was a delicate boy; your dear mother always worried about him." She drew breath. "But you are hale and hearty, and we will be your family now." She gave his arm a comforting squeeze and then grew brisk. "You will want to see Celia, of course, she was dancing with the Earl of Hyatt a moment ago. I shall find her at once."

He would have stopped her, but it had to be done, there was little point putting off the inevitable. He took a quick gulp of the champagne to settle the lurch in his stomach. He hoped she was pleasant to look at, at least.

He was suddenly bumped into from behind, forcing him to take a couple of steps to keep his balance.

"I do beg your pardon!"

He turned to find himself face to face with a young woman with pink cheeks, a merry smile and dark hair. She wore a scarlet dress with glittering beading across the bosom and hem, a bold choice in a room full of young women in whites and pastels. The only part of her clothing that was pale were her long white gloves. "Not at all," he responded.

"My shoe ribbon came untied and I tripped on it," she explained, still smiling. "You will forgive me if I re-tie it here rather than making my way to the cloakroom, I would be afraid of falling over it again." She sat down on a small gilt chair at his side and bent over to tie the red ribbons of her little red kid dancing slippers. He watched her do so, musing over whether, if Lady Celia was truly an unbearable wife, perhaps it would be wise to agree on where they should both live and when? He would prefer to mostly reside at Castle Comerford, perhaps she would prefer a town life at Comerford House in London? Slowly, he become aware that the young woman in the red dress was tying her ribbons in a strange way: her left hand moved as usual, but she seemed to only use her little finger and thumb on her right hand in an odd pincer like movement, her three remaining fingers, clad in the white gloves, seemed not to move at all, sticking out stiffly, contributing nothing to the task she was undertaking. As she finished, smoothing her skirt back down, a cold certainty came over him.

He bowed as she rose. "Lady Celia Follett." It was not a question.

She looked up at him, startled, then her eyes grew wide. "Lord Comerford!" She swallowed, evidently flustered, then rallied, putting both hands behind her back and offering a neat curtsey with a brave smile. "I beg your pardon for not recognising you at once, it has been so long since we were in each other's company."

"Indeed."

Her smile faltered when he said nothing more, before she tried again. "My dance card is full for the next three dances, but if you wish, I have the quadrille free after that."

"Certainly." He did not want to dance, would have preferred to go to a quieter part of the room and talk, but clearly there was no choice in the matter, this being a ball.

She looked over her shoulder at a young man hovering

nearby. "I – I must join the next dance, I had promised it to Mr Selsbury."

"Of course. Do not allow me to detain you."

She backed away from him, then turned and hurried to join her partner and the already-forming line of other dancers as the music struck up.

Alexander drained his glass. Of all the ways to meet again. Awkward, clumsy, flustered consternation on both sides. She was good looking, indeed her pretty smile before she had known who he was had been charming, but that smile had faded once she had realised who he was. He watched her dance. It was easy to follow her progress since she stood out in her scarlet dress. What did she mean by wearing such a bold colour? Did she think herself already married, and therefore at liberty to eschew the pale delicacy of the debutantes surrounding her? Was she someone who liked to draw attention, to flirt, even? He observed that she smiled a great deal, that her cheeks were flushed pink, her chin kept very high. She thought well of herself then, he supposed, liked to be seen and admired, to have men notice her. Were these good qualities in a woman soon to be his wife? He was unsure.

CELIA KEPT HER CHIN HIGH, EYES UPLIFTED SO THAT she might not cry. What an ignominious first meeting, indeed it was so bad as to make one think it was an omen of a poor marriage to come. She had told her mother to fetch her as soon as Lord Comerford should make an appearance. She had done this so that she might have her mother at her side when they were first introduced, to smooth over any little awkwardness and natural nervousness which might arise. And also so that she herself would be prepared, at her best, not taken suddenly by surprise. She had hoped for a pleasant first meeting, both doing their best, beginning with a dance to ease the inevitable tension. Perhaps, she had mused, they would dance so well and naturally together that it would feel as though they truly had been meant for one another, both soon at their ease, ready to begin a brief but important period of courtship, to sow those seeds which might later bring love. And what had happened instead? Oh, she had all but tumbled over him, then had to apologise. She had recognised him at once, partly from her memory but also from the portrait her mother had taken pains to show her. He was a good-looking man – tall, with dark hair and eyes, a firm jaw and well-formed nose. But he – he had stared at her as though he had no idea of who she was. He had watched her as she tied her shoe ribbons and her usually swift fingers had turned clumsy, the stupid stuffed fingers of her glove had gotten in the way and when she had finally arisen, feeling like a fool, he had said her name with a certainty which could only have come from observing her hand and had spoken as though he was appalled at having anything to do with her, had looked her up and down with disdain. She had pretended not to have known him until that moment, had gone through an absurd pantomime of startled recognition, all the while feeling like a fool caught out in a lie. Her cheeks were still hot from the discomfort of the meeting, tears threatened to overbrim her eyes. Her teeth remained clenched in an overly fixed smile to hide her embarrassment and to show the whole room – but especially the Earl who was no doubt watching her – that she was utterly unaffected by this poor start and entirely happy with her current dance partner. Mr Selsbury had uttered various pleasantries which she had struggled to answer, so wrapped up was she in what had just occurred. Shortly she must go and dance with Lord Comerford – in a quadrille of all things, where another three couples would be watching them closely, might remark on how they had behaved towards one another, whether their dancing seemed to suit each other. Oh, it was not to be borne. She wondered whether she should feign a headache or turned ankle, anything to be taken home, but that might be talked of even more, for all the *ton* would already know that this evening was to be their first evening together, if she were to suddenly go home gossip would spread. No, there was nothing to be done but to go through with it. She tried to pay more attention to Mr Selsbury, but it was hard to think of anything other than Lord Comerford. She tried to catch little glimpses of him without being caught looking. He was tall, with an aquiline nose and dark eyes and hair, she would have said he was handsome had he looked less contemptuous, his severe expression unbending even when various people spoke to him in passing. Was he that displeased with the sight of her? Was he a man who loathed parties and other gatherings? He looked as though he wished to be anywhere but here, and she dreaded their first dance together.

ALEXANDER PRESENTED HIMSELF AS THE QUADRILLE'S dancers took up their places. Lady Celia curtsied to him while the Duchess beamed at him from a little way off. He bowed his head to her and then the dance began.

The quadrille had never been one of his favourites. With four couples in each set, it required a constant swapping of partners, not allowing for any real attention to be paid to one's partner and the dance was made worse by the other three couples all staring at Lady Celia and himself with meaningful smiles throughout, no doubt aware that this was probably the first dance they had ever performed together. Why must the *ton* be obsessed with other people's business? He was not a poor dancer, but he stiffened under such scrutiny and so he was aware that he danced like a puppet and Lady Celia, who had looked so happy with all of her previous dance partners, seemed to have wiped all traces of expression from her face, which was now neither bright and carefree, nor downcast, only carefully blank, like a doll cut from paper. The whole experience was a trial, and he was grateful when the music ended, and he could bow to her. Now, perhaps, there might be an opportunity to speak together, to begin again after their awkward start.

"May I take you for an ice?"

She glanced down and away from the Duchess who had approached and was nodding eagerly. "I have promised a dance to Lord Radcliffe," she murmured.

Lord Radcliffe was a rake and not to be trusted with any young lady unless under the direct gaze of her mother and a roomful of the *ton*. He was not entirely pleased that she would have granted him a dance in the first place, but there was little he could do but bow again and allow her to depart for the other side of the room. He wondered if he should speak with her mother about the kind of partners she was allowed to dance with, for a girl her age might not know of Radcliffe's reputation, but he most certainly did, and it was not one to be trusted. A girl of her youth and inexperience might be persuaded to take a brief stroll in the gardens and then find herself suddenly alone with Radcliffe and her honour subsequently in question. He shook his head silently and accepted another glass of champagne with an impending sense of disaster. It had been a terrible start to their first meeting, and it did not seem to be getting any better.

"Comerford, good to see you."

He turned. "Mr Mowatt. Likewise."

"I had the honour of dancing with your betrothed," said Mr Mowatt pleasantly. "Delightful girl. Charming dancer and pretty as a picture. You're a lucky man."

"Thank you."

"I must go, I've promised to take Lady Honora for an ice, but I'll see you at the club, I expect?"

"Yes," agreed Alexander. His spirits rose from Mowatt's friendly exchange. It was only a first meeting, after all, he had placed too much emphasis and meaning on it. It had been a foolish notion to meet at a ball, such a public place for a first encounter. Tomorrow he would call on her at her family home and things would be easier, less formal and with fewer interruptions or other demands, so that they might talk together. Yes. He was engaged to her, and it was his duty to work at the relationship, to make something good of it. He would not be deterred by a minor setback. He spent the next two dances making conversation with her mother, a pleasant woman with a motherly air, which further encouraged him. As the ball ended, he set out to find Lady Celia and make his good intentions known.

CELIA HAD LOST HER MUFF SOMEWHERE IN THE general mayhem of the cloakroom and was now searching for it, growing overly heated in the process, for the room was warm and the other girls in it all hopelessly underfoot. Finally locating her muff under someone else's wrap, she made her way out of the room only to be immediately met by Lord Comerford, who bowed at the sight of her. Why must the man always appear when she herself was flustered or awkward in some way?

"Lord Comerford. I am on my way home."

"I will call on you tomorrow morning," he said.

"There is no need," she said.

He looked surprised.

"That is – you should not feel you must – I am sure you have much business to attend to," she stammered. "Since you are so lately returned."

"You are my betrothed," he said stiffly. "It is only right that I should call on you and your family regularly. Indeed, it is my duty to do so."

Her lips thinned, but she dipped him a quick curtsey. "In that case I shall see you tomorrow afternoon, Lord Comerford."

He bowed and walked away.

Duty? Was ever a man so lacking in social graces! She was a duty, then, was she? A tedious daily chore to be undertaken out of a dull sense of what was proper. How insufferable. Instead of her friends calling on her, being able to converse together of plays and concerts, perhaps gossip about acquaintances and speculate on who might marry who this coming season, she would have to sit in silent tedium with this man, her betrothed – all her worst expectations were coming true. She had wanted to give him a fair chance, but she was already wondering whether that was a waste of the little time available to get out of the marriage before she would be tied to him forever.

2

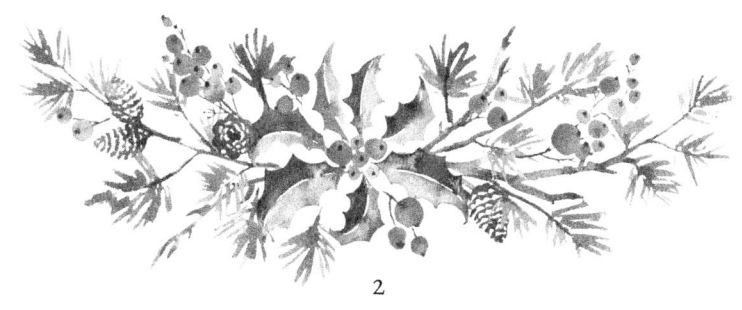

NO NEED FOR WOOING

At one o'clock precisely the next day Alexander presented himself at Follett House, only a few streets away from Comerford House. Follett House was of course a grand residence, since it belonged to a duke, but he was heartened to note that it was no grander than Comerford House, which was both newly built and furnished in the latest style, thanks to a generous inheritance from his grandmother, who had doted on John. Although Comerford House felt empty to him, at least Lady Celia could hardly complain of coming down in the world in making it her new London home.

"Alexander, so lovely to see you. You are very welcome in our home and Celia is of course awaiting your arrival," beamed the Duchess, graciously rising from her seat by the fire in the well-appointed drawing room. "I will ring for her."

A servant having been sent in search of Celia, Alexander took up a place indicated by the Duchess and accepted a cup of tea.

"Lord Comerford."

He rose and bowed as Lady Celia made her way into the room. "Lady Celia."

"Come now, I am sure we can allow first names, since you are to marry by summer," simpered the Duchess, evidently trying to make the meeting more friendly. "Celia, dearest, your cushion cover is just here, I am sure you would like to work on it while you and dear Alexander converse."

Lady Celia accepted the embroidered cushion cover, which was made up of a vacuous design of overblown pink roses and a truncated quotation – *love, the greatest of heaven's blessings* – no doubt snipped of its true meaning by the Duchess, who must have found the original quote by Plato, *the madness of love, the greatest of heaven's blessings,* far too passionate for a young lady's embroidery. Which was fair enough, what would a mere slip of a girl, barely out of the schoolroom, know about love's passions? Nothing at all. She might have fancied herself in love once or twice perhaps, overcome by a fine uniform or a sprightly dance partner but madness? Passion? No, of course not. Alexander sighed inwardly as Lady Celia began to stitch, uncomfortably aware of the Duchess positioning herself behind him, where she could easily overhear them while pretending to be otherwise engaged with her correspondence at a table by the window. However, he had come prepared with topics of conversation, to avoid just such awkward silences.

"Are you looking forward to celebrating the Christmas season?" he asked.

Her expression grew warmer. "I love Christmas," she said. "It is always a pleasure to celebrate with family and friends, to make merry together. Do you enjoy Christmas, Lord Comerford?"

He hesitated. He had enjoyed it as a child, of course, the abundance of sweet treats and games making it hard not to pass the time pleasantly. There had been snow often, with the opportunity for sledging and snowball fights. But of recent years... he had often been on board ship and the festive season, while nodded to with some better food than usual and frequent toasts, had not been given as much attention as it would have been granted on peaceful land. This year many responsibilities would fall to him, which had been weighing on his mind, never having undertaken them before. He would have to arrange and take part in the Servants' Ball, as well as give out those festive gifts to his staff which were expected in a generous household. "It is generally reckoned a pleasant season," he managed at last, aware that she was waiting for an answer.

Lady Celia's tentative smile dimmed but the Duchess, always watchful, weighed in at once.

"But you must join us at Bellbrook Manor, Alexander. We would be delighted to have you with us, especially since your family is so recently depleted. Say you will come!"

He had not expected to be asked, but after all the Duke and Duchess would shortly become family to him, no doubt there would be many festive seasons spent in their company to a greater or lesser extent. It would be part of his duty to his betrothed and part of what would make for a happy marriage; therefore, it was best to begin at once.

"Certainly," he said. "Thank you, Your Grace." He offered a smile to Lady Celia, but her expression was less than happy. He rose and bowed. "I have taken up enough of your time already," he said. "I am sure you will have other visitors. I will see you tomorrow."

The Duchess fluttered some small protest at the shortness of his visit, but Lady Celia only nodded, rose to her feet to give him a small curtsey, and returned to her needlework, all while barely meeting his gaze. Making his way down the stairs, Alexander felt the weight of the agreement again. Yes, he had been invited to spend Christmas with the family, but that was the Duchess' doing, Lady Celia had not been encouraging – indeed, she had not even been friendly – in her manner to him. He suppressed a sigh as he reached the comfort and privacy of his waiting carriage. He had a sinking feeling that this alliance would prove to be a mistake, for there was no sign of the small spark of initial affection or interest he had hoped for, neither in his own breast nor, as far as he could tell, in Lady Celia's. Still, he had been well trained by Captain Rose, one day's work meant nothing at all if it were not followed by many more such days, weeks and even years. He would continue trying.

❄

November wore into the early days of December and Alexander's days fell into a pattern which, while tedious, was at least simple enough to perform. He spent his mornings managing matters of business, followed by an afternoon or evening spent attending Lady Celia, whether at Follett House or at some social gathering, from balls to dinner parties. He made it his business to visit her each day so that she might see that he was devoted to their engagement, but they spoke little, for she was cool with him, and he did not wish to curtail her pleasures. Let her chatter with her friends or dance with whomsoever she chose. It was her first season, and she should enjoy it as a young free woman. Since their marriage was already settled, he did not feel the need to woo her – indeed he supposed that excessive attentions might prove somewhat smothering. He did not send flowers or gifts from Brown's, nor did he insist on dancing the waltz with her, he only made sure to present himself each day, faithfully following her to whatever social occasion she saw fit to attend, at which he spent most of his time observing her.

She was an excellent dancer and certainly very pretty. Her bouncing black curls and pink cheeks, her warm brown eyes, all of these were pleasing to the eye. Her vivacious manner with others and her bright clothing, while overly bold for his tastes, at least spoke of a cheerful and social character, which was to be preferred over a dull or excessively shy girl.

But... she was so young. Of course, she would grow older. But meanwhile he was faced with a girl who probably thought that balls were the be all and end all of happiness, who expected to be continually praised and courted and wooed by every gentleman in the room, who seemed, as far as he could tell by overhearing her, to chatter incessantly to her friends about clothes and shopping and little else of consequence. Frivolous. That was the word for her. A frivolous child. The idea of having her for his wife made him sigh. True, he would be able to enjoy intimacies with her, but he hoped that there might be some warmth between them to add to the pleasures of the flesh. He could only hope that she would improve over time, that with marriage and later motherhood would come a steadier character, one able to think beyond her next dress or dinner party. He could but hope, though on the rare occasions when she spoke to him her tone and words made him worry that this hope was misplaced.

"I hope you are not jealous of Mr Mowatt sending me flowers?" she asked him once, smiling.

"Certainly not," he replied. "Mr Mowatt is an excellent fellow and a friend of mine; we attend the same club. He is aware of our forthcoming nuptials, it is kind of him to pay you his compliments."

She looked away, as though disappointed by the answer.

❄

Hoping to avoid Lord Comerford visiting yet again, Celia took her horse and an accompanying groom and went to ride on Rotten Row. At least, should the Earl arrive, it would be difficult for him to locate her in Hyde Park without some effort and if he did manage to find her, she could then claim to have been out long enough, be cold or tired and return home.

"Lady Celia!"

She turned to see the Earl of Hyatt and his youngest sister riding just behind her. "Lord Hyatt, it is good to see you. Lady Sarah."

"Not Lady Sarah for much longer," said Lord Hyatt. "It has been agreed she will marry directly after Christmas. I shall miss her."

"I will be close by and visit you frequently," said Lady Sarah, smiling. "If you are riding out, Lady Celia, may we ride with you?"

"Certainly," said Celia. Privately she hoped that Lord Comerford might find her riding out with another man. Perhaps that would make him behave more affectionately with her, since his entire wooing of her seemed to consist of appearing at every gathering and staring at her with a frowning countenance, as though he could not put his finger on what he found at fault about her, but that it would come to him at any moment.

The little party rode along Rotten Row together, nodding to acquaintances as they went along.

"My brother says he will miss me, but I do not believe a word of it," said Lady Sarah. "He wishes to go traveling and I am sure as soon as I am out of the house he will do so."

"Traveling? Where?"

"Oh everywhere," said Lord Hyatt cheerfully. "I should like to follow in my father's footsteps and undertake the Grand Tour, should the war allow it, to see Italy especially. He always spoke fondly of it. He travelled all over Europe with his dear friend, Lord Barrington – when they were both young men of course, before they inherited their titles and father married. I would like to do the same."

"Before you marry?"

He flashed her a bright smile. "Perhaps. Or perhaps with a new bride on my arm. It might be an adventure to share."

His sister raised her eyebrows. "She would have to be a brave woman indeed to travel so far."

"I hope so," he replied, "I would not care for a meek woman to share my life with."

"It would be a wonderful adventure," said Celia, and she meant it. Lord Hyatt was so very different to Lord Comerford. Fair haired, with laughing blue eyes and a merry disposition, she was certain he would make for an easier husband, one who not only had exciting plans for travel, but who seemed amiable towards his sister and willing to have a woman by his side who had some spark to her. She was growing tired of Lord Comerford's apparently endless disapproval of her. It would be pleasant to ride out each day with a man who smiled, who laughed, who suggested a life full of fun and adventure to be shared, who would send little gifts and his compliments, who would dance as though he enjoyed the pastime rather than with a stiff formality.

"You will both be in Kent for Christmas?" she enquired.

"Perhaps, although since it is only the two of us this year, we may be a very small party. My younger brother has only just married himself and our two sisters are with child, so a large family gathering is not possible this season, but we shall be merry regardless, I am fond of Christmas and all its joys."

Celia reflected that Christmas at the Hyatts', even with only two members of the family at home, was likely to be more festive than at Bellbrook Manor, despite the larger numbers, if Lord Comerford was to stay with them as promised, no doubt disapproving of the many games and dances they were used to celebrating with. "I am sure it will be merry," she said, managing a smile. "And perhaps next year all of your family can be together, with its new additions."

"Indeed," said Lord Hyatt cheerfully. "I am very fond of children, I shall look forward to welcoming my nephews and nieces, there is nothing like little children for bringing excitement to Christmas morning."

Celia nodded and shortly afterwards bid Lord Hyatt and Lady Sarah goodbye, returning to Follett House, where she spent the evening sunk in despair at the contrast between her betrothed's taciturn nature and that of Lord Hyatt.

❆

IN MID-DECEMBER, WITH THE CHRISTMAS SEASON drawing close and many families now giving going-away dinners to their acquaintances until they should all return to town in March, Celia attended a dinner party hosted by the parents of one of her friends, Lady Anna Huntingdon.

To her growing irritation, Lord Comerford seemed able to secure an invitation to any event to which she herself was invited. He had stood silently behind her in the drawing room while she talked to Lady Anna. It made her conversation stilted. Usually, she would have spoken about art with Lady Anna, who was both an accomplished painter and very knowledgeable about all aspects of art and artists. But there was a new exhibition in town which she would like to attend with her friend and she was afraid that if they discussed it, Lord Comerford would find a way to be there as well, and so she fell back on speaking only of fashion, such as what clothes she might bespeak for the warmer months, a new style she had seen for trimming summer straw bonnets and how soon in spring Vauxhall Pleasure Gardens might be open without fear of cold or damp. When the announcement came that dinner was served, everyone stood to make their way into the dining room. Lady Anna was paired with a Lord Lymington, and when Celia turned her head, of course Lord Comerford was holding out his hand.

"May I escort you to dinner?"

She would have preferred not, but there was not much choice. "Certainly," she said, offering her hand.

He looked down at her hand as he took it, his eyes lingering a moment too long and a sudden anger rose up in her. "I suppose you are wondering what it looks like," she said, her voice a sharp hiss.

At once he met her eyes. "I beg your pardon?"

She looked about for people who might overhear her, but most of the room had already emptied, the only people still left were almost out of the door and were elderly, they probably could not hear her even if she raised her voice.

"My hand. You are wondering what sort of deformity it really is. Since you have never seen it."

"I was wondering no such thing."

She narrowed her eyes and pulled her hand back from his, tugged at the glove and its stupid stuffed fingers, till finally the wretched thing came off and she held out her bare hand to his face. "There. Have your fill of looking."

He kept his eyes on her angry gaze, then slowly looked down at her hand, from its thumb across the three small stubs and to her little finger. Then he looked back to her eyes. "I see."

"You are disgusted, I suppose. Don't worry, no one else in my family has ever had such a disfiguration, so it is unlikely I will taint your bloodline with it. Your children will be normal." She struggled trying to put the glove back on, the thumb space had turned inside out, and her anger made her clumsy.

"Let me help you," he offered.

"No," she said, her cheeks hot at being unable to pull the glove back on with ease. She had meant to make a dramatic demonstration that would leave him flustered, but instead it was she fumbling, while he looked on with cool interest. Finally, the stupid glove was back in place, and she reluctantly took his arm again to walk into dinner. He had been seated next to her, but she replied only in monosyllables to any conversation starters he made and at last they sat in silence while the rest of the table chattered away, and she ignored her mother's pointed looks to speak with him, giving all her attention to the soup in front of her.

He was dull. Dour. A bleak prospect of a husband, no matter his good looks or ample money. There. That was what she thought of him, and she found it unlikely that would change. He called on her or arranged to see her at some social party every day, which might speak of deep attachment and be quite romantic, were it not for the fact that when he was in her presence he barely spoke. He allowed her to dance – even the waltz – with whomever she chose and when, teasing but also wondering at the fact, she had asked did he not mind that other men should send her flowers and biscuits, he had seemed utterly unmoved, much as though such attentions were of no interest or importance, which then made it seem as though he had no romantic attachment to her whatsoever. He danced when required, stopped as soon as was possible without giving offence, his face betrayed little emotion beyond a sort of dull politeness. No doubt he thought her second-class damaged goods and would have preferred to pick his own bride, was in fact marrying her out a tedious sense of duty. And she did not want to be that second choice, she wanted to be chosen for herself, to be loved, desired, to see in her future husband's eyes a longing for her which she would feel somewhere deep inside, sparking the same in herself. Instead, their every meeting seemed to grow stiffer and less friendly.

❄

ALEXANDER TRIED TO PAY ATTENTION TO HIS DINNER companion, an elderly great-aunt of Lady Celia's, who spoke tremulously and at length about her childhood days, reminiscing about various long-dead cousins and siblings, apparently without any expectation of a response from him, thus leaving him to his sombre thoughts. He was sorry if Lady Celia had misinterpreted his glance at her hand. It was her glove he found odd, the stuffed fingers either unnaturally stiff or floppy, depending on the glove she was wearing. As for her hand, now that he had seen it – it was not so bad. She was lucky to have a thumb and finger; he had seen her tie shoe ribbons perfectly dextrously and undertake needlework. Perhaps she was ashamed of it, but there was no reason to feel so. And if she had thought he would find it upsetting or disgusting – well, then she had not been in battle, where he had seen sights, as a young boy, that had truly distressed him. As for injuries afterwards, he had seen more than one leg or arm stump. A hand with a few missing fingers was nothing to him. Evidently it caused her distress, however, since she insisted on wearing the stuffed glove fingers all the time and had so sharply reprimanded him for what she erroneously believed to be his repulsion. He wondered whether to broach the subject again, but there seemed little point in drawing yet more attention to the matter if it had so badly offended her. Better to maintain a simple silence about it, thus indicating that it was of no interest or concern to him. He glanced again at Lady Celia, sat beside him, but her eyes were kept resolutely on her plate and her expression was mutinous.

❄

"Tell him I am unwell!" hissed Lady Celia when the footman came on December the twenty-first to say that Lord Comerford was at the door.

"Nonsense, Celia, he is your betrothed, why on earth would I tell him that? You will meet with him as usual; he never stays too long as it is, he is most considerate of our visiting times." The Duchess shook her head. "Really, you are quite rude to him sometimes, I do not know why he puts up with it. He will think you an ill-humoured miss if you continue this way. You must stop reading those ridiculous novels full of romantic nonsense."

Celia acquiesced in bad humour, sitting heavily down on one of the sofas and picking up her cushion cover, stabbing viciously at it as though it were Lord Comerford's waistcoat.

Alexander entered and bowed without saying anything, then settled himself near her. The cushion cover did not seem to have progressed much in the time he had known her, he wondered whether she was in fact less dextrous than he had believed.

"I shall leave the two of you alone for a little while – I must speak with cook about this evening; you will not mind?" said the Duchess. It was acceptable to leave them here, sipping tea, even without a chaperone, since they were engaged and the wedding only months away, but Alexander still wished she had not, for conversation with Lady Celia was stilted at the best of times. Still, they would have to learn to be civil together, so it was as best to practise. Perseverance was everything.

"Your flower arrangements are very pretty," he commented.

She glanced at the three bouquets on the table. "They were gifts from my dance partners at the Selson ball," she said, her chin up and eyes fixed on him, as though daring him to protest.

"Charming," he said.

"Would you care for a biscuit?" she asked, holding out a plate on which were iced biscuits depicting roses in a delicate blush pink.

"Thank you," he said, selecting one and biting into it.

"They are from Brown's," she said, her voice still holding a challenge in it. "Lord Hyatt sent them."

He was aware of Brown's, a pastry shop whose expertise lay in beautifully decorated biscuits most frequently bought by gentlemen as gifts for ladies, something different than the standard offering of flowers. "They are very good," he said, choosing once again to overlook any attentions from other gentlemen.

"Do you really not object?" she asked sharply.

"Object? To what?"

"To other gentlemen sending gifts and flowers to your future bride?"

"Not at all. It is your coming out season. The purpose of you having a season was for you to enjoy yourself and experience the fun of social parties before your marriage. There is no harm in receiving some flowers and biscuits. Half the *ton* knows we are engaged. The other half would find out soon enough if they enquired as to your availability for marriage. I am not about to fight a duel for your honour over some flowers and biscuits."

"You are not jealous?"

"Why would I be? You are already engaged to me. I am not competing with any other gentleman for your hand in marriage."

She frowned. "Do you not think *you* should be wooing me?"

"That seems unnecessary, don't you think? I visit you daily, which I think sufficient proof of my commitment to you. I am not seeking your hand in marriage; it has already been agreed between us."

"Between our parents, you mean."

"Either way, it has been decided, and therefore I am neither jealous nor feel the need to woo you. I am bound to you, just as you are bound to me."

She stood and flung the embroidered cushion cover aside, then began pacing the room, her face crumpled into a frown. "I do not consider myself bound to you. I felt bound only to give you a chance."

"A chance?"

"Yes. To see if you and I were suited, to see whether you were someone I might fall in love with – perhaps not immediately, but that there was at least a chance..."

He sat back and observed her. Ah, so here it was at last. Here were her true colours. He had suspected as much, but she had behaved too well thus far for him to be certain. Now he saw her true feelings. "I see. And you do not think we will fall in love?"

"No! We are so ill suited! I cannot imagine why they thought we would be a good match."

"Can you not?"

"No! And I should tell you immediately that it is my intention to find another man to be my husband. And when I do find such a man, a man better suited to my character, I shall break off our engagement."

"I see."

She turned from her pacing to stare at him. "You have nothing to say? You do not wish to plead you case?"

He looked her over, her cheeks pink, her eyes wide, her barely held in outrage. "You are a child," he said. "You expected a romance. This betrothal was never arranged as a romance. It was arranged as a safe marriage for you, to save you any shame or rejection over your hand. It was intended as an advantageous marriage for me as a second son, to be linked to a duke and have a rich bride, since no-one expected me to inherit anything much from my father, as it would all go to my older brother. It was a safe match. For both of us. No-one cared about a love match."

She stared at him.

"I hoped for a marriage to suit us both," he said. "I admit I hoped there might be some small spark, some interest in one another that we might fan into flames, a chance of a romantic attachment." He shrugged. "But clearly that was my own folly. I cannot see that we are at all suited. However, that does not signify. We are engaged and I would never break that arrangement. I am sure we can come to some way of living that is not too difficult for either of us. We have Comerford Castle as well as Comerford House, we can live separately if you prefer, after marriage." He caught her look of incredulity. "Naturally we will need heirs. Therefore, the marriage will need to be consummated on occasion but otherwise I will not seek to..."

She held up her hand. "Stop."

"I beg your pardon?"

"Stop. I have just told you; this marriage will not go ahead."

"You intend to break off our engagement immediately?"

"I intend to break it off as soon as I have found a suitable man to marry."

"I am glad you have some common sense, then."

"What do you mean by that?"

"That you are keeping the engagement intact until you have found a suitable replacement for me. You are not about to throw away a perfectly good title and prospects just to make your point. It is the most sensible I have seen you be so far."

"You are intolerable. I am only not breaking it off because if I try to do that my mother and father may think I am only nervous and bring the wedding forward, leaving me no time to find a new suitor."

"Then let us hope you find an alternative suitor so that you will not have to tolerate me for much longer." He stood and bowed to her. "I think I should be going, Lady Celia, I have trespassed too long on your time already today. I will see you the day after tomorrow when we travel to Bellbrook Manor together. You will forgive me for not calling on you tomorrow, I am not sure it would be a pleasant experience for either of us. Be so good as to present my compliments to your mother."

He strode from the room, heart racing. Damn it all, but the girl was impossible. He prided himself on keeping a cool temper, but rage was rising in him at her behaviour. She was threatening to find a new husband, was she? Good luck to her, then. She was a spoilt child, wanting a different pudding than the one put in front of her at all, pushing it away in disgust when she was lucky to have food put in front of her, let alone indulgences such as sweets. He did not think overly highly of himself, did not believe himself to be wonderfully handsome or charming, but he knew himself to be loyal and truthful, an honourable man, as well as being both titled and rich, which seemed to be the only thing that mattered to the *ton*. He had not screwed up his face in disgust at her hand, had not refused her for being young and foolish. No. He had admired her pretty face and planned to be a good husband to her, to make the marriage work despite its obvious mismatch. But she? She had given up at the very first hurdle, petulantly expecting to be courted and coaxed into a marriage that had already been agreed upon, stamping her little foot when the coaxing was not forthcoming. She had issued threats which would, if brought to fruition, prove downright embarrassing to both parties, a source of *ton* gossip and no doubt borderline slander in the scandal sheets. The Duke and Duchess had not done a very good job of raising their daughter, in his opinion. This was what the pampered daughter of a duke was like, then. Whereas he, a mere second son to an earl, knew better than she how to comport himself.

Once outside in the cold air and in the saddle of his horse, he took a moment to steady his breathing. So be it. If that was her intention, let her proceed. As a gentleman, he would wait to be told he was no longer engaged to her and then proceed with finding himself a more suitable bride, one whose values matched his. Perhaps a lady a few years older than Lady Celia, closer to his age, a woman who understood honour and loyalty, with whom he could make a real marriage. He would seek a companion to whom he could be bound with pleasure instead of out of duty. Meanwhile, he would show Lady Celia what a true gentleman was. He would not be so dishonourable as to break off the engagement himself, he would continue to behave as though the conversation had never happened. When the news eventually came, he would continue to behave correctly, showing only politeness towards his past betrothed, and wishing her all happiness in her future marriage. Yes. It was the only way forward. She was impulsive, selfish and shallow. Let her continue along that path and make a fool of herself.

❋

CELIA WAS FORCED TO STOP PACING THE DRAWING room by the re-entry of her mother who expressed surprise at the sudden departure of Lord Comerford. Making a quick excuse, Celia made her way upstairs to her bedroom, where she began her pacing again, occasionally muttering to herself.

"A child! A *child*!"

She peered out of the window to see if she could see Lord Comerford leaving, but she could not spot him.

"Unnecessary! *Unnecessary* to show interest in his wife-to-be?"

The man was impossible. And rude. Hurtful, even, how dare he suggest that their marriage had only been planned to save her shame and to bring him wealth? It had been arranged because their two families were friendly with one another, she had always been told so. Thank goodness she had realised his true nature in good time, thank goodness he had made his pompous little speech and shown her who he really was. Now she could proceed with her plan to find a new husband with no qualms. She would brook no feelings of disloyalty or concern for his wellbeing or even guilt in breaking off a decades-long engagement. She felt entirely free to do as she wished, now. She would not break off the engagement just yet, as her parents would only fuss if she were left without a suitor, but as soon as she found someone appropriate, she would break off this absurdity and begin afresh with a man who could actually be loved, with whom she had the slightest chance of happiness. Thank goodness indeed. It was clear now that a new suitor was required and must be secured as soon as possible. She would, however, have to be discreet, for if she allowed her mother to know that she wished to call off the engagement she was afraid her mother would sweep aside her "romantic nonsense" as she would no doubt refer to it and bring forward the wedding. No, it would have to be done by stealth, but she would most certainly do her best to find a new suitor.

One nagging doubt about his final words remained with her, however. What had he meant by travelling to Bellbrook Manor *together*?

"Mama?"

"Yes, dearest?"

"Lord Comerford said something about travelling to

Bellbrook... together...?" she trailed off, hoping that she had misheard.

"Yes, of course. As we are such a large party for Christmas, I have invited your Aunt Louisa and her companion to travel in the carriage with your father and me on the twenty-third, while you will travel with Lord Comerford."

"Me? Why must I travel with him?"

The Duchess frowned. "Because you are his betrothed, Celia, and you will shortly be his wife. The journey will offer a good opportunity for the two of you to converse, since you barely seem to speak to him at balls and even when he calls on you."

"Because he is dull!"

"Celia, really! That is no way to speak of your intended."

"Just because he was intended by his family to marry me does not mean I intended to choose him as a husband. He is dour, and dull. He never says a word and most of the time he just looks disapproving."

"He is a man of the world, who has seen war, been injured and recently lost both comrades and family. He is not some frivolous young man with no thought in his head but to enjoy himself."

"He could enjoy himself a little, at least!"

"I will not listen to any more of your nonsense, Celia. You will travel in Lord Comerford's carriage when we all journey to Bellbrook and you will make yourself agreeable to him."

Celia said nothing more, but she was annoyed. It was bad enough that Lord Comerford should be spending all of the festive season at Bellbrook after they had all but broken off their engagement, but she had at least hoped to keep out of his way. Trapped in a carriage with no other company for several hours would be tedium indeed. She could only hope he would fall asleep if she did not provide any conversation. It would not be difficult to do so, for she had nothing to say to him.

After dinner, she made her first move, asking her mother whether the Earl of Hyatt and his sister could also join them at Bellbrook Manor for the festivities of Twelfth Night, citing her fondness of the Earl's sister Lady Sarah (whom she knew only slightly) and lying through her teeth by saying that the Earl of Hyatt and Lord Comerford were good friends, when they were only on nodding acquaintance. Her mother bemusedly agreed to extend the invitation, and Celia smiled a secret smile to herself. She did not think there could be much harm in elevating Lord Hyatt to her preferred suitor. A future of cheerful good nature, possible travel and a love of children seemed an infinitely better prospect than a glowering husband for the rest of her life. And if Lord Comerford was going to be at Bellbrook Manor for the whole of Christmas, then she would be in sore need of some more gracious company by Twelfth Night. She did not like to admit it even to herself, but Lord Comerford's comments regarding the reasons for their betrothal still came back to her with unsettling ease and regularity, making her cheeks flush at the transactional nature of the agreement, how little romantic or even friendly intentions had been behind it.

❄

THE TWENTY-THIRD OF DECEMBER DAWNED BITTERLY cold but with clear skies. Follett House was almost entirely closed up. Most of the servants had already gone ahead at first light to Bellbrook Manor, there to prepare for a sumptuous Christmas season and the many guests who would shortly be arriving. Only a small handful remained to ensure the family were taken care of on their last day. By eleven, breakfast had been served and cleared, the Duke was in his study and Celia and her mother were in the drawing room. The Duchess was engaged in completing a last few pieces of correspondence and writing final instructions for the few servants who would be staying behind, while Celia was re-reading a note her mother had received from Lord Hyatt, expressing his pleasure at being invited to Bellbrook Manor for Twelfth Night. *I look forward to our time together*, he had written, and *my sister is delighted to be able to spend time with Lady Celia, she is grown very fond of her*. Well, if that was not a clear intention of making their relationship closer, she did not know what was.

"Celia, you and Lord Comerford will be traveling to Bellbrook tomorrow after all."

Celia looked up, startled. "Tomorrow? But we are all traveling today."

"He has a few last matters of business to attend to. You will stay the night at Comerford House, and you will both travel to us tomorrow morning. If you make good time you will be with us by the afternoon."

"Stay the night at Comerford House? Alone?"

Her mother gave a laugh. "You will hardly be alone, dearest. You will have Aveline."

"I am to stay the night in the house of a gentleman to whom I am not yet married?"

"Really, Celia, there is no need to sound so prim. You are betrothed to Lord Comerford, you will be married by summer. He is a gentleman. It is only one night, and your maid will be with you. It is hardly the stuff of scandal sheets. I have already replied in the affirmative. His carriage will be here to collect you in an hour."

"Can't I stay here the night and join him tomorrow for the journey?"

"Certainly not. Nearly all the servants will be gone. Now go upstairs and let Aveline know that she should leave out an evening dress."

"An evening dress?"

The Duchess sighed. "Naturally. You will be having dinner together this evening, it is incumbent on you to look becoming."

"Dinner together – alone?"

"Of course, alone, Celia. Please stop acting like a child. Let Aveline know, would you, she will need to pack accordingly."

Celia dolefully did as she was told, then sat morosely watching Aveline complete the packing. A whole evening and dinner alone with Lord Comerford? What a dreary proposition that would be. She had hoped to pretend to sleep during the carriage ride to Bellbrook, and then to enjoy herself this evening amongst family and friends, leaving Lord Comerford to his usual silence. Let him sit in a corner and glare if he wished, she would be enjoying herself. But now it seemed she was to be forced to sit opposite him for a whole evening of silent disapproval.

Well, so be it. She would say she was tired and escape as soon as the meal was complete, they would travel the next morning when she would pretend to sleep and then it would be over. But it was a timely warning that she must secure Lord Hyatt, and soon, otherwise she really would be spending the rest of her life dining alone with a man who could not even keep up his end of a conversation, who thought her a child and could not be bothered to pay even the smallest of attentions to his bride-to-be. Thank goodness that the Earl of Hyatt would be at Bellbrook for part of the festive season. He was growing on her as a suitable alternative to her current betrothed. At least the man was merry in company. He was a good dancer, he had a fine estate, his title was the same as the Earl of Comerford's. No-one could possibly object except Lord Comerford, and he seemed only too glad to be rid of her.

"The carriage is here, Celia, come along now."

Lord Comerford's carriage was painted in a gleaming but sober black, with his coat of arms displayed upon it, a sprig of golden mistletoe bound by a red ribbon with his family motto, *fortitudo ex amore,* written on it in golden letters.

"Strength through love?" Celia huffed as she stepped in. "The man doesn't know the meaning of the word love. He doesn't have a romantic bone in his body. He should have been a monk for all he cares about romance."

Her maid Aveline tightened her lips and nodded her head. "Men know nothing of love," she pronounced with certainty. Aveline had been with Celia for over ten years. An older woman, she sometimes behaved more as though she were Celia's maiden aunt than her servant.

"Some men might. Not the Earl." Celia sat back with her arms folded. She was glad to have taken Aveline into her confidence, so that she might speak plainly about her plans. "And now I must spend a whole evening in his company, alone? It is hardly decent. How am I to break off the engagement after this without it being whispered about?"

Aveline gave a shrug. "No-one will remember it when you are safely married to someone else," she said. "As for this evening, tell him you are indisposed and eat in your room."

That seemed rude, even to Celia in her present mood. "I will go to dinner," she said reluctantly. "Then I will withdraw early with the excuse that we must travel at first light tomorrow. That will do." It was no good relying on Aveline for romantic advice. She did not hold with romance at all, having once been jilted by a footman. Her rigidly held opinion, regularly given whether it was wanted or not, was that all men were scoundrels and the best one could hope for was one who was absent as much as possible. When Celia had told her of her secret plans to marry Lord Hyatt instead of Lord Comerford, she had only sighed and said that women must put up with the necessity of marriage, no matter how unlikely it was to bring them any happiness. In her view there was little point seeking a different suitor, for men were all the same.

Celia stared sulkily out of the window as they rocked along the few streets it would take to bring them to Comerford House. It would have taken less time to walk, but that would hardly have been elegant enough for her mother, she supposed.

"Stop the carriage!" she called suddenly and Aveline rapped smartly on the roof, at which the carriage came to a slow halt. A footman's face appeared at the window.

"my lady?"

"Open the door. And stop that man!"

The footman, flustered by the dual demands, managed to open the door and take down the steps, then turned to look about him. "Which man, my lady?"

"The one holding that sack! Hurry!"

It took a few moments, but shortly a man in a tattered overcoat stood before Celia.

"Show me what is in the sack."

The man mumbled something.

"Show me, I said."

Reluctantly, he opened the mouth of the sack and Celia peered into the darkness, then reached her hand inside once and then again, pulling up two small kittens, their black and white coats dirty, both mewing loudly, one hissing at her. Celia passed both to Aveline, who looked disgusted but held them by the scruff of their necks so that they could not escape.

"Were you going to drown them?"

"Yes, my lady."

"I will be keeping them. Here is a shilling for the pair."

The man looked bemused. "Thank you, my lady," he muttered, touching his cap.

Back in the carriage, the door safely closed, Aveline put both kittens on the floor. "They are dirty! And will be covered in fleas! What were you thinking?"

"That I do not wish to think of them being drowned, Aveline. Have a heart."

"And are you going to hand them to Lord Comerford, when we arrive?"

"Certainly."

"And what is he to do with them?"

"He need only keep them overnight, they can travel with us to Bellbrook in the morning and be stable cats, if Mama will not have them in the drawing room."

"I should hope she would not have them in the house!"

Celia shrugged. "Then they will be stable cats. It is a better life than being flung in the river to drown."

"What will Lord Comerford think of you?"

"I don't care what he thinks of me," said Celia stubbornly.

Another two streets and they were at Comerford House. Celia peered up at it. It was certainly a fine house. The vast white stone façade loomed over her, while the back, she knew, overlooked Green Park itself.

Lord Comerford was standing on the doorstep to greet them. Celia stepped from the carriage holding both kittens and handed them to the waiting footman at the door. "These are mine," she said. "Have them fed in the kitchen and I will take them with me tomorrow morning."

"Very good, my lady," murmured the footman, trying not to grimace at the tiny claws pressing into his skin and the dirty coats of the two creatures.

Lord Comerford watched the exchange with a frown. "They are your pets?"

"Yes," said Celia, keeping her chin high.

The frown did not leave his face, but he held out a hand. "Welcome to Comerford House. Allow me to show you round."

They went up the steps and into a large white marble hall, where Aveline took Celia's bonnet and pelisse, handing her a shawl in return. Celia had hoped to avoid a tour of the house, for it seemed a step closer to their marriage, a viewing of the house which would become her London home if she became Countess of Comerford. Still, she could not think of a polite way to refuse, other than to claim she was too tired, which seemed an unlikely excuse in the early afternoon. It would have to be gone through, but she was determined not to be impressed. What could Comerford House offer, after all, that she had not already seen as the daughter of a duke?

"The family dining room," said Lord Comerford, guiding her into a room with a gilded dome entrance. The rest of the room was a pale yellow, with a magnificent chandelier and red-gold drapes at the windows. Red silk chairs surrounded the large mahogany table in the centre of the room.

She followed him in silence. The table would easily seat twelve. Did he intend to have many children? Perhaps she was only wanted for breeding a large family, given the sparseness of heirs in his family to date which had led to his sudden rise to the earldom. She shuddered and walked over to one of the windows.

"The terrace and garden," said Lord Comerford behind her.

The terrace was beautiful, running in white stone the full length of the house and descending via broad shallow steps into the garden, which was small, but pretty, full of evergreens which kept it green even now in winter, a few bright touches coming from the camellia bushes flowering in bold reds and the holly berries. There was one tall oak tree inside, while beyond the garden walls was Green Park itself, all towering trees and wide green spaces.

"There was no garden when the house was first commissioned, but my brother bought a small part of the park so that they could have a private garden even in town."

Celia nodded, still silent. She did not wish to ooh and aah, to exclaim over everything, for she did not want to give the impression that she was enchanted with the house, that she in any way expected it to become her home. But certainly everything was decorated in the best possible taste.

"The music room."

A pretty room in blue, decorated with touches of Greek style, including statues from mythology, a gleaming pianoforte and harp.

"The drawing room."

A room in pale green and cream, with everywhere hand-painted scenes from Greek and Roman myths celebrating love and marriage as well as gilded columns reaching up to a golden ceiling. It made her mother's choice of pink and white with gold touches in the drawing room at Follett House seem quaintly old fashioned.

"Lady Comerford's private salon for entertaining."

Here the walls were lined in red silk, the ceiling beautifully decorated with oval panels showing Venus surrounded by adoring cherubs. White orchids bloomed in gold pots. Delicate gold and red silk furniture awaited the presence of a lady and her friends to converse in private and comfort. Celia looked about the room, knowing that this would be her private domain were she to marry Lord Comerford, the room where her friends would visit her, where she would take tea and manage the household.

"And now upstairs. This floor is mostly used for entertaining."

She followed him up the white marble stairs with elaborately worked bannisters in green.

"The main dining room."

The room was vast, with multiple chandeliers, a pale primrose yellow on the walls, darker yellow marble columns at both ends, matched with two gilt console tables, featuring the face of Bacchus in the centre, with winged panthers and grape-rich vines hanging in-between. The carpet beneath their feet was evidently a quality Persian.

"The great room. For balls and suchlike."

Celia tried hard not to look impressed, but it was difficult. The great room was huge; it would easily fit over a hundred guests. The walls here were lined in green silk with long windows on one side and mirrors on the other side, but with the addition of an extraordinary, barrelled ceiling picked out in green and gold hexagons and three exquisite chandeliers.

"And the palm room at the other end of the great room. For those guests during a ball who may wish to rest and talk amongst themselves rather than partake in the dancing."

Even Celia's mouth opened. The room was all green and gold, with a vaulted ceiling and tall columns, the tops of which were decorated as palm trees, with green and gold fronds. It was a magnificent room by anyone's standards, and she saw now why her mother sometimes pined to redecorate Bellbrook Manor, which had been variously decorated over the centuries and was therefore, while grand, somewhat old fashioned in many ways. Comerford House, having been entirely built and decorated in the last couple of years, was the very height of fashion and splendour in every way. "Are you very fond of balls?" she asked, thinking back to their first meeting, when he had seemed to show little interest in the event, and the subsequent stiffness he had seemed to show when dancing at the various balls they had both attended thus far.

"It was my brother's choice," he reminded her. "The house was built to his specifications. He was a man who enjoyed socialising, he and his wife Charlotte gave parties on a frequent basis. As you can see, the whole of this floor is given over to space for entertaining, whether it be balls or dinners."

"Where is his wife – his widow – now?"

"Charlotte has returned to live with her family. She received a generous settlement including a house, but for now she is still grieving, of course." He was silent, gazing out of the windows. "They were very much in love," he said finally. "They were happy here before he died."

They stood in silence for a few moments, the two of

them dwarfed by the size, beauty and silence of the palm room. If the first earl and his wife had borne children the two of them would have lived somewhere far less grand, comfortable no doubt, but he would have been untitled, and their home would have been commensurately less elegant. Not for them golden palm-topped columns or dining rooms made to sit fifty. If the current Lord Comerford had been away for so long, did he even have enough friends to fill such a room? It was a dismal thought.

He cleared his throat. "Let me show you to your room," he said.

She followed but he paused in the corridor, indicating a smaller room off the great room. "The library."

A calming green striped wallpaper was matched with large bookcases full of leather-bound books and a vast white marble fireplace topped by a mirror which reached to the ceiling. No doubt the room could be cosy if one were a great reader, there were large green armchairs and a sofa available, but her gaze was drawn to the matching portraits of two young people in the library. Staring up at them, her heart sank. This perfect couple, this love-matched pair, one now dead and the other a widow... this house was theirs, had been planned by them and enjoyed by them. Now its echoing rooms were supposedly to be lived in by a couple whose wedding day promises would be nothing but compromise, a loveless arranged marriage to be gone through as an obligation, a dutiful following of family wishes. It did not seem right, the very house seemed to expect love and happiness to be found within its walls, gaiety and joyful meetings to be a daily occurrence. It made her all the more determined that this marriage should not be gone through with. Let the Earl choose a wife himself and be happy, as she intended to do in finding a husband she might love. It was only right for both of them.

They climbed another staircase, which led to a corridor of doors.

"I have had you put in Lady Comerford's suite of rooms," he said stiffly. "I will leave you to refresh yourself."

"Thank you," she replied, appalled, as he bowed and walked away. What was he thinking of, in a house as large as this one, with a dozen guest bedrooms, to put her into the bedroom she would occupy if she became his wife, as though the deed was already done? No doubt the chamber was next door to his rooms and (horror) probably furnished with a door between the two suites. Sure enough, as soon as she entered the bedchamber, she spotted a concealed door leading to the Earl's suite of rooms. Without hesitating she dragged a pretty dressing table in front of the door so that it might not be opened from the other side.

Aveline, who was laying out her toiletries for the night, looked up. "What are you doing, my lady?"

"There's no telling what he might attempt late at night, especially if he were in his cups, thinking himself already as good as my husband, as everyone around me seems minded to do."

Aveline nodded. "All men are the same," she pronounced with a weary sigh. "They want only one thing, and they stop at nothing to get it. I can sleep in your room with you if you wish, for added safety."

"Perhaps," agreed Celia. The door thus secured, she looked about her.

The suite of rooms comprised a bedchamber, a dressing room with a large copper bath and a small parlour. The colour used throughout was a fashionably presented green, from a deep forest for the velvet of her bed-curtains to a springlike pale hue used in the parlour, decorated with a natural scene of waving grasses and butterflies, with songbirds above in a pale dawn sky, all of it newly furbished, with a stylish sense of taste and fashion. She would have thought them pretty, been delighted to have them as her own, but she did not like the idea that being in these rooms, like everything else, clearly signalled that the marriage between them was as good as completed.

"What did you think of the house?" asked Aveline, who had already laid out a red silk dress with white ribbonwork all over the hem and sleeves and was now offering a cloth and hot water.

Celia made a face as she was undressed. "It is beautiful," she admitted reluctantly. "I can see why Mama is always nagging at Papa to refurbish the drawing room and the dining room, she says they look shabby. In comparison to those I have seen here, she is right."

"You would be mistress of this house," pointed out the always-prosaic Aveline. "You should see the kitchens, they are huge. A Mrs Poole is the cook, she was hired from the royal household itself, she is one of the most sought-after cooks in London."

"But I don't love him! And never could, he is an impossible man."

Aveline gave one of her Gallic shrugs. "You are not obliged to love him," she pointed out. "Hardly any woman in the *ton* loves her husband, especially after they have been married for some time," she added wickedly. "What matters is whether he is rich and treats you well enough to ignore."

"Well, I want to love my husband," said Celia stubbornly. "And there are plenty of rich men in London, I need not settle for one who has a sour face."

"He is handsome," pointed out Aveline unexpectedly.

"He has a good jaw, he is tall, his shoulders are manly, and his eyes are kindly." She considered. "Also, he dresses well," she conceded. "His valet does a good job."

"You are not helping!"

"But he is handsome," insisted Aveline.

Celia finished washing and held up her arms to be re-dressed in a chemise. "No-one can be handsome with that expression on their face. Enough from you," she added, seeing Aveline open her mouth again. "I don't like him and that is an end to it. Now let us get this dinner over and done with so that I can return to my room."

Aveline kept her mouth closed in a tight line which suggested she disagreed with Celia. She finished dressing her and arranging her hair in a forced silence.

❅

Descending to dinner, Celia's stomach was leaden. A whole dinner entirely alone with Lord Comerford? What were they to say to one another? After she had clarified her intentions regarding their engagement, it was hardly going to be easy to find appropriate small talk.

The so-called small dining room had now been elaborately decorated for the evening, with floral arrangements of delicate green viburnum and vibrantly pink quince flowers and candelabras shining with beeswax candles, which made the room smell of honey. It would have been beautiful were it not also absurd, the mahogany table set for only two, one of them at each end, as though they were hosting a dinner party of at least ten other invisible guests. Celia tried to choke back a laugh.

"Are you well, Lady Celia?"

She composed herself. "Quite well, Lord Comerford."

"I hope the dinner is to your satisfaction."

Celia wanted to say that it would surely be to the satisfaction of an entire regiment, for there was certainly enough food for one, with dishes laid out down the entirety of the table. Was this the dinner he would expect every evening? It was ridiculous. Even her father, a man accustomed to the finer things in life since birth, did not hold with waste or frivolously lavish displays when dining at home.

The onion soup having been served and removed; it was replaced with roasted beef. Already in place were a chicken and veal pie, tongue, Scotch collops, larks, roast sweetbreads, woodcocks, crawfish, artichoke bottoms, morel mushrooms and stewed celery, while in the way of sweet items there were preserved cherries, custards and jellies, Maids of Honour and blanched almonds and raisins. It was all excellently made, but it would have amply served a whole tableful of guests, had there been any. As it was, Celia ate what she could, but mindful of the manners expected of a lady, she did not eat her fill. Besides, having to ask for dishes to be passed to her or served by the footmen attending them was awkward, not like a jolly dinner amongst family and friends, where dishes would clatter up and down the table as desired in a pleasant manner. Here the silence was positively stifling, and Celia could not wait for the meal to be over so that she might escape the experience.

❄

Alexander could not imagine what Mrs Poole was thinking, sending up such an absurdly large dinner for only two people.

Actually, that was not true. He knew perfectly well

what she was doing. All the servants of Comerford House were walking on eggshells, for not only was he their new master but they all believed (for now, being none the wiser of her threats) that Lady Celia was shortly to be their new mistress. They wanted to please, they wanted to show off their skills so that they might not be dismissed for some real or imagined fault. Mrs Poole could best do this through providing lavish meals, the footmen were on their best behaviour, the butler and housekeeper at their most obsequious. Even the maids who lit the fires in the mornings wanted to do their best, he had never seen such roaring fires in every room he entered as had been in place this afternoon and evening. It was understandable. He did not wish to chastise them for it, but it made him look as though he had ordered all of this, as though he had no idea what was reasonable and proper. Well, so be it. If he had to suffer looking foolish so that his servants might feel they had done their best, he would bear it with patience. No doubt their overly-lavish efforts would subside once they no longer felt they were on probation.

"I have ordered the carriage to be ready for us at first light," he said, feeling the need to clarify how they would get out of this stiff experience. "Mrs Poole can pack you some items for your breakfast to eat along the way as well as something for your pets. I thought it best to depart early so that we can reach your family by the early afternoon. The staff will travel behind us."

She nodded. "I do not need food with me, though," she objected. "I can eat when we reach home. But something for the kittens would be useful."

Home. She still thought of her childhood house as home. It was natural, he supposed, but still it seemed like a rejection of Comerford House, as though she wanted no connection to it – to him – and was determined to make that clear with every word she uttered. So be it. She would refuse food, refuse to think of him or the house in a kindly fashion. It was just as well she no longer wished to marry him; it was an uphill task trying to please her. Perhaps he should view her threats as a blessing in disguise.

"Are we to be a large party at Bellbrook Manor?"

She nodded. "My family numbers fifteen. You will be there, as will two of our neighbours, an elderly couple who have often joined us." She hesitated, and her cheeks turned rosier. "Lord Hyatt and his sister have been invited for Twelfth Night," she added in a rush.

Ah. So that was how it was. She had already chosen his replacement and planned for the two of them to dance attendance on her over the festive period, before she made a choice. He would not take part in these foolish games of hers. Let her secure Lord Hyatt. He was a pleasant enough man, perhaps they would be better suited. Either way, he had lost his appetite, there was no use prolonging this uncomfortable evening longer than was absolutely necessary. He gave her a stiff nod back. "Perhaps we should retire early so that we can leave on time. The journey tomorrow will be tiring but the carriage is warm enough, there are furs and blankets for use in it."

She was on her feet before he had finished speaking and he was obliged to rise to match her, the two of them making their way with quick steps back to the hall and then upstairs. There was a slight awkwardness outside the door to her rooms which were placed right next to his, and he wondered if he had been right to have her placed in the countess' rooms ahead of their marriage, whether it had seemed too forward. But surely it would have been odd to place her somewhere else, in some lesser guest room rather than the rooms which would have been hers by rights if they had married by the summer as had been the plan? Was he to treat her only as a guest, or as his future wife? He paused uncomfortably as she hovered by her door and bowed to her. "I will wish you good night, Lady Celia. I hope you have everything you need."

She gave a quick bob of a curtsey then slipped inside the half-opened door, through which he caught sight of her maid Aveline waiting for her. He hoped that the comfort of a familiar servant might at least grant her a restful night and perhaps make her more inclined to civility on the journey. He was already dreading the many hours of silence which would otherwise ensue. Perhaps he should pretend to be asleep in the carriage. It still seemed odd to him that a young woman who seemed to be able to converse with all and sundry was incapable of managing a simple conversation beyond social niceties with her future husband. There must be some way of breaking through her frosty exterior when it came to himself. She might not regard him as her first choice of husband, but the truth was that the marriage was already as good as done, so the only way forward was to make the best of it. And after all, what was there to complain about? Two wealthy titled people, in good health, with their whole lives before them, their families in full accord that the match was a good one. If they could not manage a decent marriage between them, what hope was there for anyone? Certainly, novels and poetry liked to claim that only a love match would do, but that, to his mind, showed a lack of commitment to making an effort in a marriage. It required each half of the couple to do their duty by the other, to show care and loyalty, so that affection might grow over time as their lives became entwined and shared, such as through children.

In bed, he lay thinking for a while. It was possible that over Christmas things would come to a head. Either time spent together with her family would warm her heart towards him and allow them to try again, or Lord Hyatt would supersede him as her chosen suitor, perhaps leaving him free by Twelfth Night. He would know where he stood, at least, would no longer have her uncertainty hanging over him, and would make the best of whichever way the cards fell.

※

AVELINE SNORED BESIDE HER, BUT CELIA WAS restless. She opened her jewellery box and looked again at the note from Lord Hyatt which she had purloined from her mother's writing bureau. *I look forward to our time together...* It was possible that in a few days' time, all being well, she would be able to break off the decades-long engagement to Lord Comerford and make a new choice of her own. The thought should have lulled her to sleep, but in truth it made her nervous. This betrothal had been in her destiny all her life. To be without it would feel like a strange new landscape, a changed path that was entirely her choice – and thus entirely her fault should she make a mistake in choosing. But Lord Hyatt was a man well thought of by the *ton*, a man full of charm and poise, ready to bestow those little courtesies to a lady that showed consideration, an ability apparently entirely lacking in Lord Comerford. Surely, he would be a better suitor? And it was clear that he was not disinterested in her – he had been attentive at all the events they had attended together, had made sure to introduce his sister to her and had been more than happy to join her and her family for Christmas all the way through to

Twelfth Night, had sent the little note to her mother with a parcel of Brown's biscuits for herself, since he could not send a note directly to her without impropriety. Yes, it would not be too difficult to suggest that a new proposal would be welcomed, to allow for a private conversation somewhere at Bellbrook Manor. And once that conversation had taken place, it would be a matter of moments to free herself from Lord Comerford and shape a new path to happiness for herself, leaving the Earl to live in this beautiful house all alone, with his cold manner and his disdainful face. Yes. She would soon be rid of him.

Finally, Celia was able to sleep.

3

HOLLY AND IVY

Celia awoke in the unfamiliar bedroom to a dull light, as though it were barely dawn. She could hear Aveline chattering as she opened the curtains, but it took her a few moments to understand what she was saying.

"... and so, we cannot set out until the fog clears, it may be many hours yet..."

"What?" Celia sat up, looking towards the window, where yesterday she had been able to see the trees in Green Park. There was nothing, only a thick whiteness tinged with yellow. She climbed out of the bed and made her way over to the window.

"Fog," repeated Aveline behind her.

"But..." began Celia, pressing her face against the cold glass. She had seen many foggy days in her life, but this was not like that. There was only whiteness outside, nothing else. She could not even see down onto the terrace or into the garden which she knew were just below her window. It was as though the world had entirely vanished, starting from her window ledge.

"It is so thick no-one dares go out for fear of getting lost," said Aveline, coming to stand by her side. "There are no carriages or carts out, not even deliveries. No-one has seen anything like it."

"What time is it?"

"Nine, already. There did not seem any need to wake you, since we cannot travel."

"Nine? And not yet cleared? When will we be able to leave?"

Aveline gave one of her shrugs. "Who knows? We must hope it clears by midday, or we cannot set out at all, we can hardly drive to Bellbrook in the dark."

Celia stared at her in horror. "But if we do not travel today... we will not be there for Christmas Day!"

Aveline raised her eyebrows and nodded. "It is very likely," she said.

Dread came over Celia. To be trapped here in this vast empty house with only the Earl for company, on Christmas Day? Were they to make merry, just the two of them? She had an awful glimpse of stiffly playing charades or Blind Man's Bluff, of another elaborate silent meal... oh, it would be awful. "It *must* clear," she muttered, staring into the fog, trying to make out anything at all, but behind her Aveline only tutted and continued laying out clothing so that Celia might dress, none of which looked like clothing intended for the outdoors at all.

"I will need my coat and muff," she said, trying to will the journey into existence purely by means of her choice of wardrobe, but Aveline only shook her head and laid out indoor kid slippers rather than boots, a shawl instead of a pelisse.

Reluctantly, Celia washed and dressed, waited for Aveline to do her hair, stared out of the window again into the nothingness outside and finally made her way downstairs, the clock already chiming ten.

"Shall I serve breakfast, my lady? asked the footman in the drawing room. "His lordship did not care for it this morning, but it can be ready in a moment."

Celia sank into a chair, glad of the warm fire blazing in the grate. "Yes," she said. "I suppose there is nothing better to do."

"Would you care for hot chocolate, coffee or tea, my lady?"

"Tea," said Celia despondently.

"Very good, my lady."

Tea was served, alongside a selection of ginger cake, pound cake and a rich plum cake. Celia tried a little of each, between repeated efforts to see out of the windows. The cakes were all good, but she found it hard to appreciate them, she was so distracted. "Where is Lord Comerford?" she asked at last.

"Speaking with the grooms, my lady," said the footman. "They are trying to ascertain if it is safe to drive."

It was not, Celia could see that for herself. She made her way to the front door and peered out, but aside from the tips of her shoes, she could see no further than the next step below the one on which she was standing. There was only the white-yellow nothingness of the fog. It was becoming clear that, short of a sudden change in the weather, travel would be out of the question for the day. They were stuck here. She turned her head from side to side, willing herself to see something, anything, but there was nothing to see. Or hear. The usual clip-clop of hooves and rumbling of wheels was silent, there were no voices or even footsteps. It was as though a ghost city had overlaid London, taking away its usual sights and sounds and leaving... nothing. She shivered, unnerved by the strangeness of it.

The echoing sound of boots striding along came close by and then a sudden shadow loomed out of the void. Celia stepped back with a yelp of fear, only to find herself face to face with a frowning Lord Comerford.

"What are you doing outside?"

"I wanted to see how bad the fog was."

"It is not safe. You could be lost within a few paces."

"*You* went out."

He took her arm and guided her back inside, his grip firm. "And it is not safe. One of the grooms nearly lost his way between the house and the stables. You must not go out alone, under any circumstances, until the fog clears."

She pulled her arm away from his grasp. "Will it clear today?"

"I hope so. But if it does not clear by midday, we will not be able to reach Bellbrook before dark. For now, we will return to the drawing room."

She would have liked to refuse, to go elsewhere, so that she did not have to spend more time in his company, but where else could she go? Walk about the empty house? Sulk in her rooms? Reluctantly she allowed herself to be guided back to the drawing room, where she poured herself another cup of tea while Lord Comerford called for coffee. The servants cleared the table of breakfast and the two, still without speaking, took up places by the fire and turned to reading; Lord Comerford perusing yesterday's papers, Celia opening up a novel. For over an hour there was no sound, save the crackling of the fire and pages being turned. Both occasionally glanced at the windows, but there was no change whatsoever to the whiteness beyond. Celia kept the novel open and occasionally turned a page, to keep up the pretence that she was reading, but inside her mind she was offering up a silent prayer. Let the fog clear, let there be enough time to reach Bellbrook Manor by nightfall – it was only a few hours' drive, surely a fast carriage and a few changes of horse could make good time? If they could leave by midday, they might just manage it, or perhaps even very early the next morning? She had never seen such thick fog, usually it cleared after an hour or so of sunshine, even in the winter. It must be possible. Please, let it be possible. She could not bear to be stuck here for another silent dinner and worse, Christmas Day itself to follow. It was unthinkable.

The clock ticked on and on, occasionally chiming in an infuriatingly obvious passing of the hours, making the journey to Bellbrook Manor ever more impossible. Lord Comerford would have to own steeds with wings and sadly, fine though his horses were, she had seen no feathers in sight. A leaden weight formed in her stomach.

At last, she lifted her chin. It was no good daydreaming of horses with wings and other such nonsense. The truth was, she was stuck here. And she was not about to have a silent Christmas Day, so she must do something about it. She forgot to turn the pages of her novel for over half an hour while she made a plan.

❄

Lady Celia suddenly closed her novel with a bang and Alexander looked up, startled.

"I am bored," she announced.

Alexander regarded her with surprise. It was unladylike for a woman to say such a thing and besides, she was not a child, she should be able to find something to pass the time without expecting to be entertained. It only served to cement his opinion of her as barely out of the schoolroom, a woman in name only. He was about to suggest, in tones of reproof, that she read something more improving than her current romantic novel from the extensive library at her disposal, when she rose to her feet and continued.

"It is clear we will be spending Christmas Day here," she announced. "So we had better behave accordingly."

Alexander raised his eyebrows at her. "What did you have in mind?"

She looked about. "To begin with, the house will need decorating."

"Decorating?" What did the girl mean?

She gestured out of the window, into the white nothingness. "We will need greenery – I saw a holly out there yesterday and there was also a juniper bush, I believe. I have red ribbons aplenty upstairs in my trunk. We can fold paper flowers for the tree." She was already halfway to the door.

"You intend to put up Christmas decorations?"

"Of course. It is Christmas after all, and if we are to be stuck here then we must make the best of it. Your garden will provide enough greenery."

He rose to his feet. "As I said before, you cannot go outside, you might get lost."

She laughed. "In that tiny garden? Not possible. We will be safe; there are walls to keep us close to the house. Call one of the servants to bring tools while I put on a coat, it looks freezing out there." She left the room at a brisk pace.

Left alone, Alexander sat in bewildered silence before letting out a resigned sigh. At least the decision was now made, they would be here for Christmas, there was no way around it. Decorating for just the two of them seemed absurd, but then again, the whole situation was absurd. Sitting pretending to read while counting down the hours to a doleful day was not a pleasant way of passing the time, he would rather be doing something more active, something with purpose to it. He pulled the bell and one of the footmen, Gabriel, promptly appeared.

"We require... tools," he began, still flustered by Lady Celia's sudden decision.

"Tools, Sir?"

"We are... to cut Christmas greenery for the house..." he stumbled. "So... a saw... some kind of pruning knife perhaps..."

"Yes, Sir," said Gabriel, with no hint of surprise at the request. "Should I fetch Harris the gardener?"

Alexander nodded in relief. "And my coat."

And so it was that within a quarter of an hour, Alexander was walking out into the silent freezing whiteness, with Lady Celia close behind him, followed by two footmen and the gardener Harris, carrying tools and a couple of pails in which to place the cuttings.

The whiteness around them was complete. He turned to Lady Celia and found that he could see her and the first footman, but not the one behind, nor Harris. "Stay close to me," he ordered. "The garden may be small, but I do not want to lose anyone in it and furthermore it would be very easy to fall over any obstacles." He looked at Lady Celia. Her eyes shone brightly, even as little puffs of warm air came from her lips, which were curved into a smile. He had rarely seen her happy or excited in his company, mostly she looked bored or stiffly polite. It was an improvement, he supposed, and certainly yesterday's newspaper had been dull enough for him to welcome her plans to do something else, however odd they seemed. Decorating for just two people seemed excessive, but custom was custom after all. "What did you want cut?"

"We will need a few armfuls of greenery and some of the holly, since it has red berries, it will lend a festive air. And a tree – or at least a large branch."

"A *tree*?"

"It is what Her Majesty has. It is a custom from her homeland, I believe. Mama always has one now, since she saw it at one of Her Majesty's Drawing Rooms a few years back."

He had never heard of such a thing, it sounded far too ostentatious for just the two of them, they were hardly royalty, but he nodded nonetheless. Let her have what she wanted. He was not about to argue with her over how much greenery she chose to bring into the house, empty as it was.

"I am not sure we have any decorations to go with the greenery," he said. "Our family spent all our Christmases at Comerford Castle, everything will be stored there."

"We will manage," she said cheerfully. "I have every kind of red ribbon you can imagine in my trunks; we will use those; new ribbons can always be bought."

They began tentatively, moving slowly about the garden as a tight group, clipping the odd branch here and there, making uncertain progress and awkwardly passing the small branches one to another until they grew more confident.

"We can use laurel, holly and rosemary," said Lady Celia, beginning to take larger sections than they had allowed themselves so far. She used the pruning knife with swift movements and piled the resulting branches into the pails held by the two footmen. Alexander watched her as she pulled trailing ivy stems away from where they clung to a wall, leaving her with several long strands of the dark green leaves. She also picked up a few pine cones, fallen into the garden from a tall pine on the other side of the wall.

"If you want an actual tree there is a small juniper here," he said. "We could cut it down and place it on a table, perhaps?"

She came closer so that she could see what he was pointing at and then nodded. "Yes, that would be very fine," she said. "It will smell good, too."

Between Alexander and Harris, they quickly sawed down the small tree.

"We should have mistletoe too," Lady Celia said, peering upwards into the disappearing tree trunks rising above them. "Especially since it is on your coat of arms. There was some up in that oak, but it was very high up. Perhaps we shall have to make do without it."

"Not at all, I will climb up for it," he declared, wondering whose mouth the words were coming out of. It was utter foolishness to climb an oak tree just for a little bunch of mistletoe. But oddly he had enjoyed the practicalities of cutting the greenery so far, with the servants assisting them. It had given them something to do other than sit in silence together waiting for the fog to clear. If climbing an oak tree was what it would take to keep themselves busy, so be it.

He had Harris fetch a rope, which he flung up around one of the main branches so that he might have an additional safe hold. His boots would not help his grip, so he removed them and climbed in his stockinged feet, having already removed his coat and jacket the better to use his arms. Lady Celia and an anxious gardener and footman stood below. He could barely see them once he had climbed several feet up, so thick was the fog, could only make out their shadowy forms below him. The cold, without his outer clothing and shoes, was bitter, but energising, he felt more alive than he had for days, perhaps weeks, of huddling indoors by stuffy fires dressed in too many layers to feel comfortable.

"Be careful, Lord Comerford," came Lady Celia's voice from below. There was an anxious note to it which made him grin. She could not know how much he had always enjoyed climbing the rigging at sea, how many happy hours he had spent as a boy in the crow's nest. Even as captain, he had sometimes climbed up there, for the peace the position brought, high above the bustle below, the calm horizon the only thing to see. It had been a place to think, a place of serenity and strategy to him, for despite some early seasickness he had never been afraid of heights.

He descended holding several bunches of the mistletoe which grew abundantly on the old oak. There were little white berries, shining wet against their dark green leaves.

"Pretty," she said, her smile widening. "I did not know you could climb a tree so easily."

"When you have been in the navy since you were fifteen climbing things is second nature," he replied, tugging his boots back on. It gave him some pleasure to surprise her. She did not know him as well as she thought she did. Gabriel helped him back into his jacket and he waved away his coat since they were headed back indoors.

Alexander and Harris dragged the juniper tree up the stairs and into the great room, where after some bustling about they managed to secure it in a large metal bucket of water and put it on top of one of the side tables.

"It is plain," Alexander said, looking it over when Harris had left. "What did you say about paper flowers?"

"If you have some sheets I will show you. Be so good as to ring for Aveline and for your cook."

"Mrs Poole? What for?"

"I have need of her help."

Mystified, he rang and asked for both Aveline and Mrs Poole to join them. Her new behaviour was interesting. It made him curious to see her implementing a plan of action, so unlike her previous self in the past months when she had seemed like every other girl, incessantly chattering about gowns and balls with apparently little else on her mind.

Aveline presented herself.

"Aveline, find all the ribbons I have and bring them here, and bring my sewing box. And my paintbox and brushes."

"Yes, my lady," curtseyed Aveline.

Mrs Poole, a sturdy woman with dark hair, appeared in a fresh white apron, looking flustered at being summoned upstairs. "Was something wrong with breakfast, Sir?"

"Not at all. Excellent cake and coffee as always. But Lady Celia has need of you."

Mrs Poole turned worried eyes to Lady Celia, who shook her head, smiling in reassurance.

"I have need of oranges and red apples, if you have them to spare. I am making Christmas decorations, for it is likely we will be celebrating Christmas here after all. And with that in mind, I suppose you will need to plan for the dinner tomorrow, for you must have thought your master would be gone for the festive season."

Alexander turned to Mrs Poole, concerned, but she seemed unperturbed. "I did think this morning it might be the case, my lady. But we've ample supplies. I'll be planning a menu for your approval, and I'll send Sarah up with the fruit for your decorations."

"How are the kittens?"

"Lapping milk as though they'd fed from a dish all their lives, my lady."

"Will you ask Sarah to bring them up as well so I can see them?"

"Certainly, my lady."

As Mrs Poole left, Aveline returned, with a vast collection of ribbons of every type, from yards of scarlet silk to finely woven crimson wool and stiff red linen.

"Now then," said Lady Celia, handing Alexander a paintbox and brushes. "If you paint the sheets of paper in different colours, we will leave them to dry and fold them later, I will show you how."

He had rarely done painting, that had been for his sister, so for a few moments he struggled with the task, gazing somewhat bemused at the paints and brushes. But she took pity on him, coming to stand close to him at the golden side table. He looked down at her dark curls, her cheeks still a vivid pink from the cold outdoors, even the tip of her nose turned rosy.

"You spread out the paper on the table, then wet the brush in this pot of water and rub it over the paint block you wish to use. Like so."

She deftly turned the sheet of paper into a light blue, then handed back the brushes when the maid Sarah came shyly into the room with a basket of oranges and red apples from the kitchen over one arm, a second basket containing the kittens on the other.

"They look a great deal better than they did yesterday," said Lady Celia, smiling. "A good night's sleep and food have done wonders for them."

The kittens huddled in the basket, peeping out, but it did not take long before they clambered out of their temporary home and onto the rich carpet, taking tottering steps of exploration under the sideboard and around Alexander's feet. He layered a pink onto the next sheet of paper and kept his feet very still, surprised when Lady Celia unexpectedly knelt on the floor close to his feet, surrounded by the greenery they had brought in and began setting about it with the pruning knife. She shaped the various branches into balls and wreaths, held in place by her ribbons and adding oranges and apples to the various shapes, the bright colours bringing her creations to life. She used the trailing ivy branches and her red ribbons to shape several wreaths and kissing boughs, the smell of wet earth and rosemary strong in the room, before moving on to creating a long garland for the hall stairs. The kittens, curious, patted the greenery where it lay on the floor and sprang back alarmed when it moved, the holly leaves prickling their curious noses. He could not help smiling at their surprised faces.

"I shall name you Holly and Ivy," Lady Celia declared. "For I found you at Christmas, so you should surely have names that evoke the season." She stroked one of the kittens and began to sing.

> *"The holly and the ivy*
> *when they are both full grown,*
> *of all the trees that are in the wood*
> *the holly bears the crown."*

Her voice was sweet and clear and Alexander realised that this vast room, which had always seemed to him the most empty and ghostly with his brother's absence, suddenly seemed full of life for the first time since he had come here, what with the decorations, Lady Celia's singing, the kittens exploring and Mrs Poole, Sarah and Gabriel coming and going about their various errands.

Lady Celia paused in her song, having spotted and laughingly rescued the other kitten, which had managed to half-climb the Christmas tree, then continued with the song's refrain.

> *"Oh, the rising of the sun*
> *and the running of the deer,*
> *the playing of the merry organ,*
> *sweet singing in the choir."*

He frowned down at her, confused by something she had just said, as the kittens took turns climbing over his shoes. "Found them? Are they not your pets?"

"They are now," she said. "I found them just before we arrived at Comerford House yesterday."

"In the street?"

She shook her head, smile gone. "A man was taking them in a sack to drown them. I could not let him. They will be my pets, or perhaps my father's stables will need them to catch mice. Either way, they were better off with me."

He nudged one of the kittens away as it tried to climb up his leg, its tiny claws prickling his skin. "That was kind of you."

"My father will roll his eyes when he sees them. He says I do nothing but collect strays. Kittens, dogs, lame horses, Bellbrook Manor is full of them. He says it is a good thing I am the daughter of a duke, or I would ruin him." She stroked one of the kittens, keeping its curious nose away from the holly leaves. "It is too hard to look away when you see a creature in need."

He looked down at her, the hem of her dress muddy and wet from the garden, gloves dirty from cutting the greenery, her ribbons now engaged in decorating his house instead of her frocks and bonnets. He had thought her frivolous, caring only for her own happiness, but he was now questioning the overly fashionable appearance she usually gave.

"Their coats are dirty," he observed, painting a sheet a vivid red which reminded him of her clothing. "Perhaps they should be washed, since they have no mother to lick them clean." He had wondered last night why a lady's pets should look so bedraggled, the reason was now clear.

She nodded. "You are right. In time they will learn to wash themselves, but the gutters of London are hard to remove by yourself if you are only a kitten."

"Gabriel, have a bucket of warm water and some rags brought to the hall," he ordered the footman. "The floor there is marble, it will not suffer from being wet," he added to her by way of explanation.

"Very good, Sir," agreed the footman, leaving the room.

Lady Celia stood up and came to stand beside Alexander, looking at the coloured sheets of paper. She picked up the first sheet, now already dry, and cut from it several shapes of flowers, some larger and some smaller, then fastened each smaller flower shape onto a large one using a pin, pulling at the petals so that the flower seemed to come to life, its petals curved upwards. Turning to the little juniper tree, she adjusted the pin so that it held the little flower onto one of the branches, tutting when the prickly branches caught her fingers.

"There," she said. "It is pretty, is it not?"

He nodded.

"Now it is your turn, you have seen how it was done," she said, passing him the scissors.

He set about the task, making several more flowers, none of which matched hers for neatness, but he was not deterred and after half an hour had passed, he laid down the scissors. "There."

"Very pretty," said Lady Celia, clapping her hands at the sight of it and an absurd little rush of pride went through Alexander at his patchy handiwork, standing back to look at the green branches now holding brightly coloured flowers. "You have done a fine job of it. So now I shall recreate your family's coat of arms," she said, taking up the mistletoe bunches and holding up some of her red ribbons. She shaped the greenery into two kissing boughs, one of which she handed to Gabriel the footman who perched on a ladder to add it to the bottom of the central chandelier.

"The other is for the hall," she said.

He followed her carrying the stepladder, held it as she attached the long garland to the stairs, then climbed up to fasten the second mistletoe kissing bough, with its red silk ribbons, to the chandelier in the hall. The kittens had followed them and were now fighting one another, rolling about the floor with no care for whose feet they might bump into.

"Well," Lady Celia said, brushing some dirt off her gloves and looking up at the mistletoe and its dangling crimson velvet ribbons with satisfaction. "At least the house looks festive."

Alexander nodded. It did look better, as though someone actually lived here. And the exercise and effort had done him good, his spirits were higher. Of course there were still just the two of them and it would be a sad little Christmas, but action was better than wallowing in misery, so he gestured to the steaming bucket of water that the footman had brought up, keen to keep the two of them occupied for as long as possible in what seemed to be turning out as a friendly afternoon and evening. "Should we wash

Holly and Ivy now?" Her gloves would get wet, he suddenly realised, so he amended the suggestion. "I shall wash them, then you can dry them."

They knelt either side of the bucket and he washed first Holly and then Ivy, before passing them over to be dried. They both fought their fate, scratching and hissing, clawing desperately as they tried to escape the bucket and the water, emerging bedraggled and sodden, dripping water everywhere until they were safely wrapped up in clean rags.

"You may take the water now," said Alexander to Gabriel, who nodded. "Now," he said, addressing Lady Celia, "Let us go to the drawing room, there should be a fire so that we can warm them after their ordeal."

She followed him holding the two little bundles, handing him one as they settled down on opposite sofas by the fire. She unwrapped her kitten and rubbed it ferociously, till all its fur stood on end.

"I am not even sure they are kittens," she said giggling at the sight of first Holly and then Ivy as they staggered about the floor, looking dazed, their fur still spiky, though visibly cleaner. "They look more like hedgehogs. Perhaps they should eat now."

He rang for tea and Mrs Poole sent up hot tea with little cheese muffins and ginger biscuits, as well as scraps of ham and a saucer of milk for the kittens, who ate greedily, pushing one another away in their eagerness. Satiated, they scrambled up Alexander's leg to curl up on his lap and sleep, exhausted by their morning of new experiences. He looked down at them in surprise at being accepted as a source of comfort.

Lady Celia watched him gently stroke them, their fur slowly coming back to a softer state as it dried under his fingers with the aid of the nearby fire. "Did you have a cat as a child?" she asked.

"A tabby named Sukey," he said, smiling at the memory. "An excellent ratter, which would have been good, except that she believed it her task in life to nourish me as though I were her kitten, so I would wake to find dead rats on my bed and my nanny shrieking. They tried to keep her from the nursery, but I would leave the door ajar for her when everyone else had gone to bed. Not that I much liked the rats, but she saw it as her duty to care for me, and I could not help feeling grateful for her attentions. She was a kindly cat."

She nodded. "She must have thought your cook insufficient in her abilities," she said. "If you had a cat here it would have no need to bring you rats." She smiled. "Now, what shall we do for guests?" she added.

"Guests?" he said, startled. "What do you mean, guests?"

"We can hardly celebrate just the two of us," she said. "We shall need guests, and Mrs Poole will need to know how many we intend to host tomorrow so that she can cook accordingly, though goodness knows last night we could have been a tableful, and she would have fed us all well. Who can we invite that lives close enough to walk to us?"

He stared at her. He had been imagining just the two of them and how silent and awkward it would be. This morning's exertions had made him more confident that they would be at least able to hold a conversation, but he had still expected a subdued day. She, however, seemed to be envisioning an entirely different affair.

"My cousin Jonathan could come," she said, apparently thinking out loud. "He was going to travel today to a friend's house for the Christmas season, but he must be stuck just as we are and he lives only a short distance away, he has a set in Albany. Who will you invite? Who would you have visited over the season, had you stayed in London?"

His mind was slow under her questioning. "I... have an elderly aunt," he began.

"Excellent, let us send to invite her at once. I will write a note for Jonathan and send it with one of your footmen. Who else?"

"Aunt Mary has a companion, a Miss Smith, but..."

"We can hardly leave the poor girl alone on Christmas Day. Send for her. Are there other people you would wish to see?"

"I would have visited two captains of my acquaintance during the festivities, but they are naval men through and through, hardly fit company for the daughter of duke."

She made a face. "Invite them. I promise I shall not be shocked by rough manners."

"Captain Pemberton has a young daughter, he may have taken her to visit her mother's family, as he is a widower."

"Send a footman to ask them. If they are alone for Christmas, they would be better in company, surely."

It was a kind thought. He offered a smile. "I will find out."

"Anyone else?"

"No. I will visit Nanny – Mrs Taylor – in my own time."

"Who is Mrs Taylor?"

"She was my nanny as a child, I visit her from time to time, she is an old woman now."

"She lives alone?"

"Yes, but she has been well provided for."

"Send for her. She must be lonely at Christmas."

"She is... was... a servant," he managed, thrown by the request. "You might not wish to..."

She tilted her head at him. "I think I can bear one evening in company with a servant and some navy men."

Her determined expression made him laugh. She had never made him laugh before. "Very well then. We shall be a motley crew, I warn you."

"I promise I shall not be overcome and need my smelling salts. We shall be nine altogether then, if everyone comes. Send the footmen to invite them. I will let Mrs Poole know she must plan for a real tableful. Your small dining room will suffice, but we could play games in the great room afterwards."

"Games?"

"We should make merry, even if we are few in number," she said. "Christmas comes but once a year."

"Indeed."

He busied himself with pulling the bell, instructing Gabriel and sending several footmen out into the cold whiteness to the various houses indicated by himself and Lady Celia, each carrying a written note, then settled himself back down, the kittens swiftly returning to their roost on his knees.

She was looking at him intently. "You do not mind that I am commandeering your household?"

He had been surprised by it, but... he shook his head. "I am glad that some use will be made of it. I do not like the emptiness of it at present."

"And you are glad it will not just be the two of us, staring at one another over a goose and plum pudding?"

His mouth twisted into a smile. "That too."

She laughed. "On that we are agreed, at least."

There was a moment's silence between them. After her

threat to break off the marriage, these last few hours had changed his opinion of her more than he would have thought possible. He had seen another side to her – impulsive, yes, but with a kindly nature and intent behind her actions. Independent, certainly, she had all but taken over as mistress of his household, not asking permission before she asked his servants to carry out her wishes. But not selfish. She had considered who, in their circle of acquaintance, might be lonely. She had saved the kittens. He had seen her as shallow, only interested in her clothes and gossip, yet there was still a smudge of mud on her cheek and a small tear in the hem of her dress, her ribbons were now strewn about his house in an effort to soften its stiff formality for the festive season. She would be spending Christmas Day with naval men and a servant, as well as a lady's companion, none of them the kind of society with whom she would have been used to spending time with, yet she had pressed for them to be summoned.

"I did not expect a grown man to climb a tree with such ease," she said suddenly. "Did you learn that in the navy?"

He nodded.

"How old were you when you joined?"

"Fifteen at my first posting, under the command of Captain Rose, you will meet him tomorrow if he accepts the invitation." He had almost said "our" invitation, which he supposed it was, but that sounded too much as though they were a married couple, inviting people to events held in their home.

"Were you happy?"

She had never shown any interest in his life. Why the sudden change? He was about to shrug and say he had been content enough, have done with the question. But something about her gaze made him pause, then give a more detailed reply. "It was hard at first for a gently-bred boy, to be without my family – without my mother especially – and under the command of a man other than my father. The crew teased me, as they do all new boys, and I was afraid they would prove to be bullies, that my life on board would be a misery, but they were fair men, after a few incidents they left me be and proved to be good hearted."

"What did they do to you?"

"Oh the usual foolishness – hiding my unform in the cook's oven, tying me to the mast and making me sing a sea-shanty as loud as I might, complete with every kind of vulgar language, showing me to a hammock when I had never been in one before – I fell out the other side of course, I had no idea how one should get into it. They were most amused at my being sea-sick for the first few days."

"They sound unkind."

There was pity in her voice and again it surprised him that she should be troubled what had happened to him many years ago, when she had made it clear she did not care for him. "They did it to all the new recruits, it was part of making you one of the crew, I did not hold it against them. I think it was done in part to see your character – whether you would weep or rail or take it in good humour."

"What did you do?"

"I did my best to take it in good humour, though I am sure I must have wept once or twice, when no-one was looking, for I thought such treatment might persist. But it did not. Once we were well at sea there was no time for such things, there was first work to be done and later fighting. And Captain Rose was a good man, he allowed only what could reasonably be borne by a young man, without breaking his spirit."

"Did you fight?"

"At Trafalgar, when I was nineteen and a midshipman. As well as other battles, of course, before and after."

"Were you frightened?"

"Only a fool would not be frightened in battle," he said, though not sharply. "I was made lieutenant the year after Trafalgar and took command of my first ship when I was twenty-six."

She nodded. "I remember."

He wondered what she had been told and when, whether her family had rejoiced in his promotion, been proud of him as a future family member, whether she too had felt pride for her absent intended or only irritation at being reminded constantly of his existence.

"That was only two years ago," she said.

"Yes. Then my brother... I was sent for."

She nodded silently, then cleared her throat. "I am sorry for your loss. Were you close?"

She had never offered her condolences. "We were good friends."

"I am sorry," she repeated.

He nodded.

She looked as though she might be about to say something else but then waved her hand at the room with a small laugh, changing the topic of conversation away from such personal matters. "All this must seem overly grand after you have been on a ship all these years."

He nodded.

"Which things are most different?"

"Probably the smells."

"The smells?"

"Most of the smells here are good smells. Beeswax candles instead of tallow. Women's perfume rather than the stink of unwashed men and their tobacco. The food –

why, Mrs Poole would not consider what we ate aboard fit for the servants' table, let alone sending it up to the dining room." He recalled the joy of a good strong wind, speeding the ship across the waves. "I will say the air was a good deal fresher at sea than it is in most of London's streets."

Gabriel appeared in the doorway. "Captain Rose sends his regards, Sir, and says he will be glad to join you tomorrow, as does Captain Pemberton and his daughter Miss Pemberton."

"Excellent," said Alexander, feeling his spirits rise at the thought of seeing his old friend and his mentor. He smiled at Lady Celia, and she nodded her head, no doubt pleased that her plan was coming together.

The day came to a close with all their guests having willingly accepted their invitations, and Mrs Poole having been informed. She and the kitchen maids were busy with the many dishes she had planned, while the other servants were instructed to have ready all of the large rooms for entertainment – the dining room, the great room and the palm room as a drawing room for the day.

"We might as well use the spaces," said Alexander. "They were meant for entertaining, after all."

❄

FIRES WERE STARTED IN EACH ROOM TO TAKE THE CHILL off them for the next day, flower arrangements, side tables, cushions and other comforts moved into the palm room. Lord Comerford and Celia inspected each room, nodding at the arrangements.

"Please tell Mrs Poole I will take a tray in my room, some soup and bread and butter will be ample, for tomorrow we shall be feasting, and I am sure she has much to do tonight," said Celia.

Lord Comerford nodded. "I will do the same," he said. "It will give me time to look out a little gift for Miss Pemberton at least, I believe my mother had some pretty jewellery that might be suitable."

Celia stood. "I am sure that will be kindly received," she said. "I shall bid you goodnight, Lord Comerford."

He stood at once and accompanied her to the door, the two kittens earnestly following in his footsteps. He looked down at them, his face uncertain.

Celia could not help a giggle escaping. "I am afraid my kittens have become yours, Lord Comerford," she managed. "They seem to think you their master. Or mother, one or the other."

He did not laugh, only looked grave, as though he had been handed a serious responsibility. "They may sleep in my room, if you think it will make them feel safe,' he said at last.

She had not expected him to say any such thing, had thought he would laugh and hand them to her, or summon a servant to take them away. She looked down at their wide eyes, their gazes fixed on his face and could not help feeling tenderness at the idea of Lord Comerford carefully getting into bed without disturbing the sleeping kittens on his covers. "If you are willing, I am sure they would prefer that above all things, it will make them feel safe," she said.

He nodded, still serious, then walked up the stairs just behind her. When they reached their respective bedroom doors the kittens hesitated, looking at Celia and Lord Comerford, then obediently followed him into his rooms, one small ball of fluff behind the other while Celia stifled another giggle at the sight of them.

"What are you laughing at?" asked Aveline, who was laying out a red silk dress with a swansdown trim for the next day. "I thought you would be sulking at the idea of another day spent alone with Lord Comerford – and Christmas Day, at that."

Celia sat on the bed and undid her shoe ribbons. "It is not how I expected to be passing Christmas," she said slowly. "I cannot even send a letter to Mama and Papa; I can only hope word reaches them of how the fog has descended so that they do not fret for me. But we have made the best of it – we have guests and decorations, no doubt Mrs Poole will make a good meal – so we must be thankful, I suppose." She settled herself in the little parlour before a plate of hot beef stew with fresh bread and good butter laid alongside it. There was also cold water and two little orange puffs. It was all delicious and now she was sorry not to have eaten in the dining room. She had enjoyed hearing something of Lord Comerford's time at sea and to her surprise found she had more questions for him.

"Thankful not to spend the day facing him in silence all day, at any rate," sniffed Aveline.

Celia giggled. "You think him too serious, and so did I," she said. "But you will not believe it – he is in his bedroom now with the kittens, who will be sleeping on his bed. I did not expect him to allow it at all, but he seemed to think it his duty to care for them."

"Wait till they wake him at four o clock of the morning wanting to be fed," said Aveline. "Watch how quickly he throws them out into the corridor."

"Perhaps," said Celia. "But at any rate, he tried to care for them, and that is worth something. And he has been – well, not good humoured exactly, but he went along with all my plans for Christmas Day willingly, he was generous enough to think of the men he served with and his old nanny."

"I'll believe he is good humoured when I see him play charades and make a fool of himself, like all of your cousins like to do at Christmas," said Aveline, gathering up the empty tray of dinner which Celia had made her way through. "Shall I sleep in here again tonight, my lady?"

Celia shook her head. I will do well enough alone tonight, thank you Aveline," she said. Lord Comerford had behaved in a gentlemanly manner last night; there was no reason to suppose that would change.

Lying in bed, Celia puzzled her way through her feelings. Lord Comerford had been unexpectedly kind. He had gone along with her plans; he had not dismissed them as absurd or unnecessary. He had even set to and made inexpert paper flowers under her instruction, to make the Christmas tree pretty at her request. She had been touched by his inviting his nanny and impressed by his ability to climb the great oak. In the dark she smiled at the memory of the kittens and how they had been determined to follow him about as though he were their mother. She wished she had seen some of these sides of his character before telling him she did not wish to marry him; they might have given her pause for thought. But...

But he had also told her that she was a child for believing their engagement anything but a practical arrangement for a deformed woman and a poor second son, and that still stung, both the truth of it and the cold voice in which he had told her. One day of helpfulness and kindness could not erase that memory.

4

A MISTLETOE KISS

In the morning Alexander stood by the front door, looking out. The fog had lifted somewhat, only to be replaced by at least two feet of snow which had fallen overnight, making the world even whiter than it had been when cloaked in fog. The gardener and grooms had been out at first light, trying to clear pathways, but it was an uphill battle. It was Christmas Day, but how was it to proceed? Always someone else had managed the activities for the day. To start with, there should be a visit to church, but looking out he could not imagine that many people would be able to manage even that sacred duty. Carriages would struggle; horses might slip on icy patches and some roads would not even have been cleared. He thought he might have to lead prayers for the household staff, a daunting idea.

"Merry Christmas!"

He turned. Lady Celia was dressed for going out, in a warm cherry red pelisse over her wool dress, a cloak wrapped about her, a brown fur muff dangling from one gloved hand. Her face was bright with excitement, bringing a smile to his lips. He bowed. "Good morning. Merry Christmas to you also."

"Whatever is that?"

He looked down at the large tree trunk lying on the front steps, still covered in snow. "Harris found a Yule Log to complete your decorations. He knew of a dead tree in the park and brought it over this morning with one of the grooms. It will need drying off but no doubt it will take well enough once it is on a fire. We can have it in the great room, if you wish."

She nodded. "That was good of him. Are you ready for church?"

"Church? The carriage cannot travel safely."

"We can walk."

"To where?"

"The Grosvenor Chapel is not far," she said. "Come."

It was a smallish church close by, not a grand place like St George's in Hanover Square or Trinity Chapel which would have been more suited to their rank on Christmas Day. He hesitated, about to object that she would get cold and wet on the icy streets, but she was already halfway down the front steps, the footman holding out his greatcoat and hat. He had little choice but to take both and hurry after her, one foot almost slipping from under him as he made his way down the steps. She was already in the little road that would lead them to the chapel, walking with her feet as flat as possible, so as to avoid slipping, but as he caught up with her and she turned her head towards him one foot went out from under her, and she gave a little gasp. Swiftly he caught her arm, steadying her, and she clung to him.

"Thank you. It is even more icy than I expected."

"Perhaps we should walk arm in arm," he said. He half

expected her to refuse, but she only nodded and adjusted her hold on his arm, bringing her body closer to his. The warmth of her came through his coat, an unexpected intimacy.

They walked in silence along the little side street which had been at least partly cleared by various residents, sidestepping drifts of snow and negotiating slippery patches of ice. There were not many people outdoors, but a few passers-by nodded or called out "Merry Christmas!" to which they both responded in kind.

"It is so quiet," she said, as they reached the main road. There were only two carts far away and a horse and rider passing, nothing like the usual bustle and noise. Here all seemed silent, so that they did not need to pause for carriages or riders.

"A faithful congregation indeed to brave this weather," exclaimed a beaming vicar when he saw them approaching the door of the chapel. "Do I know you, Sir?"

"Lord Comerford," responded Alexander. "And Lady Celia Follett." He hesitated but then added, "my betrothed." He did not look at her face to see what she thought of him saying so, but he did not wish the vicar to think ill of her appearing arm in arm with a gentleman to whom she was not married.

"From Comerford House, of course, Sir, I am glad to welcome you and Lady Celia amongst my regular parishioners. Please be seated."

There were not many people, the chapel was only a third full, but there were smiles and nods of welcome and they were shown to the front pew where they sat down, awaiting the morning's sermon. Alexander missed the warmth of Lady Celia holding his arm, but as he turned his head to look at her she looked back at him and smiled.

"We got here after all," she said, "brave adventurers that we are."

He was about to reply to her jest, but the vicar cleared his throat, and Alexander turned his attention to the pulpit.

They stood to sing the hymn *Joy to the World*, the words issuing in little clouds of warm breath in the cold chapel air.

> *"Joyful, joyful we adore Thee*
> *God of glory, Lord of love*
> *And hearts unfold like flowers before Thee*
> *Opening to the sun above."*

Once again, Alexander admired Lady Celia's pretty voice. His was nothing in particular, but hers rose above the rest as though she were truly filled with joy, and it gave him pleasure to hear it. He would have liked the hymn to have gone on longer, but they all settled down for the vicar to begin his sermon, a heartfelt if lengthy affair on a cold morning.

"...and so in conclusion I ask each of you today to go forth into the world in gladness and good cheer, with your hearts filled with love, for today is the day when we celebrate the coming of our Lord into this world. Let us reach out to one another with kindness and with that love which is now within us and share it with those in our lives. Let us do good where we can and honour this joyful day through our actions in the world, just as our Saviour did. It remains for me only to wish you all a very Merry Christmas. May His blessings be upon you. Amen."

"Amen," returned the congregation.

There was much in the way of nodding and smiling, shaking of hands and salutations of "Merry Christmas!" amongst those present before Celia was able to once again take Lord Comerford's arm and leave the chapel. There was a comfort to being so close to him, a firmness in the way he tucked her arm against him that made her feel safe in his care.

"You did not mind that I told the vicar we were betrothed?" he said as they crossed the street. "I thought it best, for propriety. I did not mean to make you uncomfortable."

"Not at all," she said. She had in fact thought him wise to do so, she would not have wanted the vicar or any of his congregation to pay too much attention to the two of them, nor question their relationship. And in truth, they were still engaged to be married, he had not deceived anyone, excepting that he knew her intentions lay elsewhere. She wondered whether he was sorry that she intended to find another suitor, or whether it did not bother him one way or another. Was he secretly hurt, had he developed any feelings for her at all, or was she merely a convenience to him, a ready-made bride with good connections and a fortune to bring to his unexpected title and estate? She wondered if she should ask him, be bold enough to risk her feelings being hurt again if he were to say that no, he did not care if she married someone else. There was a chance, a small one, that he might say something else; that he did in fact care for her, that her decision to look elsewhere had cut him deeply and his current kindness to her was only a façade for a broken heart. She opened her mouth, but then closed it again, unsure what she wanted to hear. She did not want to be hurt again, but if he were suddenly to declare feelings for her, did she want to hear them? Would it make her decision harder, force her to reconsider when she had already arranged for Lord Hyatt to attend her at Bellbrook Manor – should she ever make it there through the fog and snow?

Her mind, so certain before yesterday, was now confused and so she walked in silence through the snow, the warmth and comfort of Lord Comerford's body pressed close beside her doing nothing to help her thoughts settle down. She was glad when they made it back to Comerford House that she could let go of him and have Aveline fuss over her, insisting on a change of dress now that her hem was soaked. By the time she had changed her dress and had her hair tidied, she was calmer. Perhaps Lord Comerford was showing more agreeable aspects of his character, but that did not mean he had professed love for her, nor even much interest at all. No, she would continue with her plan but meanwhile there was no harm in the two of them being civil or indeed even friendly.

A small midday meal was sent up to them of hot pease soup with cheese rolls and shortbread with tea, to warm themselves after their outing and stave off any hunger pangs till the dinner to come.

"I shall dress for our guests," Celia said when they had finished.

In her room, she allowed Aveline to dress her in one of her finest dresses.

"You are very quiet, my lady," observed Aveline. "Are you well?"

"Nervous," confessed Celia.

"About what?"

"I must play hostess; I have never done so before. And most of the people attending will be his friends and family, I have only Jonathan."

"I am sure they will be pleasant enough," said Aveline, "Though they are not the sort of people you would usually attend a dinner with," she added.

"Oh, I don't mind that," said Celia. What was really

bothering her was the pretence that she and Lord Comerford must now maintain, that they were happily betrothed and to be married in a few short months. It was a falsehood, not only for today but for that day in the future when those guests who had been here today would hear that it had been a lie, would be surprised – and shocked – to hear that she was not, after all, to marry Lord Comerford. Worse, they would know it was she who had changed her mind, since she would then go on to marry Lord Hyatt or another, while Lord Comerford, no doubt, would take longer to find a new bride. Would they think her shallow, a heartbreaker, a woman without loyalty? Or would they whisper about Lord Comerford and think him lacking, a man who could not be loved? Either way it would be unfair. She was no flighty woman, yet it was not kind to say that there was anything wrong with Lord Comerford – only that they were wrong for one another, but of course the *ton* would jump to conclusions, as it always did. But there was nothing for it. Things were as they were and all she could do now was care for their guests as best as she could and play mistress of Comerford House.

❄

ALEXANDER MADE HIS WAY DOWNSTAIRS, DRESSED IN his finest, a midnight blue suit offset with his immaculately tied white stock and stockings, the silver buckles of his shoes shining. He felt stiff, overdressed, but it was Christmas Day after all and his valet had made approving noises, which was all he could hope for.

"Lord Comerford."

He turned and saw Lady Celia standing at the top of the stairs. Perfection. It was the word that came to him without thinking. Her dark curls were set all about with tiny shining red beads, meant to emulate holly berries, while her dress was red silk. As she descended to him her every movement and breath made the white swansdown trim of her dress tremble. He had to swallow. She was truly lovely. And he had lost her. She was all but promised to another. It was only chance that she was still here in his house, that she would, tonight, act as the mistress of Comerford House, as his bride-to-be.

"Will I do?" she asked, as she reached him.

"Very festive," he answered. He wanted to say more, to express something of what he was feeling, but where to begin? It was hardly the moment to grow lyrical about her beauty when he had never mentioned her looks before. But still, he should say something. "Your dress," he began, but was interrupted by a footman, who announced,

"Lord Jonathan Montrose."

A tall young man with rosy cheeks and a shock of unruly reddish hair stood in the doorway, shaking off the snow from his boots.

"Jonathan! I am glad to see you," said Lady Celia, advancing with her hands held out.

"See you got stuck in town as I did," said the young man cheerfully. "Rum thing, that fog, never seen anything like it. Good thing you were safe here and not mid-road at some dreadful inn."

"Yes, I was lucky to escape that fate," said Lady Celia. "Lord Comerford, may I introduce my cousin, Lord Jonathan Montrose? He has a set in Albany and is stuck in London just as we are. Jonathan, this is Lord Comerford."

"Lord Comerford. Good to meet you. Husband-to-be to this young lady, eh? Looking forward to you joining the family. Heard a lot about you. Navy, wasn't it? Before –" Lord Jonathan waved his hand about them, "– all this."

Alexander nodded. "Indeed. It is a pleasure to meet you, Lord Jonathan. You are very welcome. Be seated, we have mulled wine to warm you after your cold walk here."

"Oh, I don't know. Brushes off the cobwebs, a good walk, I enjoyed it. But I'll take a cup, thank you."

"Lady Greenland and Miss Smith," announced the footman.

"Aunt Mary, welcome. I hope you have not caught a chill while reaching us," said Alexander, making his way to the older woman who had just entered, a tall young woman standing just behind her. "Miss Smith? You are welcome."

"Thank you for asking me," murmured the young woman, dropping an awkward curtsey and blushing.

"Not at all, the more the merrier and I am glad to meet you."

"Yes, yes, never mind all of this fuss," said Lady Greenland. "Jane, take my coat and bonnet, I shan't want them for now."

Miss Smith hastened to take the articles but Gabriel the footman stepped in, making sure to gather up all items from the guests and take them away, releasing Miss Smith from her minding duties.

"Aunt Mary, may I present Lady Celia Follett? Lady Celia, this is my aunt, Lady Greenland."

Lady Celia swept a curtsey. "Lady Greenland."

"Ah, you are the girl Alexander is to marry. Let me look at you." Alexander braced himself but a swift glance up and down seemed to satisfy her. "Very pretty," she said appreciatively. "And a duke's daughter. A good thing. He'll need a fine mistress for Comerford Castle and this house, hardly what he's been used to on a ship these past ten years and more. A lady will bring some delicacy to his dealings. Now show me to a fire before my feet are quite turned to ice."

Aunt Mary had barely been settled with Miss Smith at her side when there was a flurry of new arrivals.

"Captain Rose, Captain Pemberton and Miss Pemberton, and Mrs Taylor," announced the footman.

An older weatherbeaten man was introduced to all as Captain Rose and Alexander took real comfort in his old master being amongst the party, almost as though his being there would steady proceedings by means of his hand on the tiller. Only slightly older than Lord Comerford was Captain Pemberton, a good friend who had climbed the ranks of the navy beside him, accompanied by his dark-haired daughter of only twelve years, who ducked her head when spoken to, shy at attending a party filled with people she did not know in such a grand house. And behind them came an old woman, wearing a good black dress and a little pewter brooch, though the shine on the cloth indicated she had worn the same dress many times. Alexander stepped forwards, anxious that she be treated well and not be made to feel an encumbrance nor looked down upon when the rest of the party realised she had been a servant but found that Lady Celia was already holding the old woman's hand.

"Come into the drawing room, Mrs Taylor, we have mulled wine waiting to warm everyone after being out in the cold."

"It is very good of you, my lady. I am grateful to you for thinking of me."

"Not at all, we are glad to have you with us, Christmas Day is nothing without people to share it with. I know Lord Comerford was eager to see you, he said he would have visited you himself another day, but it seemed a shame that you should be alone on Christmas Day. We should have been all alone ourselves had you not all been kind enough to join us."

"Ah, my family are mostly gone, my lady, there's only me and my grandson, but he is in the navy as Lord Comerford was, and there is no shore leave this season for him."

Mrs Taylor gave humble curtseys to all those present, murmuring that she did not wish to be a trouble to anyone, but she was warmly welcomed, and Lady Celia took up a seat beside her and pressed the hot spiced wine into her hand.

"I cannot have you catching a chill, Mrs Taylor."

Now that they had all gathered it was not long before the clock chimed four and dinner was announced. Alexander led the way upstairs, into the large dining room, which brought many expressions of admiration from the guests, and in short order they were all seated.

Mrs Poole had outdone herself. There was a vermicelli soup, which, having been served to all, was removed and replaced by a fat goose, while the rest of the table groaned under the weight of roast beef, capons with stuffing, a fine sturgeon, lamb's fry and tails, potted larks, potatoes, buttered carrots, Brussels sprouts, roasted squash, mushrooms, artichoke bottoms and stewed celery. Those with a sweet tooth were well served with striped China oranges, custards, jellies served alongside Jargonelle pears cooked in sweet spices and red wine, so that they had taken on a bold pink colour, while retaining their pale-yellow interiors when cut open. Trifle and syllabub were light and creamy offerings to offset the richer taste of mince pies. Wines were poured, Alexander carved the goose, and the party, after a little awkwardness due to being strangers to one another, slowly began to enjoy themselves, passing dishes to one another and commenting on the excellence of the food.

"I have never seen such oranges," marvelled Miss Pemberton, staring at the pyramid of fruits.

"I used to beg our cook at home to make China oranges," said Lady Celia. "You cut lids off the oranges, then scoop out the flesh and make it into a fruit jelly. A second milk jelly is made, then you pour them in layer by layer, allowing each to set. When they are all set, you cut them into quarters so that you can see the orange and white layers, they are so pretty and taste very good. Try one."

The meal was a very different one from Alexander's stiff and silent first dinner with Lady Celia. Although not all the guests knew one another, all were glad to have been invited, for a Christmas Day spent holed up in their homes without festivities would have been a dismal day indeed. Aunt Mary had already met Mrs Taylor, of course, from old days at Comerford Castle, but despite Mrs Taylor being a servant, Aunt Mary showed festive graciousness at being joined at the table by her, and the two began to reminisce about Comerford Castle, sharing tales of the family and its servants. Miss Pemberton sat wide-eyed, being unaccustomed to dinner parties, while Miss Smith, set free from her usual attentions to Aunt Mary, engaged in conversation with Captain Pemberton, asking questions about his service in the Navy and the loss of his late wife. Alexander and Captain Rose were deep in conversation, but Gabriel and the other footmen ensured the dishes kept moving about the large table, so that all were thoroughly well fed.

"Now then, said Alexander, after exchanging a nod with Gabriel. "I believe it is time for the Christmas pudding."

"Sir, you go too far!" cried Captain Pemberton. "We are all as stuffed as that excellent goose, wherever shall we find space to put a pudding?"

Alexander laughed. "You shall have to find a place, Captain, for here it comes."

A large pudding was carried in, topped with a sprig of holly leaves and berries. Alexander doused it with brandy and then ceremoniously set it alight, the flickering blue flames being given a round of applause at its prettiness, before it was sliced up by the footmen and distributed to all along with a hot rich custard, and for a few moments at least there was the silence that comes from the enjoyment of good food.

"Your cook is a marvel," announced Aunt Mary. "You must give me the receipt when you are lady of the house," she added to Lady Celia. "Men know nothing of these things, but a fine cook is a jewel to be treasured. My cook ignores the finer touches; she is a good plain cook and that is all that can be said of her. But she is loyal, there's that at least, for the fine ones are always being poached from under your nose by ladies who do not deserve the name. Make sure to pay her well."

"I hope you will spend many more Christmases at Comerford House," said Lady Celia smiling. "It is a time for family, after all."

Alexander caught her remark. Did she mean it as a simple thought, that Christmas was for family and that he, as Aunt Mary's nephew, would do well to invite her each year, regardless of who his bride might eventually be? Or had she softened, was she imagining that she might marry him after all, and that the two of them would make a habit of inviting friends and family, as they had done today, to include Aunt Mary? He was unsure. For a moment he imagined that all was well between them, that their marriage would go ahead as planned, and he looked about the table with satisfaction at the happy, well-fed faces of family and friends. Lady Celia was talking animatedly with Miss Pemberton, in whom she seemed to have taken a particular interest. She looked beautiful, for her crimson dress was suited to the festive season and, sat in the position of hostess at the other end of the table from him, she looked every inch the mistress of Comerford House, setting her guests at ease, enjoying Mrs Poole's excellent fare and even, when she caught his eye, offering him a warm smile. What would it be like, to be married to her? After the past two months when he had imagined her shallow and foolish, in a matter of only two days she had shown him a kindly and spirited side, a practical nature which would suit him well as a wife. But if she had already made up her mind to find another suitor, he did not wish to force her to honour their contract, since clearly there was something in his own character she found unsuited to her temperament. What his fault was in her eyes, he was unsure, though she had suggested he was cold towards her, had not paid her enough attention of the kind that a man might when courting. He had thought her vain, but now he wondered if he had been too reserved, too cool. He had enjoyed her company these past two days, the warmth of her smiles. What would it be like, after the guests had gone this evening, to join her in the bedchamber and have the pleasure of undressing her, to lie with her and feel her bare skin against his? The idea was arousing.

"Perhaps, Lord Comerford, it is time for us to leave the table?" suggested Lady Celia, cutting into his thoughts.

"Of course," he replied, and she rose, all the guests following her lead.

They moved into the great room, where a wassail bowl stood ready to be served, filled with a warmed mixture of beer, sherry, spices and sugar, surrounded by little cups to pour it into. Alexander nodded to Gabriel, who filled each little cup and passed them around the gathering.

"I feel I should raise a toast," he began, when all had been served, and the room fell silent. He cleared his throat and hesitated. "First, a toast to my brother, who built this house. He wanted it to be a place of good cheer, and I hope today that we have done his wishes justice, even though we are but a small gathering." His voice shook, but he mastered his emotions and raised his cup. "To John."

"To John," echoed the room.

"And to all our absent family and friends, be they gone from us or only out of reach through the fog and snow – nevertheless we drink to them and hold them fondly in our hearts, hoping to see all of them again, whether it be in but a few days or in another, better place. To friends and family."

"Friends and family," agreed the group. Alexander saw Captain Pemberton put an arm about his daughter's shoulders as her eyes glistened, no doubt thinking of her beloved lost mother.

"And finally, I wish us all here a very Merry Christmas – and I thank Lady Celia, for she would not rest till we had made certain of being ready for you all to join us today. Merry Christmas!"

"Merry Christmas!" came the return.

"And now it is time for games," announced Lady Celia. "Gabriel, if you would be so good, please. I present to you all our first entertainment – Snapdragon!"

Gabriel brought forward a large, shallow dish in which lay a couple of handfuls of raisins, which he laid carefully on the table and then proceeded to fill with a pool of brandy, in which the raisins floated.

"Now the game is easy enough," began Lady Celia, her face gleeful. "All you need do is pinch out the raisins and eat them, they are very tasty. But – there is a dragon guarding them and of course, it breathes – fire!" She picked up a burning candle stood by the dish and swiftly set fire to the brandy, the blue flames spreading out in an instant. "Who is the bravest here? Captain Rose, will you brave the dragon?"

There followed much shrieking and cheering as everyone tried to pinch the raisins from the flames, some succeeding while others failed. Miss Pemberton was too scared, but her father valiantly returned twice to get both her and Miss Smith a raisin each, while Aunt Mary proved herself made of sterner stuff, pinching out well over five raisins all to herself. Lady Celia encouraged everyone to try and cheered on their efforts, but Alexander noticed she did not try herself. Her gloves, of course, might well catch fire or make her clumsy, and no doubt she would not wish to remove them if they grew soiled in her attempts. Was her good cheer in encouraging the others to partake a way to divert attention from her inability to do so, did she feel awkward in case they noticed that she had not tried the game?

"Let us play another game," he called out. "My fingers need time to heal, I think. Charades? Miss Pemberton, perhaps you would care to undertake the guessing, and we shall all try to amuse you with our inventions?"

They gathered about, with some taking seats and others standing and Miss Pemberton, excited, stood in the middle, awaiting the riddles to be set for her.

"You may lie on my first by the side of a stream," began Miss Smith.

"Elbow? Side?" guessed Miss Pemberton.

"And my second compose to the nymph you adore," continued Miss Smith.

"Poem? Valentine?"

"But if, when you've none of my whole, her esteem, and affection diminish – think of her no more!" finished Miss Smith.

Miss Pemberton, wide-eyed, was much puzzled, but Lady Celia leant towards her and whispered. "The side of a stream – or river?"

"Bank?"

Lady Celia nodded violently.

"And the second part – composing something to a nymph he adores?"

"If you were to write a..." prompted Lady Celia.

"Letter? Note? Oh! A bank – note – a banknote!"

"Very well done," praised Lady Celia and Miss Pemberton clasped her hands as they all applauded both Miss Smith's cunning and Miss Pemberton's efforts.

They continued until Miss Pemberton said her head hurt with thinking.

"Now we have a game which requires not brave fingers, but a brave face," said Lady Celia, nodding to Gabriel. "I give you – Bullet Pudding!"

There was applause but also groans, as Gabriel carried forward a dish on which was displayed a tightly packed mound of flour, on the top of which rested a single bullet.

"Now," said Lady Celia, picking up the knife that lay beside it. "I think it only right the ladies go first, and the youngest to begin. Miss Pemberton?"

Miss Pemberton took the knife and with trembling hands cut a very thin slice of the flour away, depositing it on a second dish. The bullet stayed put and she sighed with relief.

After that it was the turn of Aunt Mary, followed by Mrs Taylor, Miss Smith and finally Lady Celia. The bullet trembled and everyone held their breath, but it stayed in place and Lady Celia handed the knife with a triumphant expression to Captain Rose.

"Lady Celia, I think you have entrapped me, how will I escape unscathed?" he asked, but he completed his slice with the bullet now only half-supported by the dwindling heap of flour, yet still held aloft by what remained. "Well now," he said. "I think it only right that our host should take a turn, since he used to be my second in command."

Alexander took the knife, shaking his head. "I fear my fate is already hanging in the balance," he said. "But since Captain Rose was always a strict master, I shall accept what comes my way."

They all craned forwards to watch as he carefully slid the knife down what was left of the mound, only to cry out as the whole structure crumbled and the bullet fell into the pile of flour.

"You are undone, Lord Comerford!" cried Miss Pemberton, giggling.

"I am," he replied. "Alas, there is no hope at all." He took a deep breath and bent forwards, pressing his face into the flour, mouth open to pick up the bullet with his teeth. He almost choked but then stood upright, the bullet held triumphantly in his mouth, face entirely covered in flour. The room seemed framed with white dust from the flour on his eyelashes, and the guests fell about laughing at the spectacle of their white-faced host.

Lady Celia came close to him and took the bullet from his mouth, dropping it into the dish, shaking her head and laughing. "Your valet will be weeping tonight, Lord Comerford," she said, as she tried to wipe his face with a handkerchief, then brushed his jacket and waistcoat with her gloved hands in a useless effort to remove the flour which had gone everywhere. "I am not sure your jacket will survive such treatment."

He shook his head, laughing back at her. "I am afraid your efforts to help me are only ruining your dress," he said, for the flour had drifted onto her red silk dress. He would have helped her remove it, but he could not touch her bodice as she had touched his chest and shoulders.

She looked down at it. "Ah never mind," she said. "Aveline will scold me, but it was worth it for the spectacle." She clapped her hands together to release the flour from her gloves. "Miss Smith, I think you should declare the next game. What is it to be?"

"Oranges and Lemons!" she cried out.

Laughing, the guests formed themselves into a long line.

"The two of you must be the choppers, you know!" said Captain Rose to Lady Celia, still standing by Alexander.

She hesitated but then held out her hands to Alexander, who took them in his as they both raised their arms, forming an archway under which the guests began to slowly pass in single file, singing as they did so.

> "Oranges and lemons,
> Say the bells of St. Clement's.
> You owe me five farthings,
> Say the bells of St. Martin's.
> When will you pay me?
> Say the bells of Old Bailey.
> When I grow rich,
> Say the bells of Shoreditch.
> When will that be?
> Say the bells of Stepney.
> I do not know,
> Says the great bell of Bow."

The voices grew louder, a warning to hurry through the archway before being caught, but it was too late for Miss Pemberton, who shrieked as Alexander and Celia brought down their linked arms, catching her between them.

> *"Here comes a candle to light you to bed,*
> *And here comes a chopper to chop off your head!"*

Alexander shook his head, laughing. "Enough of these games, or we will all become children again," he said.

"Something more stately then? A dance, perhaps?" suggested Lady Celia.

"A dance? We hardly have the numbers."

"Of course we do," she rejoined. "Your aunt will play for us, won't you, ma'am?"

Aunt Mary nodded and smiled, making her way to the piano and striking up a lively tune.

"There now, it is *A Glass of Lemonade*, we only need three couples for our set. Miss Pemberton, you will have to consider this your coming-out ball, it is only a small affair, but a young lady's first ball is a great moment," Celia said, laughing. "You can hardly dance with your father, so you must take Jonathan as your partner."

Lord Jonathan bowed low to Miss Pemberton who blushed mightily but made a pretty curtsey in return.

Alexander looked on, smiling. "Perhaps Captain Pemberton will be so good as to take Miss Smith for this next dance?" he suggested, for he had seen his friend cast more than one admiring glance at the young woman and she in turn seemed to be delighted by the chance to be in society. Her days as a companion to his aunt were probably tediously dull, she might as well have a little pleasure this evening.

"Leaving you with your betrothed? Quite right," agreed Captain Pemberton smiling as he held out his hand to the bright-eyed Miss Smith.

Alexander had not really expected to dance at all, but of course they must have more than two couples and it would be seen as odd and churlish to refuse to dance, especially with Lady Celia. He held out his hand and she took it, smiling. "We will lead the dance then," he said, "so that Miss Pemberton can follow our example. Pemberton, will you take the middle place?" With the three couples laid out thus, it meant Miss Pemberton would be able to see the dance repeated twice before it was her turn, giving her a good idea of what to do.

❋

The dance began, a sprightly air. The pattern formed by the dancers was elaborate, with the first pair taking a complex set of figures around their still-standing peers, but to her surprise Celia enjoyed the dance, for she and Lord Comerford, dancing for the benefit of Miss Pemberton's young eyes, did their best to make the steps clear and tight to the tune, smiling at each other as they showed off the small twirls and niceties which only experienced dancers would know. Their display at an end, they waited while Captain Pemberton and Miss Smith danced very creditably and then all of the room, dancers and watchers alike, clapped their hands to encourage Miss Pemberton and her partner Lord Jonathan, then broke into applause when Miss Pemberton showed a good ear for music and a neat dancing style, her cheeks growing very pink with all the attention.

"Well done, Miss Pemberton!" cried Celia, clasping the girl's hands. "Why it is a great shame you will not be properly out for a few years yet, for you are an excellent dancer. You will be your season's shining star!"

Miss Pemberton ducked her head in blushing pleasure.

"Comerford, you said that you owed our merriness today to the efforts of Lady Celia," said Captain Rose. "And that being the case, I believe you owe your bride-to-be at least a kiss under the mistletoe, in thanks for her efforts."

"A kiss, a Christmas kiss!" agreed the others.

Celia's cheeks grew hot. "I – there is no need –" she began awkwardly, taking a step backwards, but when the others cheered she realised she had just stepped directly under the chandelier from which the kissing bough hung, the mistletoe bound in its red silk ribbons.

Lord Comerford bowed his head. "I can hardly refuse when I owe her such a happy day," he said, and in a few short steps he reached her, taking her gently by the waist with one hand, pulling her towards him, while his other hand brushed away her dark curls and he bent to kiss her. His lips were warm and soft, but there was a firmness in how he held her, a desire in his eyes as he let her go again to much applause, which had her heart beating fast. She wished they were entirely alone, so that she might have touched his arm, perhaps allowed the kiss to last longer so that she might have known whether she liked it or not, as it was, the applause and smiles of their guests only flustered her.

"There now, I think we have had enough merriment," said Lord Comerford, seemingly still calm and composed. "I think we should all repair to the palm room to calm ourselves and rest from our dancing. Gabriel – be so good as to tell Mrs Poole that we would welcome tea and some of her excellent lemon biscuits."

The palm room was exclaimed over, and everyone made themselves comfortable in sofas and armchairs, the hot tea and biscuits a welcome refreshment. Celia sat well away from Lord Comerford, still flustered by the kiss they had exchanged. She had not expected it at all, but he had seemed calm, even willing, had pulled her close to him and there had been desire in his eyes when he let her go. She watched him now, her cheeks still hot, as he pulled out a package for Miss Pemberton, which she opened with curiosity to reveal a wooden box, prettily inlaid with mother-of-pearl.

"Look at him all grown," said Mrs Taylor, sitting down beside Celia. The old woman gazed fondly at Lord Comerford. "He was such a harum-scarum one, you'd never have thought he'd be a polished gentleman like that, especially once he joined the navy." Her eyes glistened with tears. "It's the first time I've seen him smile since he came home," she murmured to Celia. "He wept so when he found he'd lost John, they were such scamps the two of them, always in trouble, always cheeky grins on their faces, always together. It broke his heart to lose him. He wasn't bothered about all the title and money, some people would have been greedy for it, but not him. It made him anxious, he said, for how was he to know whether people liked him for himself or because he'd become the Earl? He didn't like how suddenly every mama in town planned to break the agreement between the two of you, how all the gentleman's clubs tried to poach him from each other, he said he had hoped to be among better people, people he might trust, honourable people."

Celia listened silently. She had not seen the heartbreak behind his composed manners, had not known of his fears. She had not known that other women had planned to steal him from her. Whether she wanted him or not, it was underhand, for the whole *ton* knew of the engagement.

Mrs Taylor patted Celia's hand. "You were the only thing he was sure of," she said, smiling. "He said, she's always been promised to me, I shan't have to worry that she only wants me for my money – or the title, since she's the daughter of a duke. She'll have me as I am. It was a comfort to him."

Celia tried to smile through discomfort. Mrs Taylor was only an old, retired servant, handsomely looked after for having been close to an earl's two sons, her opinion was not one the rest of the *ton* would have paid much attention to, but she pictured Mrs Taylor's face when she heard that Celia had spurned Lord Comerford after all, had turned from him to find another suitor and why? Only because he had not paid her enough compliments? Mrs Taylor would be shocked at such lack of constancy, would sigh and say that young women were flighty, that they did not know a good man when they had one at their side.

"I suppose the two boys kept you busy, if they were such imps," she said instead, hoping perhaps to hear something about their characters which would make her feel better about her choice not to marry him. Perhaps Lord Comerford had been unkind to animals or been a naughty, disobedient child.

Mrs Taylor's eyes crinkled in fond memories. "Oh, but they were wicked. They'd scrump apples from the farmers – as though they didn't have an orchard of their own – and sneak out of the house to ride their ponies when their mama wanted them to attend to their lessons. They'd hide from me at bedtime."

Celia nodded. There. He had been a naughty child. Though she could not help thinking of her escapes from her governess and the endless tedious lectures on geography or the unpicking of embroidery that was not good enough, how she had escaped to the kitchens and begged Cook to let her make apple puffs instead.

"He was a dear boy," continued Mrs Taylor, still reminiscing. "He would bring me flowers he'd picked in the meadow and gather sweet chestnuts for us to roast and eat together, he'd lay his head in my lap when he was tired out and ask to be told stories, I never met a boy that liked hearing stories so much. And," she added chuckling, "it was no good their hiding from me when they were in trouble, for I could always hear them giggling behind a door or in a cupboard."

Mrs Taylor's words came as a wrench, conjuring up not just the child Celia had barely known, but the man she would have liked to have married, a man who would bring flowers from his walks, who would lay his head in her lap when they were alone together. She could not reconcile the boy with the man at all. How could this giggling child with his hands full of flowers have turned into a silent man who looked disapproving of everything? She opened her mouth to ask some more questions, to find out more about what had wrought such a change, but found that Mrs Taylor, comfortably full of the Christmas feast and wassail punch, was beginning to doze off.

"It is a pleasure to meet you, Lady Celia," came a voice on the other side of her and she turned to find Captain Rose taking a seat on the sofa next to her. "All these years I've known Captain – I beg your pardon – *Lord* Comerford, and known he was to marry you, but have never yet had the pleasure of meeting you myself. You must come aboard one day when we are in port, so that Comerford can show you his first posting." He gave a warm smile. "He was only a boy when he came to me, of course, but he did very well. I could not have been prouder, the day he was given a ship to command, than if he'd been my own son. He'd earnt it, fair and square."

"I heard you both saw active service at Trafalgar," said Celia, for she knew that any man who had been there was always eager to brag of it.

But Captain Rose only nodded soberly and said "Indeed. It was a hard time for him."

"What happened?"

"He was only seventeen, you understand," said Captain Rose. "I had two boys aboard my ship then, Comerford and a lad named Linton. He was not to be an officer, he was from a good enough family but poor, but he and Comerford, being of an age and having joined service together, were good friends. Comerford never had airs and graces even though he was the son of an earl." He sighed, as though unwilling to go on, then spoke fast, as if hurrying to get the story over and done with. "A cannonball caught Linton full on and tore him apart, poor lad. He had only a moment or two before he died. Comerford dashed to his side and held him, spoke with him." He sighed again. "I know he made it his business to write to his father and ask that Linton's mother be looked after, for he was her only son, and that since being made Earl himself, he has raised her pension still further." He nodded. "He is a good man through and through, he feels his loyalties deeply. I am glad to have seen him merry tonight, for I worried the Navy had taken away his cheerful disposition, with all that he had seen. I must credit you with lightening his heart."

"I am not sure I have done anything..." Celia murmured, uncomfortable.

"You are too modest. I am sure there will be a rapturous welcome for you at Comerford Castle when you return there as Countess of Comerford. I hear they have a charming welcome ritual they like to perform for each new bride."

She was not even composed enough to ask what it was, only ducked her head like a child. "I am sure Lord Comerford is glad to see you," she managed. "He speaks highly of you; I am sure he will welcome your advice as he begins his new life." *When I have chosen another suitor and he is left alone*, she could not help thinking. "He will need his friends about him," she added.

"Indeed," said Captain Rose. "And you remind me that I should speak with him now and find out how he does. You will excuse me."

"Of course."

Captain Rose got up and moved away from Celia, making his way over to Alexander and placing one hand on his shoulder in a fatherly gesture.

❄

"How goes it, Comerford?" asked Captain Rose. "How is life on land treating you?"

"I cannot complain," said Alexander.

"Complain! I should think not. A title and money, this house as well as Comerford Castle – and a beautiful woman to marry? I cannot see the hardship."

Alexander shook his head. "It is not to complain of hardship, it is only –" He trailed off, his voice lower.

Captain Rose moved closer and lowered his voice also. "You can tell me, Comerford. I have known you long enough, man and boy, for there to be no secrets between us."

"Will you walk with me, Sir?"

Alexander stood and they walked away from the gathering, across the great room, standing by a window at the far end, though it was too dark to see anything outside.

"Well, Comerford? Spit it out."

"It has all been so sudden, Sir. I was not prepared – nor brought up to it. My father did not teach me to run the estate, for it was never thought I should need to, all of that was taught only to my brother. Now I must run the estate and this house, I have a wife promised whom I barely know and – I find it hard to know how to manage any of it, yet I cannot complain, for it would be ungrateful." A sigh escaped him at the relief of admitting it.

Captain Rose nodded and took a swallow of brandy. "I understand you, Comerford. I may have twitted you for it just now, but I do understand. I felt the same when I heard of your news. Your brother lost, your whole world upended in an instant and no father to guide you."

"I would gladly accept your guidance, Sir, if you have advice to give me."

"I have never been in your position, Comerford. But I know this. You are a good man. You have never rested on your laurels, nor used your family's privilege as an excuse not to work hard and learn. I know that all this new grandeur about you – this house, the clothes, the parties you must attend, even your bride-to-be being the daughter of a duke – must feel too much after all your years at sea, and the greater burden since it all rests on your shoulders. But think of it this way. This is your new ship. Your new command. You have been given the HMS *Comerford*, and she is yours to sail now, with a new crew and a new uniform, as well as a new first mate. I know you will rise to the challenge, and though the tempests may blow, you will find your way to calmer seas soon enough and know yourself a good captain, just as you proved yourself aboard the *Vela*."

A growing calm came over Alexander as he listened to his mentor. Yes. It was a new posting, a new challenge, but one which he could face as he had faced others in his naval career. "My brother wanted to be surrounded by people talking of politics and his wife wanted to hold dinners and balls, but I am not that sort of man," he confessed. "I would like a quieter life, one where I can be among friends and family, without the need to impress. And I do not wish to hold balls and suchlike, I would want to use what I have to do some good in the world."

"The HMS *Comerford* is yours now. It does not matter that her previous captain was your brother, he had his ways about him, but they need not steer your course. A ship becomes like her master, all naval men know that, it is why each crew waits in trepidation to see who the new captain will be, they know they must shape themselves to him and his ways. Do not think of how your brother would have done things, Comerford. He is gone now, and I am sorry for your loss, but you must chart your own course." He smiled, catching sight of Lady Celia speaking with Aunt Mary. "You have a goodly first mate at your side, do you not?"

"In truth I barely know her, Sir."

"Then spend more time with her, Comerford." He held up a hand. "Not at balls and suchlike. They are no use for getting to know anyone, I cannot think why marriages are chosen after nothing but a few dances together. Spend time quietly together if you can, have a task you may share together, a common goal if you can. My wife was set on all my crews being able to read and write, it was a conviction of hers that it would make them better men and have greater advantages in life. It made me laugh at first, but I grew to like it about her and whenever we were able, she would come aboard and teach them their letters. You remember."

"Yes, Sir. She used to press gang me, as she called it, to teach them too."

Captain Rose nodded. "I recall you taught poor Linton his letters."

Alexander's stomach turned over. "Much good it did," he said, hearing the bitterness in his voice.

"Ah, now, Comerford, do not think it wasted. He was near bursting with pride at his learning from you, and his mother too. It gave them joy in his short time here on earth. And joy is all we have to share. Never hold back from sharing kindness for fear of joy being short lived. It is worth each golden moment. I still miss my wife now that she is gone from us, but I treasure the time we had."

Alexander nodded.

"And your bride does not seem unwilling to be wed to you," said Captain Rose with a smile. "She came willingly enough into your arms for a Christmas kiss, did she not? She has welcomed your friends and family, even those of us not of her rank with nothing but good humour and warmth, I would say. You will make a fine marriage between you, have faith."

Alexander wanted to ask for further reassurances in that regard, but he was too surprised by his mentor's description of their kiss. *Had* she come willingly? The moment had been awkward, but he had tried not to let it show, had moved decisively since hesitation would have been more awkward still, under the watching eyes of the gathering. He had put a hand about her waist and pulled her towards him, had placed a kiss upon her lips, then let her go, a moment and that was all... though his fingers had lingered on the silk of her dress as it slipped away from him, he had needed to steady his voice before he spoke to invite them all to the palm room. He had indeed done so only so that he might have a moment to gather the feelings which had rushed up in him at the warm touch of her lips, the widening of her dark eyes as she gazed up at him. Had she been willing? He had felt desire for her, had let her go unwillingly, had wished since then that all these guests should go away at once, this instant, so that he might kiss her again, might hold her longer this time, touch her face, feel her lips part beneath his.

"Comerford?"

Alexander realised that he had stopped speaking, had been gazing across the great room to where he could see Lady Celia. "I beg your pardon, Sir."

Captain Rose smiled. "I have every faith in your marriage," he said. "Now let us join the others, before they think us unmannerly in keeping ourselves aside."

Alexander took up a place beside Captain Pemberton. "I hope your daughter has enjoyed herself," he said. "She is a delightful girl. Lady Celia is quite taken with her." He looked over at the two of them. Lady Celia had produced a wrapped package inside which was a fur muff, by which Miss Pemberton was quite overcome. Alexander knew, since it had been impossible to go out, that the muff must have been Lady Celia's, generously given away. No doubt the daughter of a duke had more than one fur muff at her disposal, but still it was kind to give a young girl such a fine gift, something her father would have been unlikely to afford.

"She has a warm heart," observed Captain Pemberton to Alexander, nodding his head towards Lady Celia meaningfully. "She'll make a loving mother." He sighed. "I only wish my Emma might have lived to see her daughter doing so well. I am grateful to Lady Celia for taking an interest and showing her those little attentions which a mother might give, she will feel the benefit of them. I shall hope to visit you both from time to time once you have set up home together."

"By all means, we would welcome you both," said Alexander. He meant it, for he was fond of Captain Pemberton and his little daughter, but a part of him was unsure of speaking as though they would be a wedded couple inviting people to their home. Lady Celia had been so adamant that she intended to find a new suitor, and yet... and yet there had been a warmth between them, a newfound interest in one another. And the kiss they had shared... her lips warm beneath his, her eyes softening when she had gazed up at him. Was it too much to hope that she might yet change her mind? Perhaps he had been too stolidly certain that wooing was not required, that the marriage was a deal already made. He admitted now to himself that it would have done no harm to show more care, to offer her those romantic touches which after all it was only natural a young woman might dream of. He was not given to such attentions, had always held back from even small gestures, knowing himself already promised, but there was no reason why he should not try harder if it would give her pleasure. He was not a natural at words of flattery, but he could try to better show his growing feelings, even though he was unsure of how to begin. He wondered what might open her heart to him, now that he had glimpsed that it might be a heart worth opening.

"When you were courting Emma," he said to Captain Pemberton, keeping his voice low, "How did you – I mean what attentions did you show her?"

Captain Pemberton gave a chuckle. "Ah, I was so besotted it was all I could do not to altogether smother her in attentions," he said. "I think her friends used to laugh at how I conducted myself. But the usual things, you know – sent her a Valentine, danced and drove and walked with her. Got myself invited to the same dinners. Sent her flowers. I believe nowadays biscuits from Brown's are quite the thing. The usual attentions. Does Lady Celia not care for such things?"

He could not explain how it had gone between them. "It is only that I have been away so long – I feel I must make it up to her."

Captain Pemberton gave him a comforting pat on the shoulder. "She seems happy in your company, and that is all that really matters," he said. "Now, I really should take my young miss home. She has had a taste of grown-up life tonight and conducted herself admirably. I am proud of her, but she is still only a child."

Captain Pemberton's farewells proved the signal for all the guests to set out for home, each accompanied by a groom or footman with a lantern to help them find their way. Alexander and Lady Celia stood in the hall, waving to them, calling out farewells and well wishes.

"Merry Christmas!" called Alexander to the last bobbing light, then turned back towards Lady Celia. "I want to thank you," he began, not wanting the words to shrivel for overthinking them.

"Whatever for?"

"You have been an excellent hostess today, indeed, I have you to thank for making it Christmas-like at all," he said. "Had it been for me alone I would have sat alone and done little more than wish the servants a merry Christmas. But you – you made it joyful. As it should be. And I am grateful to you for including those of my acquaintances who might not usually be at such an occasion."

Her gaze was warm. "You have been a generous host," she said. "And it was right to include Miss Smith and your nanny, why should they sit alone on such a day when there is plenty to share?"

"I hope you also enjoyed the day," he said. "My friends must be rougher than the society you have been used to, but they are good men, I was glad to serve with them."

"I did enjoy the day," she said, smiling. "I have never been hostess before, I enjoyed doing things my way and seeing people the happier for it. Your friends were very gentlemanly in their manners and courtesies, and Miss Pemberton is a dear girl, I hope today's foolishness brought happiness to her after the loss of her mother, she spoke movingly of missing her greatly." Her voice wavered, and he saw a glint of tears rise in her eyes, making his emotions for her still stronger. She was nothing like his first impressions. He had too readily dismissed her, too readily judged her as what he expected – a silly young girl, when she was nothing of the kind. He wanted to tell her so, but was not sure how without insulting her.

"You were very good to her."

She shook her head, curls bouncing. "She deserved all of it and more. Perhaps when I am in London again, she will permit me to call on her and her father."

"I am sure they would be honoured." There was more to say. Could he tell her that he had wished more than once this evening that all was well between them, that they were truly to be wed? Not just when they had kissed, though her lips had been soft and desire had risen up in him, but more than that, when she had held his hand and danced her way laughing down the room, when she had dusted his face of the bullet pudding flour and sat for more than an hour talking to his old nanny, a servant she had never met before, the contentment on Nanny Taylor's face at being the recipient of such kindly attentions. He wanted... he wanted to kiss her again. But he did not wish to see her smile disappear, for her to step back in shock, so he said only, "You must be tired."

Was it his imagination, or did she glance for a second, no more, at the mistletoe hanging above them? But she dipped her head before he could be certain and said, "I am, it has been a long day."

He made her a bow. "Then I hope your night will be restful. If you require anything, any of the servants will be glad to wait upon you."

"Thank you," she said and then, in a rush just as she reached the stairs, "I was glad to meet your friends."

And she was gone, her kid shoes carrying her silently up the staircase away from him. He stood watching her, wondering again whether he should have said more, or whether he should have done what he had really wanted to do... taken her in his arms and kissed her.

5

BOXING DAY

Celia woke to a pale blue light.

"Has it snowed again?" she asked, sleepily aware that Aveline was bustling about the room.

"It has not just snowed," said Aveline, in tones of horror. "They could not even open the front door without a pile of snow came falling in. The grooms were up to their thighs in it. His lordship has sent every man who can be spared out to clear the road outside and down to the stables – but to what purpose? There is nowhere to go in this weather, that is for sure."

Celia lay back in her bed thinking over the events of the day before. So, she would be here all today as well. She turned the idea over in her mind. Yesterday had been fun, far more so than she had expected. It had been... it had been joyous. There was no other word for it. The crisp fresh cold of their morning excursion to church after being shut up indoors, the pleasure on the faces of their guests, glad not to be alone on this most festive day, the silly games and good food – all of it had been full of delight, the festive spirit truly taking over all of them. The gathering of strangers had been good natured, she had seen a new side to Lord Comerford, one which cast him in a far kinder light than she had hitherto seen him in. If that had been all, she would have looked forward to today, she would have expected a friendly passing of time – perhaps cards or an attempt at a walk, playing with the kittens and so on.

But the kiss.

The kiss between them, so unexpectedly called for and even more unexpectedly indulged...

It had felt real. Not a sham of a quick brush of the lips, awkwardly done to avoid speculation over the nature of their current arrangement, hastily performed and just as hastily forgotten. Lord Comerford's hand on her waist, drawing her to him, his lips on hers, had been firm and certain, had lingered for one moment too long. And as he let her go, there had been desire in his eyes, his fingertips had lingered on her body, she was sure of it.

But what did she know? She had never been kissed. She got out of bed and made her way to the looking glass, touched her lips with her finger. Did she look different? She did not think so. But now she must spend another day with Lord Comerford, after their kiss. Would he try to kiss her again? Or did it mean nothing to him, had it been done only in the moment so as not to seem uninterested in his supposed bride-to-be, had he thought nothing of it? She touched her lips again. The moment when he had pulled her to him, how his lips had touched her first gently but then with greater firmness, the heat that had rushed through her...

"What are you blushing at?" asked Aveline, interpreting Celia's getting out of bed as a signal to pour her a basin of hot water from the steaming jug at hand.

"Blushing? I am not blushing."

"Well, your cheeks are pink," said Aveline. "Wash and I'll do your hair. His Lordship has been up for hours; Mrs Poole will be waiting breakfast on you."

"I will wear the flower trim instead of the velvet," said Celia. Aveline had laid out a dress with a velvet trim, which seemed too grand for a day spent indoors without any visitors. She did not want to seem as though she was trying to attract Lord Comerford's attention. Why had she chosen all her dresses in red? At the time they had seemed warm and bright. Now they seemed ostentatious or even provocative. At least the flower-trimmed dress was a darker shade of red, more of a deep red plum, with tiny pink flowers about the hem and neckline, it seemed a quieter choice. "There is no need to fuss with my hair," she added, seeing Aveline approaching with a mouthful of hairpins. "Something simple."

"It takes this many pins just to keep those curls of yours in order," mumbled Aveline through the pins, but she obliged so that Celia eventually made her way downstairs with her hair plainly pinned up and no jewellery.

She found Lord Comerford in the drawing room, where cake and coffee had already been served. He rose and bowed as soon as he saw her. To her amusement the kittens were with him, one of them asleep by the fire, the other attempting to climb onto the table by means of scrambling up the wooden legs, which it was finding difficult.

"Good morning, Lady Celia."

"Good morning, Lord Comerford," she returned with a curtsey. It was hard to meet his gaze, but she did not want to seem awkward, to make more of the kiss than it had been. Perhaps to him it was nothing, only a polite gesture at their guests' urgings so as not to embarrass either of them with awkward questions. She would behave in a friendly manner. But nothing more.

"Shall I call for tea? Or chocolate?"

"Tea, thank you," she said, turning towards the table and helping herself to cake, then moving on to coo over the kittens, so that she need not face him.

The footman duly rung for and dispatched for tea, she settled down by the fireplace, opposite Lord Comerford. There was an awkward silence and all she could think of was an obvious remark about the weather.

"I gather it has snowed a great deal in the night?"

"It has," he said. "I am afraid travel is out of the question."

She nodded. "We must resign ourselves to a quiet day, then," she managed, with a small smile.

"Not really."

"No?"

"It is Saint Stephen's Day," he reminded her. "I must make up boxes for the servants – and it was to have been the Servants' Ball tonight. I must find out from Mrs Poole whether she has enough supplies to lay on a good spread for them, for I would not wish them to do without. If she cannot, I suppose they will have to postpone it, though that does not seem very merry. She has already said that milk is in short supply now, for no deliveries can be made."

She had forgotten. Of course. At home the Servants' Ball was a great occasion, when her mother and father would arrive at one of the great barns on the estate and her father would dance with the housekeeper, her mother with the butler. She had not been allowed to take part as such, being young it was considered not appropriate for her to dance with, say, one of the footmen or a groom, for fear that they might afterwards not treat her with the appropriate decorum expected. But last year she had danced with the steward, a man of many years who could be relied upon to maintain a gentlemanly air in their subsequent meetings.

"What can I do to help?" she asked.

"Nothing," he said, looking startled at her asking. "You need do nothing at all. You may – read or sew or – whatever you wish. I will take care of everything."

"Have you already packaged up their gifts?"

"Not yet," he admitted.

"Let me help. I have nothing else to do. I am good at wrapping gifts," she insisted.

They found themselves once again in the great room, now with gifts of cloth and money neatly laid out all over the carpet. As she parcelled up each one, adding flourishes such as a colourful ribbon or sprig of greenery, she would pass it to him where he stood at one of the side tables with pen in hand, writing the name of each servant onto the paper and laying it to one side, ready to be given out.

He had been generous, she could see that in the quality and quantity of the cloth he had given for clothes and no doubt with the money for each as well, though that was placed in folded up notes fastened close with his seal, the spring of mistletoe pressed into the red wax.

"I am sure they will be grateful," she remarked.

"I hope so," he replied, and she heard anxiety in his voice. "I spoke with my steward about what might be expected and added a little more – they have had to welcome a new master and had much additional work this year, with... with everything."

She lifted away a kitten who was attempting to play with a neatly folded length of blue wool cloth. "I shall have to lock you downstairs if you cannot behave," she told it. "I think the servants probably deserve a gift just for all they have had to put up with these past few days – my visit, unexpected guests for Christmas Day, kittens..."

He looked down, smiling as a kitten played with his shoe buckles. "I believe they will have found it more interesting than looking after one man all alone, it is hardly a good use of their time to keep a whole house in readiness for just one person." He looked about the room. "Indeed, I cannot imagine how such a house might be used if one is not inclined to constant balls and dinners. I am fonder of Comerford Castle, it is large but it feels more like home to me and of course it is surrounded by the estate and that has a purpose of its own."

"You would not give it up?"

"No, of course not, it is a splendid house. But it seems empty to me."

"When you have a family, it will feel full enough," she said and immediately regretted her words. They had come out without her thinking, but were overly familiar, their future children the sort of thing a young couple might tease one another about before their marriage or as they started out in married life.

A silence fell between them. For while they only wrapped packages and addressed them, until the task was complete.

"I will ask –" he began, just as she said, "Would it –" and then fell silent.

"Please, you were saying," he said at once.

"I was only going to ask if I might join you at the Servants' Ball this evening, to help them make merry," she said. "Where will it be held?"

He looked awkward. "I was thinking I might offer them this room – it is only sitting empty, after all."

"That is very kind."

TO WIN HER HAND

He gave a shrug. "What is the good of a large room if not for parties?"

She nodded as though this were entirely logical, but in truth she could not think of many noblemen who would turn over their ballrooms to the servants. It was a generous gesture, and one which, yet again, spoke well of his character.

❆

CELIA MADE HER WAY TO HER ROOMS TO BE DRESSED for the occasion, choosing a dress in a plainer style than she might usually pick for an evening's event, for she did not wish to outshine the servants. They would wear their best clothes, which would pale beside one of her more elaborate evening dresses. She waved away Adeline's attempts to decorate her hair, opting instead for simple curls at the front and the rest pinned with a red ribbon threaded through it.

The ballroom looked its best, with bright candles and a roaring fire which still sported the Yule log in it. The servants had begun to gather, all of them stiff and nervous in their very best clothes, some of them, like the footmen, almost unrecognisable when she had only ever seen them in uniform. The maids stood in little groups as though for safety, wide-eyed at being allowed into the grand room, too scared to move in it now that they were not doing chores. Celia sensed all eyes on her. The bobbing and bowing that followed her across the room made her all too aware that her very presence would curtail their fun for the evening, unless she could find a way to set them at ease. The doors at the far end were open into the large dining room, which had also been granted to them for the evening, and there she could see Mrs Poole hovering in a fine green wool, her hair for once not hidden away under a white cap but more elegantly presented with a green wrap that matched her dress.

"Good evening, Mrs Poole," she said. "You must show me the dinner you have prepared for this evening's festivities."

The fare, she saw at once, was more than plentiful but less dainty than what had been served for the master's table, more suited to the appetites of working men and women. Here were generous golden pies of ham and of beef, a thick pease-pudding, a calf's head served on a bed of rice and peas, a large dish of tripe, cheese and loaves of bread served alongside Indian pickles, with cider and ale to drink. For sweets there were dozens of small mince pies as well as a great apple pie served with hot sweet custard and preserved plums along with a vast bowl of walnuts to crack.

"It is a fine spread, Mrs Poole," she told the cook. "I hope you will serve me some of that ham pie, it looks very tempting."

Mrs Poole flushed with pleasure and hurried to serve Celia with a large slice, which Celia tasted and offered generous compliments for, which came easily since it was quite as flavoursome as any of the dishes she had been served at Comerford House.

"Here comes the master," murmured Mrs Poole, and Celia turned to see Lord Comerford making his way through the same bowing and curtseys she had done, he also well-dressed but without too much in the way of ostentation.

"Lady Celia," he said, bowing. "Mrs Poole."

They both curtseyed.

"Mrs Poole has been busy as you see," said Celia. "And this pie is most excellent; you should try some."

He nodded and smiled as Mrs Poole passed him a slice.

"It is delicious," he pronounced. "I hope you will serve it at one of my own dinners one day."

"Thank you, my lord," said Mrs Poole, her cheeks by now rosy with all the attention and praise being lavished on her.

Lord Comerford moved towards the ale and Gabriel, watchful, hurried to serve him, but Lord Comerford waved him away.

"Now, now Gabriel, you do not need to serve me tonight, I am quite able to pour a glass of ale."

"Yes, my lord."

The glass full, Lord Comerford returned to the ballroom, Celia and Mrs Poole following behind him.

"Let me raise a toast," he began. "I thank you all for your hard work in these past months. You lost your master, your mistress returned to her family and you have had to grow used to a new master in me. You have all conducted yourselves admirably, most of all in these last few days when the fog and snow caught us all unawares. I thank you for being of good cheer and of taking such good care of not only me, but Lady Celia and our guests on Christmas Day. It is only right that you should enjoy the comforts of Comerford House tonight for your ball. I know Mrs Poole has seen to it that you will eat well, and I see that Jack and Edward are ready with their flute and fiddle. Here's to your good health!"

"Good health!" called the servants, raising their glasses.

"And now it is time to dance. Mrs Pratchett, may I have the honour?"

He held out his hand to the housekeeper, a narrow woman with pinched features, who gave a bright smile and accepted.

"I hope Sanders will accompany me?" asked Celia, approaching the butler.

"It would be my honour, Lady Celia," he said in his dignified way and the music struck up a stately quadrille.

The dancing went on for more than an hour, the music and servants growing ever bolder and more jolly, so that the last dance that Celia took part in was a country jig, with much in the way of whoops and clapping to the tune, with Lord Comerford choosing Sarah the kitchen maid as a partner and she herself being twirled about by Gabriel.

"Enough, enough," called Lord Comerford at last. "We are both worn out, but I am sure you still have much to celebrate, and besides you have not yet had your dinner. We shall leave you now, so that you can be as merry as you wish. Good night to you all."

"May I raise a toast, Sir, before you leave us?" asked the butler.

"Certainly, Sanders."

"I only wished to say that we all felt the loss of the late Lord Comerford deeply, Sir, but we're grateful to have you as our new master and hope to serve you and Lady Celia these many years to come. Three cheers for Lord Comerford and Lady Celia! Hip! Hip!"

"Hooray!" cried the gathering.

The cheers rang out three times with much applause to follow and Celia, not knowing what else to do, offered a curtsey before she saw that Lord Comerford, having bowed to them all, was now holding out his hand to her to lead her from the room. Blushing, she took it, and he guided her downstairs, back to the hall.

She turned to him, letting go of his hand. "I think they will make merry long into the night. I hope they will, at least. They deserve it."

He nodded. "Thank you for being such a good part of the evening."

She smiled, as though surprised, took a step away from him up the stairs towards her bedchamber. "I only danced."

He looked at her before replying, the words coming out of his mouth almost without thinking, a simple truth. "You make duty seem joyful."

They were both silent, before he cleared his throat, embarrassed by the declaration, returning to trite topics. "It is possible the snow will melt by morning, if the temperatures rise."

"And if not?"

"If not, we will be stuck here until it does," he said. "I am afraid there is very little choice in the matter, no carriage nor horse could travel safely in such conditions."

"I am sure we will manage," she said and to his surprise she was smiling. It looked as though she were actually happy with the predicament in which they found themselves. "We have done well so far between us, have we not?"

"We have done very well," he said, looking up at her. "I have been surprised by how well, in fact."

"So have I, Lord Comerford," she said quietly, her expression grown serious. Her lips parted, as though she was about to say something more, but then she gave a shake of her head. "Good night," she said, and turned away, walking quickly up the stairs.

He stood watching her walk away from him for the second night in a row and wanted to follow her, to catch at her hand and ask her – what? He was not even sure. To reconsider her plan to marry someone else? To begin again, pretend they had only just met after these past years and see whether they might manage to make a better impression on one another? How was it possible, after two months of disliking one another, that barely three days together at Comerford House could have them celebrating together, being friendly, even, perhaps, something more, a spark that might have enough heat in it to burst into flames, were it given more time?

But she was gone, she had reached the landing and turning into the corridor leading to her bedroom without a backward glance. Perhaps he was wrong, perhaps it was only he who felt anything for her, perhaps she was only making the best of a bad situation, her training as a nobleman's daughter allowing her to appear well mannered and even pleasant under pressure.

Or perhaps, and he allowed himself a smile at the foolishness of the idea, perhaps Comerford House had been built for love and was determined that it should be found within its walls. Every part of it cried out for happiness in marriage, from its paintings to the decorations and symbols used in all its furnishings. Perhaps the house itself was coaxing even the tiniest sparks of interest out of its two inhabitants, growing progressively warmer and brighter between them, the longer they were held within its walls.

He could still hear the fiddle and flute, the laughter and thumping of feet from the great room. At his feet, a shadow moved, revealing both kittens, who had anxiously roamed about the house until they had found him. Holly mewed and Ivy sat down to wash her face. Absent-mindedly he patted both on the head, their fur soft and warm under his fingertips.

"Aye, she'll make a right good mistress to the master, an' he deserves her," he heard from the corridor above, as two of the footmen carried up a new tureen of hot custard and some clean dishes. He stepped out of their sight, quietly opening the front door and standing in the silent snowbound street. Looking up, all was darkness, with a clouded sky. The servants approved of her, then, they saw in her their future mistress and were glad, considered them a good match. He was beginning to agree with them, but how to mend matters? The last time they had spoken of the engagement, they had agreed to break it. How was he now to propose that it be kept in place – and what if she were to refuse? He was unsure whether speaking now would only return them to a place of stiff civility, just when their enforced days together seemed to be bringing them slowly closer.

"It is possible the snow will melt tomorrow, and then we will be free," he murmured to himself, echoing his words to Lady Celia. And then, in the silence of the empty road, certain that no-one could hear him, he looked upwards into the dark sky, as though saying a tiny prayer and spoke again, barely audible except to himself.

"Let it snow."

6

GINGERBREAD

Whether through the efforts of Alexander's prayer or not, the next day everyone awoke to another foot of snow that had fallen overnight, and the certainty that they would be going nowhere at all.

Alexander managed to make his way to the stables, where he spoke with the grooms and inspected the horses. The inability to get about London was a nuisance, certainly. A horse might be able to pick its way about with some difficulty, but none of the carriages would do well, there was a real risk of slipping and overturning, which would not only hurt the passengers but might well harm the horses. But there was little anyone could do. He headed back to the house, stamping his wet boots in the hall, the footman on duty rushing to fetch his indoor shoes. Once changed, he stepped inside the drawing room, to find Lady Celia standing by the windows, her shawl wrapped about her, looking out at the garden and Green Park below, both so deeply covered in snow that only the vaguest of shapes was visible – bushes here and there, the dipped terrace indicating the steps down to the garden. The white snow outlining all the dark-barked trees gave their bare silhouettes a stark beauty, but Alexander's focus was all on Lady Celia. He admired again the dark curls, her rosy cheeks, her figure, dressed today in a dark red wool that was almost burgundy, a more sombre choice than her previous days' outfits, but its shade echoed the hue of her lips, which he found it hard not to linger over. As he watched, she shivered.

"Good morning. You are warm enough, I hope?" he asked, glancing at the roaring fire in the fireplace.

Startled, she turned to him. "Good morning, Lord Comerford. I am very comfortable, thank you. I was only thinking of those less fortunate; it must be a harsh winter for them. I have never seen so much snow fall in so little time."

He nodded.

They stood together in silence for a few moments before she spoke again.

"Let us go down into the kitchens. We can make gingerbread."

Alexander was entirely thrown by this idea. "Gingerbread? I am sure Mrs Poole will make you some, if you have a hankering for it."

"Not for me to eat. For the children."

"Children?"

"If we make gingerbread this morning, we can ice it later and then tomorrow when it is well set, we can take it to the Foundling Hospital, for the children there. I doubt they enjoy much in the way of treats at this time of year." She waited expectantly, her bright eyes on his face.

Decorations were one thing, but the kitchen was Mrs Poole's domain and Alexander had never been there. "I am sure the kitchen staff would be glad to make gingerbread for the children," he began, uncertainly, "there is no need for you to do it yourself. A footman can be sent tomorrow to deliver it. The carriage cannot be used, as you know, and it is fully a mile on foot."

"But we have nothing to do, and I would rather be gainfully occupied," she persisted. "A mile's walk is not so far. You and I can easily go together tomorrow. I would like to see the children's faces for myself. Charity at a distance is all very well, but it does not fill the heart, nor seem particularly caring to those to whom it is offered, it smacks of charity for show, done without any trouble to oneself rather than rising from any real concern. The children would like to have some visitors to brighten their days. There will be fewer visitors than usual, given the weather. And a walk will do us both good. Will you show me to the kitchens?"

Alexander stared at her, but she did not seem as though she would brook reluctance. Why was she always catching him off guard with suggestions which seemed demanding and yet were so kind-hearted in nature and intent as to bring a rush of fondness for her? It was unsettling. He nodded and silently lead the way to where a concealed door, he knew, led down to the kitchens, though he had never been anywhere near them. "They will not be expecting us," he said, as he opened the door from the white marble and polished dark woodwork of the grand entrance hall into the plain whitewashed stairwell leading downwards.

"They will not mind," she said gaily, starting down the stairs ahead of him. "Mrs Poole said I was to ask for anything that would make me feel at home."

He followed her down the cold stairwell, his emotions in turmoil. He was growing to think of her as a sweet-natured, practical young woman, with a kind heart and a generosity of spirit that frequently caught him unawares, all of which he would very much like in a wife. Now she was speaking of Mrs Poole as a confidante, a woman to be relied on and turned to with confidence, as a lady of the house would turn to devoted and well-respected staff, certain of their willing assistance. Mrs Poole, in turn, was speaking of her feeling "at home". And yet she had made it clear that she did not wish to marry him. He did not know how to feel about her; it was like being pulled about in two directions at once.

She was proved right in her certainty of being welcomed below stairs, for Mrs Poole, suddenly confronted with the master of the house and his supposed future wife appearing in her domain, did not show any consternation, only listened to Lady Celia's plan and nodded.

"That's kindly of you, Lady Celia. I can do it myself but perhaps you're feeling restless with little to do?"

"I am," said Lady Celia, making her way to the fireside, where Holly and Ivy lay asleep, their sleek black and white bodies curled around one another. "If you'll guide me, I shall be glad to turn my hand to something useful." She looked back at Alexander, who hovered in the doorway. "Lord Comerford can keep us company, he is probably unused to baking."

He felt in the way, awkward, but then Lady Celia gave a little laugh. "Here. Take that stool and sit near me while Mrs Poole fetches me an apron. How might we decorate them, once they are baked? I was thinking of anchors and flags, ships and dolphins, things from your time in the navy. What do you remember from your time on board?"

He sat on the little stool, now lower than she, having to look up at her smiling face.

"Stars," he said, the word coming out of his mouth unexpectedly.

"Stars?"

He ploughed on, despite feeling awkward. "At night, keeping watch, there were stars so bright... in London you cannot see them so well, there is too much light and the air is dirty. But at sea..." He cleared his throat. "The men used to like to look at them and imagine their loved ones were watching those same stars. It made them feel closer to home." His voice had gone husky, and he stopped, remembering the loneliness that would rise sometimes, sudden as though it had been shot from a cannon into your chest, the pain of it. It always faded, there was too much to be done at sea and in wartime to be moping about pining for home and family or friends, for thinking of lost comrades, but still it would rise from time to time when it was least expected and each time it was sharper than seemed possible. Often a man would look up at the stars when tears were threatening to fall, doing his best to master his emotions in front of his fellow men. If they were truly still engaged, he might, over time, have unburdened himself to her of some of his past experiences. The sad memories might have softened over time while they built happy memories together, from their new shared life. And indeed, he might then be able to look back on his time in the navy as the good times that they undoubtedly had been, without the sad memories overwhelming him.

She was watching his face, her eyes steady on him. "Stars," she said, her voice gentle as though he had told her of the loneliness, though he had not. "Stars would be beautiful on gingerbread; the children will think of the star that led the wise men to the stable where the baby Jesus lay. And we will think of those men who did not come home but were comforted by them in the sky."

He had to look away, pretend to notice the boot boy gathering his supplies to get about his work for the day. The cannonball had hit him again in the chest when he so rarely allowed it to overcome him. Her simple kind words had found their way to his heart in an instant and opened it up to feelings he made it his business to forget about whenever he could. He cleared his throat again and nodded brusquely without answering her.

"You'll have a cup of tea, Sir? While you sit along of us?" offered Mrs Poole.

He nodded and a kitchen maid set about making up a tray, which she deposited near his elbow with a timid curtsey, unused to waiting on the master.

"Thank you," he said, noting the incongruity of the delicate flowered china he was used to sipping from in the drawing room. Here in a working kitchen, it did not seem sturdy enough to survive.

Mrs Poole was gathering the necessary ingredients on the long kitchen table, from pounds of flour and sugar to butter and treacle, all in large quantities, for there would likely be more than four hundred children at the Foundling Hospital. There were more than five pounds of dried orange peel to be cut into tiny pieces and jars of spices to be emptied out entirely. Ginger, caraway, cloves, mace and allspice were carefully weighed and ground by one of the kitchen girls, while another buttered tin plates ready to bake the biscuits once the dough should be ready. And amidst them all was Lady Celia, apparently entirely at ease, pouring melted butter into a bowl with the treacle and stirring it thoroughly with a large wooden spoon, ready to add all the other ingredients, apparently uncaring that her gloves were growing dusty with flour. She began to sing, her voice sweet and joyful and the two kittens peeped out of their basket at the unexpected sound, their eyes round with wonder, paws clinging to the wickerwork rim, eager for further exploration of their new surroundings now that they were certain of being well fed and cared for. Noticing them she laughed and reached out one finger to dab flour on Holly's head so that the kitten appeared to wear a crown of white on her black fur. Holly shook her head and sneezed at the flour coating her nose, then scampered away to the boot boy, who was offering both of them little scraps of bacon fat.

> *"The holly bears a blossom*
> *As white as lily flower*
> *And Mary bore sweet Jesus Christ*
> *To be our dear Savior."*

One of the kitchen maids joined in quietly and suddenly they were all singing the final verse, Mrs Poole could barely hold a tune, but her face was full of smiles, while the boot boy, who had crept in to listen, had a high voice that would have graced any choirboy.

> *"The holly and the ivy*
> *When they are both full grown*
> *Of all trees that are in the wood*
> *The holly bears the crown."*

Lord Comerford suddenly stood up. "I have something I need to see to," he said, to no-one in particular, and strode from the room, his boots clattering into the distance as he took the stairs two at a time.

※

CELIA CONTINUED CUTTING OUT GINGERBREAD AS though she was unbothered by his departure, but she was disappointed. He had been willing for her to come and make the biscuits, had even shared confidences of his life at sea, speaking with real emotion about the loneliness that the men sometimes felt, the homesickness that would have come over all of them at one time or another. He had sat amongst the kitchen staff and drunk tea, stroked the kittens and smiled when she sang. It was romantic. If she had been shown such a scene and asked whether she would like her marriage to be like this, she would have fervently agreed. A little fun whilst undertaking a practical kindness towards others... she had been enjoying herself, had found it a happy use of the morning. No: more than that, if she were truly honest with herself. She had been enjoying Lord Comerford's company, had sung because he had admired her singing voice a few days earlier, had played at being the mistress of Comerford House and enjoyed it. And now he was gone, with no real explanation, only a vague and muttered excuse. Had she been mistaken? Had he only begrudgingly come downstairs, appalled at her lack of propriety in doing the baking for the children herself, had he left because he could stand it no longer? She was sure there had been more than mere politeness between them. There had been a warmth beyond an effort to be civil, beyond even friendliness. But it had suddenly gone.

"There's no more room on that tray, my lady," said Sarah the kitchen maid. "Let me pass you another."

Celia looked down at where she had, unthinking, placed one biscuit on top of another. She waited until Sarah had changed over the trays, leaving her with a newly empty tray, then continued cutting the biscuit dough and placing it on the tray, all the fun gone from the activity.

"Perhaps you can finish the last tray for me, Sarah," she said. "Mrs Poole, I will be back in the morning to ice them."

"Yes, my lady," said Mrs Poole.

❄

CELIA SAT IN THE DRAWING ROOM, GLOVES NOW changed for fresh ones, downcast. She had been the mistress of the house but now was an interloper, an unwanted guest left to sit here in this empty room, her host gone who knows where. Gabriel inquired whether she would like a midday meal, but she only shook her head. She did not feel like eating. She *was* unwanted, after all. She had told him she did not want to marry him, that she would find someone else, had even indicated Lord Hyatt as a suitable alternative and he had only agreed with her. Then she had seen another side to him... or thought she had before it had disappeared again. Why was he so difficult to get to know? Every time she glimpsed something warm and friendly about him, it was gone again, leaving her uncertain of how to proceed. If she ever did get to Bellbrook Manor in time for Twelfth Night, which was looking less and less likely, should she proceed in gaining Lord Hyatt's affections and indeed proposal of marriage? Or should she hold back, speak with Lord Comerford again and try to ascertain his true feelings for her? If he was only being polite while she was his guest and was still hopeful that she would remove the engagement between them by forming a new alliance, then matters would be clear between them. But... but she could not believe that he still felt as he had done just before Christmas. Her feelings towards him had changed a great deal, was it not possible that his had also? But if she were to confess her misgivings about breaking off the engagement, would he turn cold and distant again and remind her that there was nothing between them except for a decades-old practical arrangement between their two families? She did not wish to hear that again.

She tried to read, aware that several hours had passed. Where had he gone? Words swam before her eyes and she re-read the same page more than once.

The door suddenly flew open to reveal Lord Comerford. "I have a surprise for you," he said, his eyes bright, his lips half-smiling. There were snowflakes in his hair and he seemed full of a new energy.

"What is it?"

"I have hired a sleigh for the horses to pull; it had to be driven across London to get it here. It will make for a pleasant ride around the park, or even further beyond, should you wish it. The horses will manage as far as the Foundling Hospital tomorrow, I believe. But it is ready to drive now, if you wish to try it out."

She was already on her feet. "I will get my coat."

"Wrap up warm," he reminded her. "I will ask the servants for footwarmers and furs, but it will still be very cold, especially when we are moving fast."

She nodded eagerly, her previous gloom gone in an instant. In her room she did not even bother to ring for Aveline, only grabbed at a thick coat of red wool and a bonnet decorated with berries. She looked about and found a large grey fur muff in the oversized style that was all the fashion. Usually she found it excessively large, but it would be needed in this weather. She hurried back down the stairs, excited at the prospect of being outdoors again. And his sudden absence from the kitchen now made sense, perhaps he had not been annoyed or bored by her company, rather he had gone to secure the only means of transport available just now and he had been successful, had found a way for them to enjoy the outdoors as well as make their planned journey to the Foundling Hospital with all the gingerbread easier – he had tried to make her plan come to fruition. Happiness rushed up in her, partly in excitement at going out, yes, but also warmth towards Lord Comerford. She had misjudged his actions, and been proven wrong. He had acted to please her, to make her happy. And she was.

Stepping outside she gave a gasp at the cold air. Snowflakes were slowly falling. A groom stood holding the reins of two bay horses who stood stamping their feet, behind them a fine sleigh, in carved wood painted a bold red, the tresses bound with little brass bells, which jingled as the horses moved. The seats in the sleigh were heaped up with blankets and furs.

"Let me help you in," said Lord Comerford, holding out his hand.

She took it, his firm grip guiding her into the sleigh until she was safely seated, finding a welcome footwarmer at her feet. She arranged the furs and blankets as he made his way round the sleigh and climbed in beside her. The sleigh was not large, so their bodies were close together. Celia held herself stiffly apart, so that they would not touch, for it seemed very intimate. But it was warm and comfortable and when Lord Comerford took the reins from the groom and clicked his tongue to the horses, she felt a thrill as the sleigh moved forward, slipping at first on the icy road and then more smoothly as the horses stepped neatly outwards to the edge of Green Park, leaving the road behind.

And then they were flying, the cold wind rushing by, the horses growing more confident as they found the untrodden snow firmer beneath their feet than the packed ice of the street, moving beyond a trot to a full gallop. Celia let out a giggle and then a laugh at the exhilaration of it, at the wild freedom after the days spent locked indoors or trying to walk London's snowy streets – suddenly they were free to gallop, to rush through the snow. It was breathtaking. She glanced at Lord Comerford and saw that he was smiling at her, before returning his eyes to the horses, to keep them safely on track in the hard-to-see terrain.

There was no-one else out in Green Park, it was only a white landscape stretching out beyond them. At full gallop, the sleigh skimmed the fresh snow, while Lord Comerford lightly steered them away from obstacles in their pathway. At a distance Celia could see Buckingham House, the home of Queen Charlotte, and wondered if the Queen might see their little sleigh rush past in the snow and wonder at who was daring enough to brave the deep drifts.

They swept past the river and circled back, but when they came close to Comerford House, a groom standing waiting for them, Lord Comerford looked down at her and she shook her head, laughing.

"Again! Please let us go back round again!"

He gave a quick nod, and they were flying again. Their bodies grew close, pressed together as the sleigh swerved around tight curves. The furs and blankets created a warm nest, until suddenly –

"Oh!" she cried. A low-hanging branch of a tree along their pathway had snatched at the blanket covering them, so that it was unexpectedly ripped away. Even her woollen coat and bonnet were not enough to protect her from the sudden rush of cold.

"Whoa," called Lord Comerford. "Whoa there."

The horses came to an uncertain stop, the sleigh still

slipping forward as it slowed. Lord Comerford jumped out on his side, then strode round to where the blanket was hanging precariously from the branch. He unhooked it and shook out the snow that had fallen onto it, then came round to Celia's side.

"Let me re-cover you," he said, smiling. "It is too cold to be without it."

She nodded and he bent over her, gently laying the blanket over her furs, then carefully tucking it around her body so that it could not be lost again. His hands were all about her, pressing against her arms, her thighs, wrapping the last part close to her shoulders, one hand brushing the nape of her neck. Her lips parted as she looked up at him, warmth spreading through her at his touch, his closeness to her as he busied himself.

"Thank you," she murmured.

He paused, his face very close to hers, one hand either side of her, one on her arm, one close to her thigh. He paused there, his eyes searching hers, as she gazed up at him, his face asking a question she did not know the answer to.

"Thank you," she murmured again, but this time she almost breathed the words, so quietly were they spoken, and his eyes flickered to her lips as though he were hungry for them.

Then one of the horses snorted, and stamped its feet, growing cold in the snow without moving, and the sleigh slipped forward a few inches. Lord Comerford placed his hand on the side. "Whoa there," he commanded, and his voice was hoarse. He paused for another moment, his eyes still on Celia, before he strode round, back to his place beside her, his body once again warm against her. This time she did not try to hold herself apart, only relished the sensation of it, her mind full of the silence that had just been between them, his expression when he had looked at her mouth, the moment that had come and gone too fast, leaving her heart thudding.

❄

BACK AT COMERFORD HOUSE THE SILENCE BETWEEN them remained as servants hurried to meet them. The grooms led the horses and sleigh away, Gabriel took Lord Comerford's hat and coat, while Aveline exclaimed over Celia, removing her coat, muff and bonnet.

"It's too cold to be out for so long, my lady, shall I have your dinner brought to your bedchamber so you can stay warm and have an early night? I can't have you catching a chill."

"Y-yes," said Celia, the words reluctant. She was unsure of what she wanted, but at this moment being close to Lord Comerford was both all that she desired and something to be escaped at once. It was easier to accept Aveline's insistence, not to think about the choices open to her.

Lord Comerford stood watching her. When he saw her take a tentative step towards the stairs he gave her a small bow. "Good night, then, Lady Celia," he said.

"Good – good night, Lord Comerford."

She knew he was watching her as she mounted the stairs, wanted at each step to turn back and say that no, she would eat dinner with him instead, but every step she took made the changing of her mind seem less possible and now she was on the landing, following Aveline like a child. She turned her head for one last glimpse of him and saw him still standing there, watching her, his expression unreadable.

7

A SLEIGH RIDE

Celia awoke early after a night of troubled sleep. She had woken several times, and each time she had revisited her choice the previous evening, to escape to her room and have hot soup and an early night, Lord Comerford's face as he had quietly accepted her choice. In between she had slept, though badly, and in her dreams her blanket had escaped her more than once, more than once she had seen Lord Comerford's face come close to her, his hands touching her body as he tucked her back in, warmth rising up in her during the pause when he had looked into her eyes, the choice hanging between them. She felt overheated even in the cold room, before returning to her dreams, summoning them back to hold them fast to her.

As soon as she saw the sky grow light she summoned Aveline with the excuse that she must ice biscuits if they were to be ready for the Foundling Hospital. Seated before her mirror as an unusually silent Aveline pinned up her hair, she looked at herself in the mirror and saw pale cheeks and shadows under her eyes. Even Aveline grimaced at the sight of her when she was finished, unlike her usual nod of approval over a job well done, then leant over her and pinched her cheeks without saying anything, though even this home remedy did little for her complexion.

Back in Mrs Poole's kitchen, two kitchen maids were assigned to help her ice the biscuits with stars and anchors. There was a quietness to this morning, with no singing. She had a cup of tea by her side, but it slowly grew cold. The kittens were asleep and showed little interest in joining in the work, while Mrs Poole was busy trying to change menus to suit the shortages now taking effect, for with day after day of first fog and then snow, deliveries from the countryside had been badly affected, such that the milk was now almost gone and vegetables were growing scarce. Delivery boys were not making their usual rounds, so most of the footmen had found themselves pressed into service to act as such and had left the house to visit butchers and grocers about town. Comerford House was well equipped with preserves and root vegetables, but the myriad of dainties which Mrs Poole was accustomed to commanding were now sadly absent.

"And this is why grand folks ought not to live near St James," was her opinion, muttered under her breath as she looked through her recipes and the contents of the larder and other food stores. "For all the traders will favour the palace of course, before they serve the likes of us. Times like these, even an earl's household will not be good enough for them, begging your pardon, my lady."

"I am sure we will be looked after by you, Mrs Poole," soothed Celia. "Where is Lord Comerford this morning?" she could not help adding. She wanted to see him again, indeed she could think of little but his face last night and their closeness when they had been out in the sleigh, but she had committed to going to the Foundling Hospital with gingerbread for the children and so that must come first. Besides, it gave her an excuse not to see him, for she was not at all sure what she would say when she did. She tried over a few greetings in her mind, all of which sounded too formal or too expectant of something between them. None of them sounded right. What did she want? She was not sure. The longer she spent with him, closed up here together, the more she liked him, the more she wanted to spend longer with him, perhaps indeed to spend their lives together as had been the plan all along? But it had been her choice to say that she did not want to marry him at all and so now – what? Was she to retract her threats and instead offer herself as his intended bride after all – was she, in so many words, to *propose* to him? It seemed absurd, certainly unladylike, desperate even. But there was beginning to rise in her a desperation, a need to see him, a need to always be close to him and if that were the case then surely it was madness to continue her plan, to look elsewhere for what was right in front of her?

But he did not *fight* for her. He allowed her to walk away from him, time after time, as though he was entirely unbothered one way or another about whether she stayed or went from his life.

"We're done, now, my lady," murmured Sarah and Celia looked down to see that the biscuits were indeed all iced, though she was sure the two maids had done the lion's share of the work while her mind had been elsewhere. The biscuits were neatly laid out drying now, their icing pretty, if not up to the standards of Brown's, but no doubt the children they were destined for would not care about such niceties, they would only be glad to have a sweet treat brought to them to make the festive season special.

"Thank you. Sarah and Mercy, if you would be so good

as to package them up when they are dry, then Lord Comerford and I will take them to the hospital."

"Yes, my lady."

"Thank you again, Mrs Poole."

"Not at all, my lady, I'm sure the children will be grateful."

She climbed the stairs out of the servants' domain and then further up, to her room, where she changed her gloves again, dropping the icing-smeared ones for Aveline to clean and pulling on a fresh pair, her movements clumsy, her mind elsewhere.

❄

An hour later, Alexander stood waiting by the sleigh as two of the footmen carefully attached a large travelling trunk filled with layers of gingerbread neatly stacked with brown paper to keep them from damaging their icing. He nodded to them as they finished. Always these two steps forwards and one back with her, it threw him into confusion. Was she warming to him or not? Always it seemed so – until it did not. Yesterday she had laughed out loud beside him, her face alight with pleasure, had begged for the sleigh ride to go on for longer. When the blanket had caught on the branch and he had tucked it about her again he had grown suddenly aware of his hands on her person, the intimacy of it, and looking at her face he had seen a waiting there, a desire that had matched the desire rising in him. He had wanted to take her face in his hands and kiss her upturned lips. But then the horse had moved, he had needed to control it lest the sleigh pull away and the moment had been lost. When they had returned to the house he had been about to speak, to ask her to come into the drawing room and discuss their future, ask her if she was sure she wanted to break off their engagement. He had tried out a few phrases in his mind, reminding her of the pleasure they had seemed to have had in one another's company these past days, asking whether it was worth them trying anew to be a couple in more than just name or expectation. But she had hesitated in the hall and then all but run away with her maid to her bedchamber for the evening, and he had yet to see her this morning. He could not make her out at all, but his feelings for her were growing day by day. He believed they could do well together, he felt for her more than duty or loyalty.

What he felt now was... love.

He had not known it before in his life, but he recognised it nonetheless, as though it had introduced itself formally by name and title. What else could it be, that had him look upon her with desire, that made him want to kiss her lips and hold her close, to know her and care for her as his own? Yet every time he felt the certainty of it there was uncertainty in her behaviour, as though she did not feel it at all.

He did not want an uncertain wife, one who blew hot and cold, who made him feel doubtful. He wanted her to feel as he did – that to lose this chance of happiness would be the action of a fool. Perhaps there were other women of the *ton* better suited to him, but he could not imagine it. Before, he had thought a marriage needed only duty and loyalty, the effort made to be a good husband or wife, that these would suffice. But now they seemed like pale shadows of what he really wanted. And what he wanted was...

"Lord Comerford."

What he wanted was Lady Celia, stepping from the house in her red coat and dark furs, her eyes not meeting his, her demeanour awkward. Here it was again, the step backwards so that he could not be sure of her. He did not wish to force her into marriage if she did not feel as he did, but surely there was something in her that had changed? How else could she be so merry and warm in his company, at least on some occasions, when before Christmas she had been so determined to leave him in the past?

"Good morning, Lady Celia. I trust you are well rested?"

She nodded without answering, stepping into the sleigh. He did not tuck her in as he had the previous day, leaving her to make herself comfortable as she saw fit. He could not bear that intimacy again and the feelings it provoked in him if she would only run away from it.

The drive through London was slower and less exciting than their time in Green Park. Despite the thick snow, some streets had been cleared of drifts, though they were still icy, and men and women made their way about, walking or riding with excessive care, mindful of icy patches in the roads. The driving took up all of Alexander's attention, trying to guide the horses so that they would not slip but allowing the sleigh to move easily without getting stuck. Lady Celia sat in silence beside him. He glanced at her occasionally, but she seemed to be looking only ahead, her face carefully devoid of expression.

❄

It was strange to be in the sleigh again after the previous day. At first her heart had fluttered at the idea that Lord Comerford would once again tuck her in, his hands touching her body, his face close to hers.

But he did not. He looked briefly at her to see that she was settled and comfortable, then turned his attention solely to the driving, and she was disappointed. Had he decided her actions after yesterday indicated coldness on her part? Perhaps. Or perhaps he had not felt what she had, had only been mindful of her comfort, without any further intentions, perhaps anything more had all been in her own mind. She sat in silence beside him, watching the snowy streets going by, still uncertain of what path to take.

The matron of the Foundling Hospital was surprised to receive visitors, since the streets were so quiet, but naturally enough welcomed them with great politeness and gratitude for their interest in the children. Lord Comerford was taken for a walk round the building with the chaplain, while Celia was offered the chance to hear the children singing in the chapel.

"As you know one of our great benefactors was Handel, who composed music especially for the Foundlings to sing, and held many recitals for their benefit. I will leave you in the chapel to hear them perform."

Celia sat quietly at the back of the chapel as the children were put through their paces by the choirmaster. Their soft voices rose to a crescendo, filling the space with music and bringing tears to her eyes, touched by their earnest little faces. She hoped that they might all find good homes one day.

The matron returned to collect her, and the children filed past, casting curious glances at Celia.

"When do they leave you?"

"About fourteen years of age, usually," said the matron. "They will be apprenticed or sent for service. We try to find good positions for them."

Celia nodded. In her pampered life, at fourteen her hardest task had been to make her sewing sampler neat and keep her frocks tidy, to stay quiet of a Sunday church sermon. By the time they were fourteen these children would be expected to work hard for many hours a day, even in a good household or business, and they were the lucky ones who had been taken in by the Foundling Hospital as babies. Here they were fed and clothed, trained for work and kept clean, but she doubted their lives contained much in the way of fun or pleasure. She was glad that at least today they would have a festive treat to eat, to make the season brighter.

"If you come this way I will show you round some of the building," said the matron. "Lord Comerford has been so good as to take two of our girls for Comerford House to serve as kitchen maids and five boys for Comerford Castle, two as grooms, three as gardeners. It is a great opportunity for them, and we are most grateful for his generosity," she added as she showed Celia around the girls' sewing room. "He says when he has spent more time at his estate he will look out further opportunities. It is men like him who show others that charity is a duty that all great men should undertake. Many think a small donation will suffice their conscience, but few men think to take the children directly into their care, yet it is a very great chance for them to be part of a lord's estate."

Celia nodded, thinking. Lord Comerford had not made a great show of his generosity, had the matron not spoken she would not have known of it at all. But he had acted with true kindness, not just delivering the gingerbread as a festive treat, here and gone again in an instant, but making permanent provision for those children to whom he could offer employment and a good life. A man of few words, but to whom good deeds and generosity seemed to come naturally. She imagined the two of them married, how they might visit the hospital each year, perhaps, bringing something to cheer the children, but also taking away those children to whom they might offer a new life when they were ready to leave. They could do good things together, she was sure of it, they would not feel like tedious dutiful expectations, but rather be suffused with the joys of the season, shared with those who were most in need of it.

"May we take the children into the field to play?" she asked suddenly.

"Play, Lady Celia?"

"There is snow outside and we have a sleigh. I imagine they spend their days without much festivity. We would like to help them make merry."

She thought the matron would refuse, but after all Lord Comerford had proved himself a possibly valuable benefactor and the matron was clever enough to know that the whims of such benefactors must be curtseyed to. "As you wish, my lady."

❅

AND SO ALEXANDER FOUND HIMSELF ON THE ROAD outside the Foundling Hospital, driving the sleigh back and forth, each time filled with a group of overawed children, while on the field beside the building itself he could see the red-coated figure of Lady Celia, running about playing snowballs with the other children, more than one hundred of them laughing and calling out to one another, while fifty more stood waiting patiently for their turn in the sleigh. He could not imagine how this had come about, but there was pleasure to be had from seeing the wide-eyed children take their turn in the sleigh, he remembered such rides with his brother when they were children, the eager exhortation to go faster, still faster, to go round once again. One of the boys, a lanky dark-haired child whom he had chosen to come to his estate took the horses' reins each time children came in and out of the sleigh, holding himself with a gravity of manner that made Alexander smile.

"I can see you'll be a fine groom one day."

"Yes, my lord."

"What is your name?"

"John Tavistock, Sir."

Alexander looked the boy over. A foundling, given the name of a local street in the absence of any other. He would not know, of course, that the street had been named for the Marquis of Tavistock, a nobleman unwittingly passing on his name to a child devoid of family.

"I hope you'll do well at Comerford Castle," he said gently. "It will be a big change for you, but my staff are good people, and the countryside will be a healthier place for you to grow up in than here in the city."

"Yes, sir."

"Are you the oldest of the children I've chosen?"

"Yes, sir, by six months."

Alexander tried not to smile at the pride taken in just six months' precedence. "Then I shall have to task you with looking after them, John. They will be unused to their new lives. But I know that you will take care of them and be a good leader to them as they settle in."

The boy straightened. "Yes, Sir," he said proudly.

"Now, I believe we have two more rides to run and then I must take Lady Celia home, or she will be catching a cold. Sit by me and I'll let you take the reins as we ride."

"Truly, Sir?"

"Well, you must begin to learn some time."

The next two journeys were considerably more bumpy, having a less experienced pair of hands on the reins, but the boy was beaming by the end and Alexander patted him on the shoulder. "Well done. Now, hold the horses for me while I fetch Lady Celia."

He found her kneeling in the snow behind a hastily erected fort made of an old barrel, shaping snowballs for the children to throw, ducking her head to avoid being hit. Her pelisse was wet through, but her cheeks were pink, and she was laughing. He stood and watched her for a few moments, overwhelmed by the rush of his feelings for her.

He loved her. The woman he had believed to be tediously young and superficial, selfish and childish, had revealed herself to him these last days together and his emotions, so long held back, had flowered at her touch, her very presence. He knew for certain now that he wanted her by his side, wanted to marry her and make her happy. He wanted her laughter and bright eyes, her warm heart and kissable lips to be a part of his life for the rest of his days. But how to tell her that?

"Must we go already?" she asked, catching sight of him.

He pulled off his coat. "We must. Your pelisse is soaked; you will catch a chill. Take this."

She shook her head, though she smiled as she did so. "I cannot take that, you will freeze."

"I will do well enough. Come."

She turned first to wave at the children, now being ordered back indoors by the watchful staff. "Goodbye!" she called, and they enthusiastically waved back to her, their small voices half swept away by the wind.

"Goodbye, y'ladyship!"

She moved back to him, cheeks and the tip of her nose pink with the cold, nodded acceptance at his coat. She peeled off the sodden pelisse, wrapping it into a wet bundle that she laid where her feet would go on the sleigh, then turning her back to him so that he might help her on with his coat, which more than wrapped about her, trailing slightly in the snow since it was far too long for her. "Thank you."

He stepped back. In placing the coat about her, he had caught her scent again and it brought heat rushing up in him, so that he was glad not to be wearing his heavy overcoat. Too full of feelings to speak, he held out his hand to help her into the sleigh, then walked round to his own side and got in beside her.

"You must not catch cold," he said, leaning over to better tuck in the furs about her, their closeness bringing back the memory of their sleigh ride the day before, the moment when he had been about to kiss her. For one moment he suddenly imagined her undressed, wrapped only in the silky soft furs, how it would feel to slip his hands under her dress, to touch the nakedness that lay beneath. It left him flustered, unable to return her smile.

"Thank you," she said. "I should be cold, but I am not, it is the exhilaration of the drive, I think. That and your warm coat."

❉

HE ONLY NODDED, HIS FACE SERIOUS, THEN DROVE AWAY from the Hospital. Celia sat back in the comfort of the sleigh, enveloped by the furs and blankets, which she did not notice. About her was Lord Comerford's coat, still hot from his body, and each time she breathed in, she inhaled his scent, warm leather and the festive spices of the season. They turned down a smaller street and the sleigh slowed as the horses walked carefully through thicker snow that had not yet been cleared away. There was no-one about.

"Lord Comerford?"

He turned his head at once. "Yes?"

"Would you stop the sleigh?"

He reined in the horses, his face concerned. "Are you well?"

"Yes."

They sat still, looking at one another. It was very quiet and Celia almost lost her nerve, but then she swallowed and said, "It was very good of you to take the children."

The frown did not leave his face. "I could do more, I think, but until I have spoken with my steward..."

She pulled her hand out from the heap of covers and laid it on his arm. "It was very good of you," she repeated. "You are a kind man."

He looked down at her hand on his sleeve, and the frown softened on his brow, when he met her gaze again his eyes were warm. "Thank you," he said. "For taking me there. For thinking of them at this time of year."

"We did well together," she said, her voice too small and quiet for what she was trying to say.

He did not answer, instead his eyes left her gaze and he looked at her lips, then back to her eyes. His voice was low when he replied. "Lady Celia – I –"

"Please, Sir, spare a penny?"

Celia turned her head, startled by the interruption, to see a child, perhaps ten years old, dressed in many layers of shabby clothing, holding out her hand. One of her feet, she noticed, was turned in on itself, so that the toe of her broken boot did not face ahead, but inwards almost to the heel of the other shoe.

Celia looked back at Lord Comerford, who looked shaken by the interruption, but was already feeling in his pocket for some coins, which he gave to the child.

"Thank you, Sir. God bless you, Sir."

The girl child began to walk away from them back up the street, one foot dragging.

Celia looked back at Lord Comerford, wanting what had been lost, their few words perhaps about to lead to something greater but she could not forget what she had just seen and instead she twisted in her seat, knelt up on the cushions and called out. "Girl!"

The child turned, her body already cringing in fear as though she thought the precious coins were about to be taken away. "Miss?"

"Come here," said Celia.

The girl shuffled back to her. "Miss?"

"What's your name?"

"Eliza, Miss. Eliza Southam."

"Where do you live, Eliza?"

"Just there, Miss. In that house," she added, pointing to a shabby crooked house wedged between two newer buildings.

"With your family?"

"Yes, Miss, and another." Eliza looked down, then said, "Only there's no work, not for more than a week. The menfolk sells vegetables and me mam sells hot potatoes, but there ain't no deliveries from the country, so there ain't no money coming in. I – I wouldn't normally beg Miss, but a few coins would buy us some bread – what bread there is to buy."

Celia was already climbing out of the sleigh. "Take me to your mother," she demanded.

8

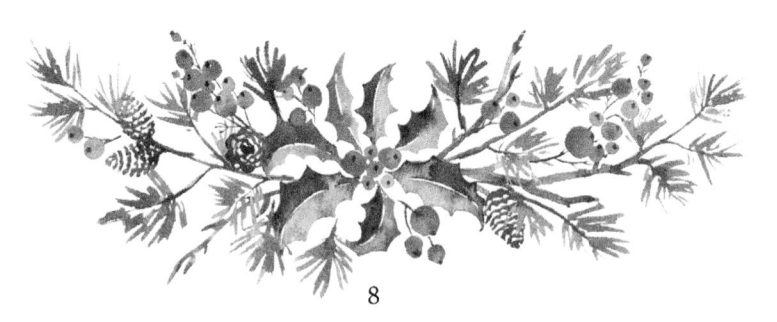

THE SOUTHAM FAMILY

The house was tiny and smelt thickly of tallow candles, but Alexander, following Lady Celia in, could see that there was an ongoing effort to keep it clean, blankets neatly folded in a corner indicating that the room where they were presently standing must be also used as a bedroom at night for the children.

Lady Celia was already talking with two women. One very elderly, who sat in bemused silence, one an anxious-faced woman who, finding herself suddenly faced with nobility standing inside her house, was clutching at her apron with nervous hands.

"We took in my poor sister's husband and their two children when she died," she was saying. "We have two working men and the boys pick up errands and help out, so we do better than most when they can work. They sells vegetables and I sells strawberries in summer or hot potatoes in the winter, but there's been no deliveries, see, not for a week now. All the snow means everyone stays indoors and so we've very little. We're very grateful to his lordship for the money, of course we are, but I don't like the children to beg, it's not right when there's others worse off. But Eliza can't do as much as the other children, on account of her leg."

"She did not mean any harm by it," said Lady Celia soothingly. "It has been a very harsh season. May I send round some food for the children this evening, something simple? It would give me great pleasure to be able to help."

"Thank you, my lady. But I don't want to take charity."

"It is not charity," said Lady Celia. "It is a Christmas gift. I would have taken boxes on Saint Stephen's Day to my father's tenants, but I have been stuck here in London instead, so I would be grateful to keep up the tradition with your family, if you will let me."

Mrs Southam hesitated, no doubt not wishing to give offence, but Alexander could see her pride being dented by receiving the act of charity, however sorely it was needed.

"I think you said you had two working men in your family?" he asked suddenly.

"Yes, your lordship."

"If they cannot work their vegetable business for a few days while the snow stays, might I hire them? I have need of extra hands at Comerford House, clearing snow and in the stable yard. I can pay them wages for a few days if they have nothing better to occupy them – and your boys, too, if they are willing to run a few errands about town? I'm having difficulty managing my affairs with the post not working, I'd hire them as messengers until the weather returns to normal."

He saw her brow clear at once. "They're right good workers," she assured him. "We'd be glad of the work, your lordship."

❅

They returned to Comerford House with two men and three boys in tow, and Celia watched as Lord Comerford disappeared with all of them, finding them work which any of his own servants could have carried out, while she went indoors and asked Mrs Poole if she could make up a large batch of mutton stew and apple dumplings to be sent to the Southam's by the end of the day. Then she retreated to the drawing room to think about what she had just seen and how she might better help. She had offered charity, which was much needed, but Lord Comerford had given dignity through work, and that had been graceful, she realised. When he rejoined her, she rang for tea and for the housekeeper.

"Mrs Pratchett, do you have some old linen that I might use? A bedsheet or suchlike will do very well. I wish to make some rag dolls and some sachets of lavender; do you have dried lavender to spare amongst your stores? And a salve, for hands?"

Mrs Pratchett gave a decided nod. "Certainly, Lady Celia," she said. "I shall look out a piece of linen myself and send one of the girls to you with dried lavender."

"Mrs Southam had such red hands," said Celia to Lord Comerford when Mrs Pratchett had gone. "I am sure she has little in the way of creams for them."

A jar of dried lavender flowers and an old sheet having been provided, Celia took out a pair of scissors and set about the linen with an assured air. "You can help me, if you wish," she said to Lord Comerford, who was regarding her with a curious air. "Now that I have cut out some little squares you put a scoop of lavender in and tie them up like this with a scrap of ribbon, you see? It will make a little scented parcel which the women can add to their clothing to keep it smelling sweet."

"I've seen such parcels at the backs of cupboards my whole life but never thought about making them," he said.

She laughed. "I will teach you."

Clumsily, he managed the first few, his fingers growing more assured as he progressed. Meanwhile Celia was cutting out two larger pieces of the linen and stuffing it with some straw from the stables, which was falling all over her skirts, although she did not seem to mind.

"I felt sorry for those families," she said, voice soft. "We think such weather is for huddling indoors, but for many it means no work at all. I hope we can help them."

"We will send the food you ordered tonight," he said. "I will ensure more is sent when the provisions are readily delivered, until they get back on their feet. And the men will be paid tonight, as will the boys."

She looked up at him and her eyes were warm. "Thank you," she said.

"You need not spend all evening doing that work if you do not wish to," he added. "I am sure that the food and work will suffice."

"Food is a necessity for all of course," she said quietly. "But a poor child rarely has a toy, and a poor woman rarely has something of her own to bring her a moment of comfort in a hard day. These are not much, but they are something. And it is not as though I do not have enough time."

She had finished stuffing the rough shapes she had made: a head and a swaddled body. Now she painted each little face, giving them different expressions with only a few strokes of her brush, eyes and mouths, a suggestion of a nose, little buttons down their fronts a wisp of hair under a cap, the semblance of tucked in arms.

They were simple poppets, but they had a warmth to

them, a liveliness that he imagined would be delightful to a child who rarely played with toys.

"I have a collection of marbles somewhere," he said.

She looked up. "Have you? Did you like to play with them as a child?"

"Yes. I could give them to the boys."

She smiled. "You do not need to feel obliged to give them away."

He shook his head. "They are sat in a box somewhere doing nothing, I will search them out." He rose and left the room, while she continued painting the two little dolls, placing them in front of the fire to dry.

"Let us eat what the Southams are eating," she said, when he arrived with the marbles and she had placed them into little bags, one for each of the three boys. "As a child I used to beg my governess to let us have a pudding-dinner as we called it and apple dumplings were one of our favourites. We are not too grand to eat mutton stew and apple dumplings, are we?" she added, glancing at him with a smile.

"No, indeed, if you wish it," he said, seeming surprised by her choice.

"Did you have such dinners?"

He nodded. "If my brother or I felt unwell. Mrs Taylor would bring a tray to the nursery with steaming hot rice pudding, full of spices and sugar, with stewed apples or plums according to the season." He smiled, remembering it. "We would eat in our nightshirts, and I swear the milk of the rice pudding made us fall asleep faster. Probably why she offered it."

Celia rang the bell and informed the footman of their wish, who bowed without allowing his undoubted surprise to show on his face and returned in a short while with a tray on which sat steaming bowls of the stew and dumplings.

"There is nothing so comforting as the smell of cinnamon," Celia said, taking a mouthful. "Mrs Poole's apple dumplings might even be better than our cook's, you are lucky to have her."

"She has been with us all my life," he said. "I cannot recall any other cook at Comerford House. She even travelled with the family to Comerford Castle when we were there. My mother said more than one guest tried to poach her for their households, but she never deserted us."

She nodded. "Loyalty should be appreciated," she said, and when she met his gaze there was something that spoke of more than faithful servants.

"Shall we return to them tomorrow morning with your gifts?"

She nodded, smiling. "I would like that, thank you," she said.

The door opened to reveal Aveline, who gave a curtsey. "Your bath is ready, my lady," she announced.

Celia wanted to protest. She wanted to stay here in the firelight with Lord Comerford, to ask for more stories of him as a child, but Aveline was waiting. "I look forward to visiting the Southams tomorrow," she told him, and he stood and bowed as she left the room. She glanced back to see him still watching her.

9

A FIRESIDE TALK

The morning of the thirtieth of December dawned bright and sunny, though still sharply cold. Visiting the horses in the stables at first light, Alexander heard from the grooms that there was skating in Hyde Park, where the river had frozen over. He sat at breakfast, hoping Lady Celia would soon join him, but became aware of Gabriel hovering.

"Yes?"

"Mrs Poole wishes to see you, my lord."

He nodded. "Certainly."

She stood in the doorway, flustered at being above stairs, hands tugging at her clean apron.

"You wanted to see me, Mrs Poole?"

"Begging your pardon, my lord, but supplies is beginning to run low, there's not many deliveries coming in from the countryside yet. We won't starve, of course, Sir, but the food I send up may be plain fare, and I didn't wish to disappoint you and Lady Celia."

He smiled at her anxious face. "You have done very good work so far, Mrs Poole, I am certain you will continue to do so. Lady Celia and I will be content with whatever you send up." He thought, remembering how good the simple food of the day before had been, especially after the hardship they had witnessed. "Indeed, why not send us up a picnic this evening. Simple fare, as you say. We will spread a rug by the fire and eat there; there is no need for all the formality of the dining room."

She looked surprised but did not comment, only bobbed a curtsey. "As your lordship wishes, of course, Sir."

She bobbed again on her way out as Lady Celia entered. Alexander stood, then waited until she had been served toast and tea.

"Would you like to go ice skating when we have finished with the Southams?" he asked.

She smiled at once. "I am a poor skater,' she admitted. "But I am a willing learner, if you will be patient with me."

He was ashamed that she should not expect patience from him as a given, he had been too quick to voice stern words rather than kind, perhaps it came from giving orders to his men on board, but it was no excuse, he must learn to speak more softly with her, she deserved nothing less.

"I will keep you steady," he promised, and was rewarded with another of her warm smiles, which he was beginning to look for, indeed more and more he found himself trying to make her smile.

❄

THERE WAS A NEWFOUND SENSE OF HOPE AT THE Southams' tiny home. The men and boys were working at Comerford House, but the two girls, Eliza and Betty, were awestruck by the gift of the poppets and Mrs Southam, dignity restored by the menfolk's working wages, was grateful for the gifts, her face less anxious, even managing a small smile as she served them both a weak cup of tea. Alexander listened as Celia asked about Eliza's future.

"Her foot is all twisted, m'lady, she cannot walk well nor stand for a long time, so she cannot work with the others. She might be able to learn lace making, but it's hard on the eyes."

Alexander looked down at the little girl's bowed legs, one foot turned so severely inwards that it sat awkwardly in the way of the other stepping forward. He saw in the girl's face the shame of not being able to earn her keep as the other children did, of knowing she was a burden and might suffer as she grew up, unable to make a living if she were not married. Lady Celia nodded, then beckoned to the girl to come closer.

"Would you like to see my hand, Eliza?" She did not wait for an answer, only tugged at her right glove, exposing her hand, which the girl and her mother both stared at.

"You can learn to do plenty of things that will not require you to walk," she said. "Look, let me show you something." From her reticule she pulled out a tiny leather notebook and a silver pencil, with which she drew a small doll, her thumb and little finger deftly gripping the silver pencil. "I will send you paints and paper, and you can learn to draw and paint paper dolls," she told Eliza. "They can be sold for a penny each, but a doll with a wardrobe of her own can fetch three shillings. And I will tell you a secret – dressmakers for fine ladies often give their best clients such a doll with costumes that match whatever new clothes they have ordered, as a gift for their children. My modiste – my dressmaker – is called Mrs Gill and if you practise, I will send you to her and see if she can give you regular work."

Eliza gazed up at Lady Celia with wide eyes and

Alexander saw that she was suddenly imagining a future for herself that she would not have dared to dream of. "Yes, m'lady."

Lady Celia stood up and spoke to Mrs Southam. "I will send you cloth for a clean dress and apron for her, so that she can look her best when she goes to Mrs Gill, it will help her chances of being employed. I will send everything over tomorrow with one of the maids and will enclose a note to be given to Mrs Gill in one month's time. Meanwhile she must practise every day: let her sit somewhere where she can see ladies passing by and have her copy their clothes as best she can. Can you do that?"

"Yes, m'lady, I'll do that right gladly. I'm grateful to you."

Alexander had to look away at the rush of feelings inside his chest. There was something magical about Lady Celia and himself as a couple, he knew it so strongly now that it could not just be his imagination. Each of them saw something that might be done to spread kindness in this world and then the other would use that first step as a ladder to do something greater, and so it went on. The fear he had undergone in being suddenly raised up to his new position, the desire to do good but not knowing where to start – all that fell away when he was with her, for he saw how the two of them might do something truly worthwhile in their lives together.

If they could only stay together! He wanted to laugh at the idea that he had almost let her go without a fight, had not much cared, thinking her a poor choice of wife anyway. Thank God he had seen her for who she really was in time. He was sure now of his feelings and even of hers, she could not be wholly indifferent to him. He must secure her, must bind her to him before she made a choice that he would regret for the rest of his life.

"Are you ready to skate?" she asked, as they left the house.

"Ready," he said, offering his arm.

They walked through the streets, still quieter than they were usually, although there were now a few more people walking along and the odd horse and cart rumbled by. He liked the warmth of her close to him, the way she had taken his arm without hesitation as soon as they had left the house.

Once arrived at the Serpentine they found the idea of skating was a popular one. There were children of all ages, but also adults testing their steadiness on the frozen river. They were accosted at once by various stallholders who had set up there, some renting skates, which Alexander procured for them both, others offering hot drinks or food, which he waved away. A band played by the side of the river, lending the place a festive air. A little boy knelt before Lady Celia, helping her strap on the skates over her boots, while Alexander managed by himself before giving the boy a penny for his trouble. Lady Celia stood up, shakily, her feet clumsy beneath her.

"Take my hand," he said, and to his pleasure she did so at once with a firm clasp, trusting in him to lead her to the water's edge, now turned frozen white. She stepped down onto it and immediately slipped with a frightened gasp, but he pulled her firmly upwards so that she regained her footing.

"I thought I would fall at my very first step," she laughed.

"I will not let that happen," he reassured her.

She regarded him, her face suddenly serious. "I know,"

she said softly, before her smile returned. "Then let us strike out and hope for the best!"

She struggled at first. More than once he had to tighten his grip on her to keep her upright, but slowly she began to feel her way to a smoother movement which allowed her greater freedom.

"How is it that you have such good balance?" she asked after a while. "It is most unfair. Did you skate a lot as a child?"

He shook his head. "I think it must come from being at sea, you must keep your footing no matter how the ship dips and rolls. It is never steady beneath your feet even in fair weather. In storms – it is every man for himself, and it is far harder to stay on your feet than this."

She nodded. "It has stood you in good stead," she managed, before slipping again. "I thought I was improving!"

"You are," he told her. "Look." Gently he disengaged himself from her.

"Don't leave me!" she implored at once, her eyes widening.

He wanted to clasp her to him, but instead he shook his head, smiling. "I know you can do it," he told her. "Follow me." He skated ahead of her, looking back, one hand outstretched so that she might grab at it if she needed to.

He saw her swallow in fear, but then she lifted her chin and stretched out her arms for better balance, following him with dogged determination along the ice. Once she slipped and gasped again and he reached out for her, but she found her balance again and gave him a triumphant grin.

"I did not fall!"

"You did not," he agreed. "You are becoming quite the

proficient. Are you tired yet? There is hot chocolate and mulled wine on the riverbank, if you wish to rest."

She nodded. "I think I have done enough for today."

Carefully he helped her off the ice and summoned the boy to help her out of the skates. Once their feet were back on solid ground, he led her to a stall where he purchased spiced hot chocolate for them both.

"Feed the birds, ladyship?"

A woman was selling stale bread with which to feed the ducks of the park, their usual home on the water suddenly gone.

"By all means," Alexander agreed, paying for two little paper cones of the bread and passing them to Lady Celia.

They walked towards a little grove of trees where most of the ducks were grouped around a few children feeding them. Along the way they nodded to acquaintances hurrying to take part in the fun of skating.

"We should bring Miss Pemberton here," said Lady Celia.

He nodded. "She would be most entertained. It is not often one gets the chance to skate."

Lady Celia began to break up pieces of the bread. She offered him some to throw to the ducks, but he only shook his head and stood back to watch her. She seemed happy. She spoke with some of the children and called out softly to the ducks, urging them to come closer.

"Comerford?"

Alexander looked over his shoulder to see the Earl of Radcliffe approaching. Not a man he took any pleasure in spending time with. Radcliffe was an inveterate gambler and rake, having little care for the broken hearts and honour of ladies he mistreated.

"Radcliffe."

"Ah, Comerford, it *is* you. And your future countess, I see. No chaperone? Does her mother know you are out here all alone? I heard she actually stayed at your house over Christmas, is that really so?"

Lady Celia turned and gave a curtsey, then continued feeding the ducks, ignoring his comment. Alexander liked her for it; she showed dignity in the face of Radcliffe's insinuations. He kept his mouth closed in emulation of the choice she had made.

Radcliffe watched Lady Celia as she scattered broken up pieces of bread. "Pretty thing," he said to Alexander, then lowered his voice. "Shame about the hand."

Alexander stiffened. "She manages quite well as she is," he said.

"I'm sure she can do embroidery and all that nonsense. Different matter once you're wed, though."

"I don't catch your meaning," said Alexander.

Radcliffe made a vulgar gesture. "Won't be able to perform all her wifely duties with a hand like that, will she? I suppose she'll have to learn to use the left one. Not the same though, is it?"

The pain that shot through Alexander's hand as his fist met Radcliffe's jaw was well worth the look on Radcliffe's face as he staggered backwards.

"What the devil?"

Alexander stepped closer to him and lowered his voice to a hiss. "Do not let me hear Lady Celia's name in your mouth again, Sir, or I shall require satisfaction."

He thought Radcliffe might persist in his behaviour and find himself facing a duel, but to his surprise he only grimaced and then backed away a few steps. "Damn you, Comerford. The navy's left you with rough ways. Hardly gentlemanly."

"I've known better manners from a midshipman in his cups," Alexander snarled back. "You're a disgrace, Sir, be on your way."

He stood and watched Radcliffe as he walked away, heart still thumping with anger, when a hand gently tucked itself into his arm and he looked down to see Lady Celia looking up at him, her eyes warm.

"I imagine he deserved that," she said. "He is no gentleman. Shall we walk back to the sleigh? The ducks are full, and my feet are growing cold from standing on the snow so long."

They walked back in silence together and when they returned to Comerford House he gave instructions that her shawl should be brought and that the picnic dinner should be served in the drawing room, the fire built up to keep them both warm. With the shawl, Aveline brought down a piecework bag, from which Lady Celia pulled knitting she was undertaking in a dark blue wool. She sat quietly with it while the food was brought and laid out on a large flowery rug that had been brought into the room for the purpose.

Mrs Poole's ideas of plain fare were generous. There was fresh made bread and sliced ham, cheese, hot baked potatoes served with little dishes of potted shrimps, and stewed pears served with a treacle sauce rather than custard or cream, milk and cream having been some of the first supplies to dry up. She had sent up an ale, as well, and it went better with the bread and cheese than the fine wines stocked in the cellar.

"Mrs Poole is mortified at serving us such a simple dinner," he told Lady Celia.

She laughed, shaking her head as she did so. "She should be proud of managing so well when we have been snowbound so long," she said. "Besides, you must be accustomed to worse. What did you eat on board?"

He smiled at the recollection. "As captain, I was lucky enough to eat off fine china and have a half-decent cook," he told her. "I did well enough. There was a great deal of mutton, corn beef and potatoes, though our puddings were better, being made from preserves we could have plum, cherries and even gooseberries. And there was food from the sea aplenty – turtles, sharks, dolphins. Some of the men were fair shots at birds, I cannot much recommend the taste of seagull but sometimes it is better than having mutton again. We took livestock on board as well, of course, everything from pigs and goats to hens for their eggs, cows for their milk. In ports, the locals would sell us fresh provisions – when we sailed in the Mediterranean there was an abundance of fresh lemons and oranges, which were much pleasanter than the bottled lemon juice with which the men had to be dosed to avoid scurvy. But the men ate food Mrs Poole would throw up her hands in horror over."

"Such as?"

"Oh, their breakfast consisted of burgoo – coarse oatmeal boiled in water, although some preferred Scotch Coffee – that is burnt bread boiled in water and made sweet with sugar."

She wrinkled her nose.

"Lobscouse was a common dinner – boiled salted meat with onions and ship's biscuit, stewed together. All the men were dosed with lemon juice daily, to protect them from scurvy. And I am sorry to say that if the ship should be infested with rats the men would catch them and have them cooked – they said they were every bit as good as rabbit, though I did not care to try them for myself."

She grimaced. "You were lucky to be an officer, then."

"I was."

She helped herself to the stewed pears. "And we are lucky to have Mrs Poole who can make a meal out of anything, it would seem."

"I would have been infinitely grateful to have her on board with me, as would the men."

"Do you miss that life?"

"I did at first," he said. "It was all I ever wanted, and all I knew for the last thirteen years. My life's path was set." He paused. "It was not an easy life," he went on. "I lost good men along the way and being captain I was responsible for all the men in my service. But I knew what I was doing."

She stopped her work and looked up at him. "Do you not feel that now?"

No, of course not. Here he was with the woman he had been destined to marry, the one constant in all the changes that had happened to him in the past year, and he was still not certain of her feelings for him. He shook his head. "It has been a big change and all this – the estate, my new position – it can feel overwhelming if you were not raised to be ready for it."

She nodded and was silent. Then, without looking at him, she said, "Your care of those around you shows your good intentions. A good man will always do well if he lets his heart guide him."

He did not reply, for his voice would have emerged choked. She had just called him a good man. He clung to that praise – not in relation to how he might be as the Earl, but in how she thought of him. She had not been of that opinion before Christmas; he was sure of it. He only gave a nod and rang for Gabriel to clear away the food.

The meal having been cleared away, Mrs Poole sent up little ginger biscuits and tea. Once it had been served and the servants had left the room, Alexander seated himself opposite Lady Celia, cup in hand. He was peaceful, content to sit in silence without the need to make conversation, the stiffness of their first encounters gone.

Some time passed, during which the only sound was Ivy snoring quietly and the click-click of the knitting needles.

"My mother has always made me wear gloves," Lady Celia said quietly at last.

He said nothing.

"Both inside and out," she continued, bitterness in her voice. "Both in front of guests and when we are only family. I have worn them all my life and they have always had these stupid stuffed fingers, as though everyone would not notice – as though everyone would not look anyway – and as though the servants would not whisper to other servants, so that everyone knows what my hand looks like though they have never seen it. I heard a girl telling another girl what it looked like at my very first ball and I had never even met her." Her voice cracked and she fell silent.

He gazed into the fire and then looked down at her hand, hidden in its little silk glove. "You do not have to wear gloves here," he said. "Nor any home of which I am master, nor any other place where I am by your side, if you do not wish to."

She looked at him, held his gaze, almost as though testing him, her eyes very bright with unshed tears. Without looking down, she drew off first her left glove and then, after a brief hesitation, her right glove, her chin held very high.

He held her gaze until she looked abruptly back down and resumed her knitting, the needles clicking.

In the silence he looked down at the dark blue wool taking shape between her hands. He looked at her right hand, noted the shape of it, the little stubs of ungrown fingers between her shapely thumb and little finger. He had never really noticed what she was knitting before, it was women's work, hardly of interest, but now something about it caught his attention. It was a sock, he saw, in a thick blue wool, sturdy and large, larger than her feet.

"What are you making?" he asked.

She looked up, frowned as though he were making fun of her, but then swallowed and looked back down at the three needles engaged at once so that she might make the curved shape necessary for the heel. "A sock. I have made almost fifty pairs this year, I was hoping to finish fifty-two by tomorrow, since it is the last day of the year. It would make one pair a week, but I am behind. Still, there is always next year."

"*Fifty* pairs? Whatever for?"

"I send them to the navy, for men who do not have families to knit for them. It seems sad that some men might receive little comforts from home and others not. We have a groom who used to be a sailor, he limps and can no longer serve but he is good with animals, so my father took him on. He said once that receiving a parcel from home was always a moment of joy even when times were hard, and that when he lost his mother and stopped receiving them, he found it very hard to see the other men receive theirs, however humble the contents. So now I knit socks." She laughed. "Mama insists I keep the embroidered cushion cover close at hand, for she says knitting socks looks inelegant in society, so when we have company, I must work on that, but I confess it progresses slowly, for as soon as everyone leaves, I return to my socks." She paused. "I did not think you would mind if I worked on them now, while we are talking, since it is for the navy and since I am so close to my goal."

He shook his head. "I do not mind."

"Good," she said, and continued her work, the sock growing in her hands as she worked.

He thought of the embroidered cushion cover with its insipid pink roses and misunderstood romantic quotation. Shame washed over him: he had judged her for having chosen it, thinking her foolish, shallow. Yet it had all been for show, something chosen so that the judgemental *ton* would approve. This was the real Lady Celia, this young woman who listened to those around her and, hearing lack, took it upon herself to provide comfort and sustenance, by whatever means were available to her. He wanted to stop her work, to lift her hand and kiss it, to share his newfound feelings for her and ask her to marry him after all. But it was late, and he wanted to find the right words, he did not want to stumble or appear presumptuous that her feelings, too, might have changed.

"Tomorrow morning," he began slowly.

She paused in her work, looked up at him, perhaps drawn by the change in his voice, which had grown husky. "Yes?"

How warm her eyes were. A deep brown, with tiny flecks of hazel. He gazed at her a moment too long, then cleared his throat. "Perhaps tomorrow I could speak with you of... of our – your – plans."

She did not ask what plans, she only gave a slow graceful nod of her head, almost as one might at the beginning of a dance, an acknowledgement of the partnership about to begin.

Relief flowed through him. She understood him, there was an understanding building between them, he was sure of it now, and that gave him confidence. "Then I will bid you good night," he continued, rising to his feet, eager to have the next day come quickly – at once, even. "I will look forward to our conversation tomorrow."

She nodded, still silent, then rose and met his gaze once more. "Goodnight, Lord Comerford," she said softly, and left the room.

❄

She could not sleep. She was certain of what he would say to her in the morning. She had wanted to ask him to speak then and there, by the fireside, but she had been too nervous to do so. But she wanted him to speak. To say that things had changed between them in these few short days they had been together, that his feelings had changed, to ask if hers had also. In the dark she lay and mouthed words to indicate that they had, indeed that her feelings had so greatly changed that they were beyond recognition. She wished that she might go back in time and start again, to wipe out the unkind words that they had both uttered, spoken in haste and anger, but also perhaps out of feeling unwanted, rejected by the very person whom they had expected to care for them – love them even. It had seemed that all was lost. But now there was something between them, a kindness, a tenderness, even – and she blushed though no-one could see her – a rising desire that could not be denied. Tomorrow morning he would speak with her, he would say that they must begin again, that he wanted her as his wife. She was sure of it, wanted the morning to come quickly, yet she could not sleep. She wondered if, when she confessed that her feelings had changed, whether he might kiss her again, and the thought of it kept her awake for more than two hours though her eyes ached with tiredness, the clock chiming in her room to remind her that she must sleep, until at last she fell into a restless doze.

※

IN THE MORNING, SHE WAS OUT OF BED BEFORE Aveline had even reached her, then changed her mind about her clothes.

"The cherry wool – or no! Perhaps the beaded dress?"

Aveline looked doubtful. "That's more of an evening dress, my lady, it'll look odd at breakfast."

"I want to look my best."

Aveline looked her over. "Why is that, my lady?"

"N – nothing. Just I should like to look well."

"You look tired," said the unhelpful Aveline. "Did you not sleep?"

"Just put me in the cherry then," said Celia, desperate to go downstairs. "Quickly."

"Quickly is not how long it will take to do your hair," tutted Aveline. "It looks like a crow's nest."

Celia did her best to sit still under Aveline's hands, but it was difficult. At last her hair appeared passable, and she hurried down the stairs, intending to seek out Lord Comerford in the drawing room, but was met in the hall by Gabriel opening the front door to visitors.

"Lord Hyatt and Lady Sarah Hyatt," he announced, just as Lord Comerford came out of the drawing room.

"Lady Celia! We are delighted to find you here. We are at last on our way to Bellbrook Manor, having been delayed, as you have no doubt also been, by this inclement weather," smiled Lord Hyatt, on spotting Celia. He bowed low over her hand, planting a discreet kiss on her glove.

Celia pulled her hand back. "Lord Hyatt," she said,

offering a quick curtsey. "I am glad you and your sister will be able to travel."

Lady Sarah advanced on Celia, offering a quick embrace. "We have come to collect you!"

"Collect me?"

"Naturally! We can hardly travel to your family's home without coming to fetch you, why, we would miss your company terribly! Ah, Lord Comerford, so good to see you."

There were more greetings, Lord Hyatt and Lady Sarah full of charm and good cheer, Lord Comerford polite but restrained in his manners. He gestured to them to follow him into the drawing room, which they did, chattering and laughingly recounting their own experiences of having been stuck in London.

Celia trailed behind. Why could the weather not have obliged her by providing icy roads or further snowfall, keeping Lord Hyatt and his sister well away from both Comerford House and Bellbrook Manor? Instead, here they were, all smiles and charm. No doubt they had discussed the invitation at length, saw it for exactly what it had been – a hint that his attentions would be favourably received, a chance to meet her family and perhaps even seal the deal should all go well – a quick word to her father to collect his blessing, a private murmuring of intentions to her, followed by a joyful announcement to round off the festivities. Yes, of course, they had come with this aim in mind and curses, it was she who had brought this situation on herself. Now she must find a way out of it.

"And so here we are! Yes, Lord Comerford, a cup of tea would be delightful, it will give dear Lady Celia's maid time to pack her things."

Lord Comerford frowned. "Pack her things?"

"But of course! We are here to collect her and travel to

Bellbrook Manor with her. If we hurry, we will be there before dark, even with the roads poor as they are, carriages are beginning to run again, thank goodness. And of course, the dear Duke and Duchess will be wondering where their daughter has got to!"

"She has been safely in my care," Lord Comerford said slowly, the frown still on his face as he rang for the footman. "Tea, Gabriel."

"Of course she has, thank goodness," rattled on Lady Sarah. "Lady Celia, do ring for your maid and tell her to pack, we must make haste."

She was unable to think of a way out. She could not refuse to travel with them to her family when they should all have been there for the past week together. She looked at Lord Comerford, hoping that he might intervene, that he might say that no, he would travel there with her himself, in his own carriage, but he said nothing, would not meet her pleading gaze. Reluctantly, she pulled the cord that would summon Gabriel and instructed him to find Aveline.

"Yes, my lady?"

"We are to travel to Bellbrook Manor."

"Now, my lady?"

"Yes. Please be so good as to have my luggage ready at once."

"Of course, my lady."

The following half hour passed in unending small talk, with Lady Sarah continually saying what fun they would all have at Bellbrook Manor and Lord Hyatt recounting their various adventures during the past week, from the servants having to shovel snow just so they could even get out of the house, to a Christmas Day spent only with an elderly uncle who slept throughout most of the festivities.

"We shall be grateful for good company," he finished with a smile. "Will you be joining us, Comerford?"

Celia waited, breath held. Now was the moment when he could say that most certainly he would do so, in his carriage, that he would bring Celia himself just as soon as he had spoken with her on a matter of some importance… but he only shook his head.

"I have business to attend to as soon as the new year begins," he said, his voice as stiff as his shoulders. "But I hope you will all be merry."

Her heart sank but there was an anger in her too – was he not going to fight for her at all? Was he going to allow Lord Hyatt and his chattering sister to carry her off to Bellbrook, breaking last night's promise to speak with her today? Had she been wrong in what he had intended? It seemed so, for he avoided her gaze until Aveline appeared in the doorway with Celia's pelisse, hat and muff, declaring that all was ready for their immediate departure.

"We shall bid you farewell, then, Comerford, said Lord Hyatt, holding out his hand for a hearty handshake. "I shall hope to see you at the club one of these days."

"Indeed," agreed Lord Comerford, without a hint of a smile. He bowed. "Goodbye Lady Sarah, Lady Celia."

Was that all? Only a stiff goodbye whilst barely meeting her eye after the past week they had spent together, her name last on his lips?

"Goodbye, Lord Comerford," said the ever-smiling Lady Sarah. "Enjoy Twelfth Night, I hope you have something pleasant planned. I cannot wait to see everyone at Bellbrook," she added, taking Celia's arm and pulling her along in her wake, while Lord Hyatt strode out of the front door and Aveline trotted along behind.

"I must just –" began Celia, unhooking her arm. "I must just mention something to Lord Comerford before I go. You will excuse me; I will be with you momentarily."

"Of course," trilled Lady Sarah, making her way through the door, followed by Gabriel carrying some of Celia's luggage.

Celia faced Lord Comerford alone.

※

SHE HESITATED. HE SAW HER GLANCE UP AT THE mistletoe ball still hanging from the chandelier above them before she blurted out, "Are you certain you will not come with me to Bellbrook after all, Lord Comerford? And – and stay until Twelfth Night?"

There was no reason why he could not, it would be easy enough to travel there, to take the time to know her family better, to tell her that his feelings had changed, that he was ready, if she would have him do so, to woo her as she deserved to be wooed, without taking the engagement for granted. She was asking him to go with her, surely that counted for something, gave some indication of good will towards him – towards their supposed betrothal. But a stubbornness had set in, jealousy overtaking any sensible course of action.

"How long is Hyatt staying?"

"I do not know – a – few days, perhaps."

He could see it now, all the family gathered there, the Earl no doubt having brought along his sister to have her make Celia's acquaintance, wishing to tighten whatever bond there might already be between them. Anger grew in him, a desire to grip her close to him and demand to know her feelings for him, but that was not how a gentleman conducted himself, so he only bowed his head stiffly, holding down his feelings. "I am sure you will enjoy yourself."

She started to reach out a hand but did not touch his arm. "My family would be glad to see you."

He wanted to ask, *Will you be glad, that is all that matters, do you want me there? I do not care what your family wants, it is your heart's desire that I seek to know.* But that sounded too dramatic, like something from a foolish novel and too much like begging for her favour. He was not sure he wanted to hear the pause before she hurriedly said that of course she would like to have him there. He did not want to feel the hurt of her dismissal again, so he only repeated, "I have much to attend to in London."

She nodded, eyes still searching his face, then lifted up the hood of her cloak, hiding her face from him, lifted one hand in a gesture of silent farewell before turning her back on him and making her way towards the carriage, where a footman stood waiting, the door held open for her. Another few steps and she would be gone from Comerford House, would be on her way to spend a happy few days with the Earl of Hyatt.

He let out a curse and strode forward, caught at her hand and as she turned, startled, he pulled her hard against him and kissed her. It was not a soft kiss, this, not a gentle courteous kiss for a watching audience who supposed them engaged. No, this was a kiss of desire and desperation, a last chance to claim her as his own, his mouth on hers, her lips parting, her hands coming to rest in his hair, on his neck, a willing kiss, a breathless kiss.

And it was over. As the footman turned towards the

house, Alexander pushed her away from him, her eyes wide, cheeks blushing pink, lips still parted from their encounter. It was all he saw before he turned and walked away from her, strode through the corridors and into his study, slamming the door behind him.

10

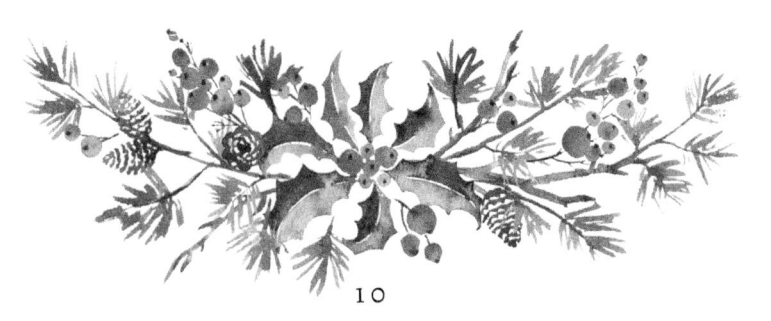

TWELFTH NIGHT

The carriage proceeded slowly through the streets, for the horses must still be guided with care through icy patches. Celia sat in silence, looking out of the window. They were only a street away, two streets away, three streets, there was still time to command that the carriage return to Comerford House, only it was not her carriage to command, what excuse would she give for her strange request? The streets passed by and more than once she was about to call out, to ask that they retrace their route, yet her thoughts were so confused that before she knew it they were already beyond the centre of London, changing horses for the first time at some coaching inn or other before taking once again to the road, now making faster progress as there was hardly any traffic. It was too late.

Lady Sarah kept up a stream of conversation, but Celia barely answered, lost in a misery of confusion and reproach.

Why had she been so hasty? Why had she judged the Earl of Comerford?

Because he had hurt her feelings. She had wanted

wooing and charm, and he had provided neither. She had goaded him, and he had told her the truth. Which had stung. But the truth had not been his fault. Enraged by the humiliation of what he had told her, she had pushed him away, only to discover...

A man of deeds not words. A man who would climb a tree without hesitation if she expressed a desire for mistletoe. Who had opened his house to stray kittens and a rag-tag of acquaintances to ensure they all had somewhere to go at Christmas and to make the season festive, as it should be. Who had found a sleigh in snow-bound London, whose warm hands had touched her skin.... whose lips had found hers not once but twice... and who had then pushed her away. He had taken her at her word of finding another husband and left her to deeply regret her actions. Now she would have to keep Lord Hyatt at bay during the festivities to come, without even knowing if she could win back Lord Comerford's favour. He had kissed her but then turned away, left her standing in the cold hall, shaking with desire. She looked down at her hands, which still trembled, despite being clad in warm woollen gloves trimmed with a dark fur, overcome with what had passed between them.

At the last change of horses both Lord Hyatt and Lady Sarah descended from the carriage, leaving Celia alone. Aveline came to look in on her from the servant's carriage which was following behind.

"I thought you'd changed your mind about Lord Comerford," ventured Aveline as she changed the foot-warmer for one worthy of the name.

"Be quiet," snapped Celia and then, sorry to have lost her temper, "I believe I may have made an error, Aveline."

"He was a good man," said Aveline quietly.

To hear this from Aveline, whose horror of men was so

ingrained, was a bitter blow. Celia only shook her head and stared out of the window, wishing she could turn the carriage around, but it was too late now. Bellbrook Manor was less than an hour away.

❇

By late afternoon that day, Bellbrook Manor was positively bursting at the seams, for not only had the entire family gathered, but there were several guests staying who had not yet been able to depart after Christmas Day and who now had decided they might as well stay for Twelfth Night on the fifth of January, since it was now only six nights away. Celia was welcomed with embraces and exclamations over the weather that had kept her away so long, but everyone was too jolly to enquire after Lord Comerford's absence after she had muttered something about his being too busy to join them.

The days between her arrival and Twelfth Night passed slowly, more slowly than Celia could have believed. How could the same number of days fly by in Lord Comerford's company and drag on so here? She avoided everyone, especially Lord Hyatt and Lady Sarah, making visits to the poor of the parish and estate to give them tardy Saint Stephen's Day boxes of clothes and food, paying calls on local acquaintances, even claiming headaches when all else failed.

"You can't stay in your rooms all day," chastised Aveline. "If you don't care for Lord Hyatt, better tell him so at once."

"There is nothing wrong with Lord Hyatt," muttered Celia.

"Marry him, then. He's eager enough, him and that

sister of his following you about everywhere they can," said Aveline with a sniff.

There was indeed nothing wrong with Lord Hyatt. He was sociable, cheerful, kindly in manner, attentive to Celia and to his sister. It would be easy enough to walk closer to him, to take his arm, to smile warmly. It was only that she did not blush in his presence, did not wait, breathless, for him to kiss her. Her hands did not shake when he was close to her.

And yet Lord Comerford had not come to Bellbrook, had not declared himself. She had been so certain of wanting him and he had turned away. Now she was alone and Lord Hyatt would no doubt press his suit and she must... choose.

Why could Lord Comerford not send a missive of some sort, or come in person? Why must she decide all alone?

❈

ALEXANDER SAT IN THE DRAWING ROOM OF Comerford House on the fifth of January, the drapes closed, a fire burning low. He had already snapped at a footman for opening the curtains and a maid who had come to build up the fire. He had refused breakfast and then rung in a temper to demand coffee, which he had left to go cold. A midday meal had also been refused and now the short day was drawing to a close, the room growing darker as twilight fell upon the city. It was too late to ride or drive to Bellbrook now. If he had set out in the morning, he could have joined in with all that the Duke and Duchess had arranged, but it was not to be. He would be all alone tonight.

Gabriel entered. "Sorry to disturb you, Sir, but the

housekeeper has instructed that we take down the Christmas decorations."

"Leave them."

Gabriel hovered.

"What is it now?"

Gabriel looked embarrassed. "Only... it's bad luck, Sir."

"What is?"

"Leaving up the decorations past Twelfth Night, Sir."

"Get out of my sight."

"Yes, Sir."

Twelfth Night. A night of merriment and feasting, of games and sweet treats, time to bid farewell to the festive season and look towards the coming of spring. No doubt there would be dancing at Bellbrook, there would be the selection of the King and Queen of revels... the Earl of Hyatt might well try to make sure that he and Lady Celia were chosen. He could have been with them all, could have asserted his rightful place by Lady Celia's side and yet he had sullenly held back, unwilling to humble himself to her, to open his heart up to her scrutiny and possible rejection. The days since she had left had been lonely and empty, the house had gone back to echoing silence. The pristine snow had melted into dirty slush and dangerously slippery ice, but he had sent the sleigh back to the stables where he had sourced it, not caring to leave the house even for a ride in Green Park – which no longer lived up to the name, being only stirred-up mud and barren-branched trees. New Year's Eve had come and gone without his paying any attention to it, for what was there to look forward to? Only an imminent social embarrassment to be got through whenever Lady Celia chose to make an announcement that she had chosen a new husband-to-be and after that? No doubt the mamas and daughters of the *ton* would close in on him until one of them caught him in their net, whether he liked it or not. He would go along with it, for it did not make any difference who his bride was, when what he wanted was Lady Celia, and she would now be promised to another.

He watched the dancing flames and saw her dancing in her red dress, laughing as she held his hands, singing in her sweet voice as she set out to try and make the world around her a better place. The touch of her lips, her pink cheeks and the tip of her nose pink from cold. The scent of her when she was close to him, something bright and fresh like lemons but with a softer vanilla that made him want to nuzzle into her neck and have his fill of her. How had he lost her? How had he managed to allow such a woman to slip through his fingers when he was practically married to her? Through pig-headedness, he chastised himself. For want of wooing, kindness, for want of opening up to her, he had lost her entirely and now he was left alone. Stubborn fool.

"Enough," he said out loud. "Enough." He put a hand to the bell pull and gave it such a violent tug that Gabriel appeared alarmed at being so vehemently summoned back.

"Sir?"

He was not a boy; he was a man. He was the Earl of Comerford, dammit all, and he was conducting himself like a child. He knew what he wanted, and he was not going to get it by moping. Nor by wishing bad luck on his household. Whether he believed in such superstitions or not, he did not wish to dishearten his staff.

"I shall be taking down the Christmas decorations myself and you will help me."

"Yes, Sir."

"We will burn them in the garden."

The footman looked startled but clearly thought it best

to accept his master's wishes, contrary though they might seem. "Yes, Sir."

They made their way through the dining room, drawing room, ballroom and hall, collecting the greenery as they went, pressing the boot boy into additional service to carry armfuls of the decorations. Alexander flung open the doors to the garden and they piled up the greenery in a heap before dispatching the boot boy to fetch the wherewithal to set the fire. Meanwhile the footman set about removing the red ribbons holding the boughs together, and when he was done, handed them to Alexander.

"They were Lady Celia's," he said by way of explanation.

Alexander looked down at the handful of ribbons. Scarlet silk, cherry linen, a deep ruby red wool. Tiny though they were, he could not but think of her dresses when he looked at them, her always-red wardrobe of fashionable styles that had made him think her nothing but a thoughtless popinjay. How readily she had given them up, these ribbons, in order to make the house ready for Christmas. How little she had cared for her fashionable clothes being ruined by flour when she had donned an apron to make gingerbread or set out into the snowy streets to deliver it to the children of the Foundling Hospital. How willing she had been to spend her evenings painting the faces of poppets to give to poor children or dancing to please the servants. How much he had misjudged her; how much he wished she were still here. "Thank you," he managed, and thrust the ribbons into his pocket, turning his attention to lighting the fire with the hot coals brought up from the kitchen by the boot boy. It took little effort for the flames to start, for the greenery had had many days in warm rooms to dry out. It drew the fire into itself and after a few billows of smoke, a fast crackling sound began, and the bonfire was well and truly underway.

"You may go in now," he told the footman and the boot boy. "Bring me my greatcoat and I will watch over it."

"Yes, Sir," they chorused.

Clad in his warm coat, he sat on the steps that led back into the ballroom and watched the fire for the next hour as it built higher and higher before settling into a dull roar and then slowly lost its strength, fading into glowing coals with the odd spark still being thrown up into the darkness. It was fiercely cold, even close to the fire, but there was something soothing in the ritual, a burning away of his worries and frustrations, an unbending of his prior certainties and a glimpse of something new to come, of a fresh path glowing before him, one which might lead him to a greater happiness than he had hitherto thought possible for himself. Above him he heard the occasional flutter of night wings and saw the stars emerge to illuminate the sky above the darkness of the park beyond. The red of the fire was all but gone by the time he stood up and made his way back into the house, up the stairs to his room and a deeper sleep than he had enjoyed for some days.

❉

THERE WAS FRESH SNOWFALL BY MORNING, BUT Alexander chose to ignore it, striding out into a newly refreshed London, enjoying the bracing cold and the walk to a fashionable glovemaker, where he spent almost an hour bespeaking the exact gloves he had in mind. The glovemaker's work arrived two days later in a small blue box tied with a white ribbon. He did not open it, trusting that his instructions had been followed, only had it sent on by the first post to Bellbrook Manor.

※

The Twelfth Night cake stood upon a side table in Bellbrook Manor's ballroom, and all who entered the room spent time admiring it, a vast confection in thick white icing, studded all over with gems made of paste, the whole intended to resemble a crown, with intricate modelling. Somewhere beneath it all was a rich fruitcake, ready to be cut to reveal the monarchs of the evening.

"Now let us cut the cake so that we will know who our king and queen are!" called the Duke.

Everyone gathered round, jostling, to see the knife plunged into the elaborate decorations, a slice carefully brought out and placed on a plate and passed to the first guest.

"Remember, if a gentleman finds a bean, he is our king, if a lady finds a pea, she is our queen!"

There was lots of laughter as forks were poked into the slices to try and find the hidden items and a sudden cry from Lady Sarah. "I knew it! Brother, I greet you!" and she gave a deep curtsey to Lord Hyatt, who held up the bean from his slice.

There was much bowing and curtseying. Celia's stomach tightened. As she had feared, Lord Hyatt was now king of the revels for the night, and she dreaded being made the queen. Hastily she chopped her cake into small pieces and relaxed when she failed to find a pea.

"Hold my plate, would you?" whispered Lady Sarah. "I must tie my shoe ribbon."

Celia took Lady Sarah's plate, who bent to tie her shoe

ribbon and then stood again, neatly taking back, not her own plate, but Celia's.

"Oh, that is –" began Celia, trying to return the correct plate.

"*There* it is – we have found the pea, and it is dear Lady Celia who is our queen. Your Majesty!" and Lady Sarah swept her a curtsey, followed by the rest of the guests. "Brother, I have found your queen for this evening!"

He bowed. "I am much obliged. May I furnish you with a crown?" He held out the little paper crown that had been supplied with the cake and pulled on one of his own. "There, now we are properly dressed for this evening's merriment."

Celia did her best to smile, offering a curtsey before seeking to retreat. "Shall I play the pianoforte so that you may all dance?"

The guests began to pair up, but Lady Sarah held out her hand. "You must join our set," she called. "We cannot have our king and queen not dance together. Come!"

Celia tried to demur, but a younger cousin was promptly installed at the pianoforte in her stead, and she was left with a beaming Lady Sarah and her partner, as well as Lord Hyatt.

The dancing went well enough. Lord Hyatt was light on his feet and conversed with charm whenever the dancing permitted him to, but Celia found her mind wandering to those few days ago when she had danced with Lord Comerford on Christmas Day, laughing as they encouraged Miss Pemberton down the line. The silly games being played here tonight seemed forced, when Christmas Day had been nothing but ease and joy, even though she had been in a strange home and mostly amidst strangers. She finished the dance with relief and suggested a game of cards.

"Ah, now, before we left London, I made certain to collect some very special cards from the confectioner, so that we might amuse ourselves," said Lady Sarah. From her reticule she pulled out a neat deck of illustrated cards. "Now then, we shall each draw a character and then we shall be bound to behave as our new name demands. Brother, draw a card first."

He obliged, looking down at the card he had pulled from the pack. "I am... Sir Constant. I shall do my best. To whom should I be constant?"

"Why, to your queen, of course, who else! See to it you do not leave her alone all evening."

He bowed his head to Celia. "Why would I even seek to go elsewhere?"

"Very pretty," agreed the Duchess, smiling.

"Your Grace, will you pull a card for me?" asked Lady Sarah.

"You are.... Miss Candour!"

Lady Sarah laughed out loud. "Ah, then what can I say but that... It is high time my brother made a good match for himself... and I believe the lady in question is not so far away!"

Celia tried to smile at the giggles and winks amongst the guests that Lady Sarah's declaration evinced, but inside she wanted only to run away. "It is my turn to be given a character," she said, hoping to stop Lady Sarah from making any further comments. She pulled at a card and looked down at it, heart sinking. "Lady Flirtation," she said, her voice flat.

"Oh, you cannot be," said Lady Sarah giggling. "For my brother here is named Sir Constant and surely, he cannot be seated next to Lady Flirtation? He will have to keep you in line, madam."

Celia stifled a sigh. The good-natured Lady Sarah was

proving a difficult matchmaker to foil, so stubbornly was she set upon her pathway. No doubt she had stacked the deck with great care, just as she had succeeded in passing her Twelfth Night pea on to Celia. She meant well, no doubt, had taken a fancy to Celia and was now eagerly helping matters along so that she might soon claim her as a sister-in-law, but it was a wearisome campaign to evade.

※

THE EVENING WORE ON. THERE WAS DANCING, THERE were games, the character-cards forced everyone to behave like fools. Celia found herself more and more alone, seizing any excuse to fetch a shawl and tarry in returning, to take a breath of fresh air without anyone noticing her, to summon servants for some imaginary service she wished them to perform. She thought longingly of the picnic by the fireside she had shared with Lord Comerford, how he had told her more about himself, shared deeper feelings than she had yet known him capable of. How simply they had eaten – bread and cheese and ale, eaten with their hands! It was laughable compared to a tableful of dainties and only the finest tableware... and yet it had tasted good and they had been happy together. Would she willingly give up tonight's entertainment and company, the fine food and drink, for such another night as that had been?

Yes. She knew the answer was yes.

She knew, now, with utter certainty, that she wished to marry Lord Comerford, but how had she only been certain of it now that she was many miles away and with no means of seeing him again for months? The Duke and Duchess would not return to London until the season proper began, in March. March! She could not wait that long. She must make amends to him, be clear in her feelings.

"Lady Celia, there you are! I had thought you lost." A beaming Lord Hyatt had in fact found her with ease, half-hidden in the doorway to the orangery. "Might I walk with you?" He paused and then added, meaningfully, "alone?"

Ah. The request had come too soon. Although at least it had not come sooner when she might still, foolishly, have welcomed it. She swallowed. "Lord Hyatt," she began.

"Please call me Robert."

She shook her head at once. "That is too kind. Lord Hyatt, I fear I may have been too forward in my attentions in your regard, that I may have given the impression that your advances would be welcomed when in fact..."

He took a step backwards, though his smile remained in place, only dimmed. "Has your stay with Lord Comerford changed your mind in his regard?"

She grimaced. "You are a clever man. Yes."

He nodded. "I shall have to blame the fog and snow for losing me the opportunity to secure a very fine wife, then," he said. "We have not known each other long, but we would have been well suited. My sister will be most disappointed; she had set her heart on you."

"I am sorry," she said awkwardly. "I would not have... I did not know my mind. But it was wrong of me to give you hope when I was not yet certain myself."

"Ah, no harm done, Lady Celia. You had not yet broken my heart. I would have been glad to let you try, but perhaps it is for the best. You will be going ahead with the engagement to Lord Comerford, then?"

"If he will have me." The fear rose up in her again that she had lost him, that he would have seen that last kiss as only a farewell, would by now have turned his face away from a future together, set his heart against her.

"It is time to burn the decorations!" called the Duke. "Come along, we must all take part if we are not to incur bad luck next year! Everyone take some of the greenery and follow me."

All the guests, helped by the footmen, took hold of the various decorations around the ballroom and hall, then followed the Duke out into the grounds, where a bonfire had been set and was already burning fiercely.

The guests took turns throwing their decorations into the flames where they spat and threw up sparks, causing shrieks from some of the ladies and applause from all the guests. In the darkness Celia touched the little mistletoe berries of a kissing bough and remembered Lord Comerford's coat of arms, the motto, *Strength Through Love*, and the moment when his lips had first touched hers, how he had held her to him...

"Throw it in, Celia!" encouraged Lord Hyatt. His manner continued to be friendly, she was glad to see. "For good luck in the year to come!"

She nodded and let go of it, throwing it into the burning flames, watching the mistletoe leaves curl and darken, disappearing into the heat.

❄

THE GUESTS GONE, LADY SARAH SORROWFUL BUT LORD Hyatt still kindly, Celia woke to the first morning without snow in days and the arrival of the first post in over a week. While her father read his business correspondence and her mother settled into the drawing room with a copy of the latest Belle Assemble, she retreated to her room, holding a small parcel with Lord Comerford's seal on the back. A parcel? What could he be sending her? Her cheeks flushed at the memory of that last kiss, a kiss that had made her want to run after him and tell him she had changed her mind, that she wished to marry him after all, but he had seemed almost angry, had pushed her away as though the kiss was intended as a farewell, an acceptance of there being no future between them after all.

Seated on her bed she broke his seal and tugged at the brown wrapping paper to reveal beneath it a little blue box tied with a white ribbon and inside…

Gloves. Gloves in softest kid leather, stained scarlet and trimmed with white swansdown, beautifully laid out, one on top of the other. She stared down at the top glove, the left hand, unsure about the gift. They were exquisite. But gloves? She had spoken to him of her mother's constant insistence on her wearing gloves even indoors. His subsequent reassurance that he did not mind her hand, the moment when she had removed her gloves and sat alongside him knitting, the freedom of it, had been sealed upon her heart and now… what? Had he forgotten? Had he not truly understood how deeply his words had touched her, what they had meant to her? Or had he not meant them after all? There was something leaden in her, a sadness sinking downwards. She picked up the topmost glove and pulled it on. It was a perfect fit, a beautiful thing. She gave a tiny sigh and looked down at the second glove, then stared.

It was…

It was made for her.

The glove for her right hand did not have the stuffed three fingers that had shamed her all her life. It did not have empty floppy fingers either. It had a perfect thumb. A perfect little finger. And in between… a slightly longer space for her hand. Slowly, she drew it on. Inside, her three tiny fingers found a soft padded space in which they could make their own indentations, resting comfortably in a silken lining.

She sat for a long time staring down at her hands in the gloves before she looked back at the box and its emptiness finally told her what she needed to know about Lord Comerford. She had hoped for a missive from him. But he was a man of deeds, not words. He had cared for her. He had matched her actions, step for step. When she had desired to break off the engagement, he had agreed to let her do so. When she had shown warmth, he had responded in kind. Now, he had sent these gloves, which expressed more than any fine words. If she wished for pretty words, there were many who might provide them – and even those who might mean them, good men, like the Earl of Hyatt. But this was a man to whom pretty words might not come easily but whose every deed she might trust and be cherished by. She heard again the solid thud his fist had made punching Lord Radcliffe for his impertinent and insulting remarks, smiled at the look of astonishment on that gentleman's face. Not that he was worthy of the name gentleman.

❄

"Back to London? Certainly not. The roads will be barely passable, and no-one of any importance will return till March."

Celia shook her head, hands pressed tightly together. "I must return to London, Mama. I wish to see Lord Comerford."

"Why? Has something gone awry between you?"

"Yes – no – that is, I was not – I did not – oh, Mamma,

please do not ask questions. I wish to go to London to see Lord Comerford. Please send me."

The Duchess narrowed her eyes. "Celia – I hope nothing – *untoward* happened over Christmas? There was no..." she cleared her throat. "Unwarranted intimacy? There is no..." she looked Celia over carefully, focusing on her waistline, "...reason for the wedding to be called forward?"

"Oh no," said Celia hastily and watched the Duchess' shoulders drop with relief. "I fear I may have offended him. I should see him so that I – we – so that our misunderstanding can be mended."

"A misunderstanding?"

"We had a dispute," managed Celia. "I called into question our engagement."

"Celia! I expressly forbade you from mentioning your absurd notions of breaking off the marriage."

"I did not call it off exactly," muttered Celia. "I was only – there was a dispute, that is all that matters, and I wish to mend it."

"You can write a letter."

She was tempted. But no, he was not a man of words and letters, he was a man of deeds, she understood this now. She felt the need to see him in person, to show, by her return to London, that she wished to undo the harm she might have caused between them, that she wished indeed to be his wife after all, that the kisses they had exchanged, his manner of behaving over Christmas, had changed her mind. She was only anxious that she would be too late. He had kissed her and she had departed anyway, she had stayed away from him, silent, when he knew full well she was merrymaking with Lord Hyatt and his sister at Bellbrook, he might well have decided that she was by now no longer his and that therefore he was no longer hers, that he was a free man, free to pay his attentions elsewhere, to love elsewhere. She had not given him much reason to love her, first in declaring she did not wish to marry him, then in all but pointing a finger in Lord Hyatt's direction as a suitable alternative. She shifted from foot to foot, wishing she might climb into the carriage now, at this very moment, drive through the night back to London. An impossibility, but... "I need to see him," she insisted. "You must let me go back to London."

❄

It took three more weeks of begging before the Duke and Duchess gave in, followed by two cold and miserable days of travelling in a stony silence which was almost colder than the air outside. Rugs, footwarmers and furs did little to keep them warm, and they stopped frequently at inns along the way to stand in front of fires and drink hot soups and broths, tea or mulled wines, in an attempt to stop their teeth chattering. The fields they passed were overlaid in an endless whiteness, from which only vague shapes emerged: far off hills, shapes which might or might not be houses and barns, the occasional church steeple rising above the unchanging white.

Her mother was not entirely correct. More people than usual for the time of year were returning to London, drawn by word of the River Thames having frozen over and the subsequent erection of a Frost Fair and all its delights, for few people had seen one, the last being almost twenty years back. Those families within easier reach of London had been lured out of their recently enforced solitude, keen to see the world again after being bored at home. So Bellbrook

Manor was left behind them and the servants had been sent ahead to prepare Bellbrook House against their arrival. Even so, the house felt chilly when they arrived, the whole of London locked into an icy winter that took Celia's breath away as she dismounted the carriage.

Once installed in her room she paced, thinking. What she really wanted was to go now, at once, across the oh so short space between them, to Comerford House, there to demand to see Lord Comerford at once and make all right between them. She would say – what would she say? That she had been mistaken, that she wanted their engagement to stand, that she wanted to – to be kissed, was what she really wanted to say but that was impossible – no, she would say that she had been mistaken and hasty, that she wished for them to spend more time together in anticipations of their nuptials, that she felt – she felt so much, it was impossible to speak it into words, how did one even begin? She leant against the windowsill, looking down on the dirty slush built up around the streets, so different from the glistening white snow that had been their lot over the Christmastide. Could she find it again with Lord Comerford, that sense of wonder and joy that had slowly crept up on her? Or was that final kiss the last she would ever see of him? No. She must not let that happen. She had seen another side to him, a kind and caring side, but also a man who could laugh at himself and make the lives of others happy. And she wanted that man as her husband.

At last, she sat down and took up a pen. It was scandalous to write to a man, of course, but then again he was supposedly still her intended. One piece of paper after another ended up on the floor around her, crumpled in frustration, as she sought to make sense of her feelings and communicate them to him. In the end she gave up. Half of them sounded too sentimental coming from a woman who had sworn not to marry him, the rest too formal or complicated in their explanations. Finally, she wrote only a handful of words. *Meet me at the Frost Fair tomorrow after noon. Celia.* If they met in person, she would be able to find the words that had so far eluded her, she was sure of it. She hesitated over her name, thinking that perhaps she should write Lady Celia Follett but how many Celias did Lord Comerford know? And she did not want to be Lady Celia to him, she wanted to hear him say her name as a husband might to his wife, with love and desire in his voice.

11

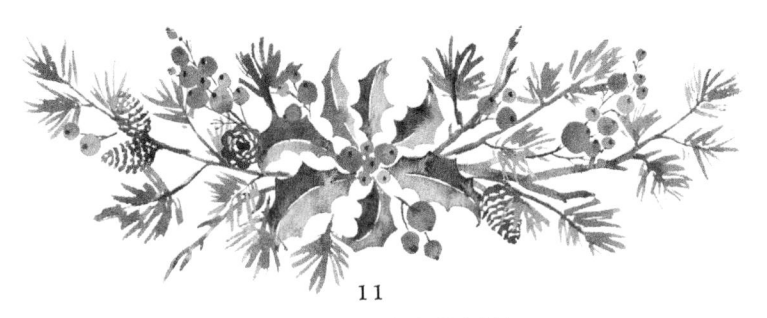

THE FROST FAIR

He tried to control himself, to seem indifferent to the silver tray which was being proffered, the little heap of cards and letters laid on it. He nodded and gestured for it to be placed next to the coffee pot, continuing to eat the toast with preserves he had already started. But his hand shook as he reached out, picking up each item and opening or reading it, then laying it aside, frustrated.

Nothing.

No word from her.

He had sent a gift that might show something of what he felt for her and after three weeks still there was no word. Was she offended? Had she felt embarrassed by the little glove made to the shape of her hand, had she been unwilling to let the world see her as she truly was? He had not meant it that way. He had wanted to say so many things. None of them would come to him when he had tried to write to her. Instead, he had sent only the glove. He hoped it said, *I love you*. He hoped it said, *I love you as you are*. He wanted it to say, *I love you as you are and you will always be safe with me*. But perhaps it had not said those things. The tray was empty and still she had not replied. He had failed yet again with her, had not found a way to break through these endless barriers that seemed to rise up between them.

He poured another coffee and drank it, harsh and bitter.

Very well, then. He had promised himself he would not mope about, would behave like a man and not like a boy. So be it. There was much in his life that was good, that could not be denied. What could he do with this title, the estate, this house, his life? He had many years ahead of him as Earl of Comerford, or at least he hoped so, he could at least do some good in this world. He rang for his secretary and settled down to his correspondence.

"Tell the Marine Society they may hold their event here at Comerford House."

"Very good, Sir."

The Marine Society placed boys from poor backgrounds into the navy, training them and giving them an honest career. It would make men of them, and they would be paid a decent wage. From time to time such charities would hold a ball or dinner, at which they would encourage the attendees to support their work. It was the least he could do to offer Comerford House for such an occasion, for given its size it was well equipped to offer a grand event which might raise funds for their valuable work.

"Write to Mr Jones at Comerford Castle and tell him I shall visit in March, that I will want to discuss the rebuilding of the farm cottages, they are in a poor way and I would have my tenants well housed. And while you are writing to him, ask if he would be so good as to request that the vicar's daughter might want to be schoolmistress, if we had a school for the farmers' children. They should at least learn their letters and numbers."

"For the boys?"

"The girls as well. They will make better wives and mothers if they have some learning."

"Yes, Sir."

He rolled his shoulders in the stiff shirt and cravat, once again feeling hemmed in by the new clothes, the new life.

No. He did not have to put up with this nonsense, he was his own man. "Ring for my valet."

The valet duly presented himself.

"Tell the laundrymaids not to starch my shirt and cravat so much. I feel like a trussed-up chicken at table. A man should feel comfortable in his clothes."

"Yes, Sir."

"That will be all."

The valet disappeared. The secretary's pen scratched away, and Alexander's eyes drifted back to the missive that had most rattled him. Lady Sarah Hyatt, sister to Lord Hyatt, was now married, as expected. Would Lord Hyatt shortly announce his forthcoming nuptials to Lady Celia, not having wished to overshadow his sister's wedding until now?

"Sir?"

He realised he had crumpled the card in his hand and unclenched his fist. "Nothing, it is nothing. Continue. Remind Mr Jones that I will require a horse, my brother's was too sedate for me, it was like riding a plodding carthorse. Tell him to look out something with spirit."

"Yes, Sir. Anything else?"

"No, that will do for now."

"Should your coat of arms be repainted on the second carriage, Sir? The steward sends word to say it has grown somewhat shabby."

The mistletoe bound by her red ribbons, formed into

kissing boughs by her determined hands, the two kisses they had shared beneath them. *Strength Through Love.* He had not found any such thing, love seemed to him to be nothing but a weakening of a man, leaving him bereft of her presence when she was not with him, perturbed by her when she was. Broken at the idea of life without her.

A patting on his leg drew his attention and he looked down to see one of the kittens, Holly, attempting to climb up him. He hoisted her onto his lap, where she purred loudly and promptly went to sleep, while her sister Ivy investigated the room, poking her head into every available space, no matter how small. How easy their life was – except it had not been, they had been moments from death when she had rescued them, had insisted they be saved.

"A letter, Sir."

Gabriel in the doorway, holding out a small, folded note.

"But the post –"

"It was delivered by hand, Sir."

He did not wait for Gabriel to reach the table, he sprang out of his chair and all but grabbed at the note, turning away from them both to open it, stared down at the few words written on it, his mind whirling, heart thudding in his chest.

Meet me at the Frost Fair tomorrow after noon. Celia.

She was here. In London. And she wanted to see him. A smile grew on his lips until a sudden thought filled him with dread – perhaps she meant to tell him in person that she was now engaged to Lord Hyatt? Perhaps she considered it only fair to do so, in view of their longstanding arrangement? But no, no, that could not be possible, she had signed herself *Celia*. Just Celia, no Lady, no Lady Celia Follett. *Celia.* An intimacy they had never yet used, one which now seemed significant.

"Is everything well, Sir?"

He realised he was holding the crumpled little note to his heart and carefully lowered his hand, rearranged his face to hide the elation he felt before turning back to his secretary. "Yes, yes, all is well. I – will have to attend to a matter of business tomorrow at – at noon, we must wrap up what matters we have today, I shall be otherwise preoccupied."

"Certainly, Sir."

❄

THE NIGHT WAS ENDLESS. HE WOKE OVER AND OVER, each time lying awake in the darkness until he drifted into uneasy dreams of reaching out for Celia's hand, only to feel her slip away from him, as though on unsteady ice. He heard the hour being chimed every hour, and when the clock finally told him it was five, he gave up on sleep and instead rang for hot water. A startled maid delivered it before his equally surprised valet was roused from his sleep to help him shave and dress. No doubt his early waking had put the whole household into confusion, although his morning coffee and cake arrived with commendable swiftness.

And then he must wait.

He was not sure if it was worse to wait in bed in the darkness or fully dressed in the early morning light of his drawing room. By mid-morning he had decided both were insufferable. He reached eagerly for the morning papers once they arrived, hoping for some distraction, but everything he read was so dull that it did not serve his purpose at all and the clock's hands moved so slowly he got up twice to check it was working at all. His foot was on the ice by noon, eyes already searching everywhere for Celia.

TO WIN HER HAND

❄

The Frost Fair was an icy wonderland, a hubbub of noise and excitement, with everywhere new enticements promised. The whole of the riverbank was full of people gazing in awe at the great River Thames solidly frozen over, hurrying to make their way down onto the river itself to partake in all the delights that had been erected for their pleasure. Those who wished to gamble were already lost, for there were men and women calling out to come and play Rouge et Noir, Te-totum or the wheel of fortune, each game hosted by a tent, from which music and loud cheers or groans emerged. Patrons entered eagerly and then emerged some time later without even a penny to pay for the wooden planks that brought patrons safely to and from the Thames, each new person teetering down the planks trying to not overbalance, arriving on the ice and taking their first steps as unsteady as any baby fawn, wide-eyed at the new world that had sprung up almost overnight. No-one with so much as an ounce of business acumen had ignored the opportunity that the Fair had brought – there was no rent to pay for premises and no-one to say what might or might not be offered in the way of enjoyment and so there were swings and horse-drawn sleighs for children beside women of a certain reputation touting their wares in lascivious murmurs, thick slabs of roasted ox next to dainty gingerbread hearts and everything in-between. A city of tents and stalls, decorated with ribbons and streamers, had created little winding lanes between the amusements and through these winding lanes came thousands of Londoners seeking pleasure, delighted at the novelties surrounding them. There were large fires everywhere, around which sat men and women drinking grog and rum, ale and punch. From inside some tents came the sounds of fiddles and singing, the dancers inside occasionally emerging, hot and sweaty, to be cooled by the cold air outside. There were plays being put on, using boats embedded in the ice as their stage, groups gathered round to hear the stories being told. Skittles, puppet plays, football pitches and bowling matches were all at play and everywhere darted little children, shrieking with excitement, though some, more silent, made it their business to relieve gentlemen and women of their purses, their little hands darting into pockets and reticules to retrieve coins too quickly to be caught, for even if the person turned on them, they were off, vanishing down icy alleyways too fast for chasing.

Alexander walked amongst it all seeing and hearing nothing. He wanted only to see Celia, and everything that surrounded him was only a hindrance to finding her. He looked everywhere for her red clothes. But there were red clothes everywhere – women's cloaks and officers' red jackets. Vendors called out to him offering oranges, cakes, roast goose, even a shave or a new pair of boots, for it seemed there was no business in London but had found a space on the ice, it was a wonder the ice was thick enough to hold them all.

"A hot toddy, Sir, on this cold day?"

"A souvenir of today, Sir – a book printed here on the ice celebrating the Frost Fair?"

"Sir! A gingerbread heart for your Valentine?"

He turned his head this way and that, frustration mounting. How was he to find her here, amidst all this confusion? It was impossible. Had she played him for a fool, was her note only a jest, that she might laugh at him? All his old feelings about her rushed up in him unbidden. A foolish girl, a childish selfish being… perhaps he had been right all along and these new feelings for her were only a dream, an illusion of the festive season, now gone even as the snow had turned from sparkling white to dirty grey.

"The elephant! The elephant is coming!"

Heads turned, his with them. A little way off, slowly lumbering onto the ice, was the vast grey shape of an elephant. He had heard the promise of it, some circus owner knowing the sight of such a creature on the ice would bring plenty of spectators to the show tonight. The crowd watched wide-eyed, breath held as it moved across the ice. Would it break? Were there sounds of cracks, or was that just the creaking of the swings, the turning of the roasted ox? No, the ice held, the elephant was safe. A cheer went up and the spell was broken; people rushed forward to stand closer to the animal.

He caught sight of a familiar frame in the crowd: the tall elegance of the Duke of Buckingham, with his cousin Miss Seton beside him.

"Buckingham!"

The two turned at once, Buckingham offering a warm smile. "Comerford! Here all alone?"

He felt alone. He must find her. He must. He wondered if he would always be alone, it was a fear that was growing in him, the fear that he would indeed find Celia but that it would be too late, that she would have already allowed her heart to be claimed by Lord Hyatt, leaving him to retreat to a cold and lonely life. He tried not to grimace but knew his face must be showing something of his distress. "I am supposed to be meeting Lady Celia Follett, but I have yet to catch sight of her." He remembered his manners. "Miss Seton," he added, bowing.

She curtseyed. "Lord Comerford."

He tried to think of something useful or polite to say,

recalling only that the word around the *ton* was that Buckingham and Miss Belmont, daughter of the Godwin family, were likely to marry. "I've seen the Godwins," he said. "They're over by the swings."

Buckingham gave a polite nod with no sign of interest, not even glancing towards the swings. "Thank you."

"Lady Celia Follett is just there," said Miss Seton, pointing. "In the red coat."

His heart beat fast as he looked where she had indicated and caught sight of Celia's black bouncing curls touching the shoulders of a crimson pelisse trimmed in fur. He tried to keep his countenance calm. "Ah yes," he managed. "Much obliged. Good day to you both," he added as he strode away. He was being abrupt, he knew it, almost rude in fact, but he must find her at once, must get to her quickly.

❄

Celia stood by the swings, uncertain. She should have been more specific in her note to him, she should have chosen a meeting place, but she could not have imagined the sheer size of the Fair, how it stretched out in all directions around her, everywhere sights and sounds to confuse her eye and ear. Coloured streamers fluttered, catching her attention every time she tried to make out his familiar shape. Vendors nudged her, reached out to her, called their wares louder and louder, so that all her senses were assailed.

"He'll be somewhere about I expect," said her cousin Jonathan, in a jolly mood. "Have some gingerbread, it's very good."

"No thank you," she said, turning her head this way and that.

"Hot chocolate? You need something to warm you."

She took the unwanted drink, hoping to stop him offering things, but he was delighted with the surroundings. "I say, a whole roast ox! You'd think the fire would have it sink through the ice, wouldn't you? Astonishing! Do you want some?"

"No, thank you, Jonathan. I do not need anything more."

"Good Lord, an elephant! I heard they were going to bring one, but I didn't quite believe it – but there it is! Astonishing, isn't it? Shall we move closer?"

"Yes – no," she said, still distracted. If she moved, she might find him more easily but if he was also searching for her and they both kept moving – she was not sure what to do, only stood clutching her cup, feeling the heat of the chocolate within seeping through to her cold hands. Where was he?

"Coming?"

"No," she managed at last. "You go, I shall stand here, you can return to me when you have seen it first-hand."

He hovered, uncertain. "You'll be alright here? By yourself?"

"Of course," she reassured him. "Nothing can happen here, we are in broad daylight and there are plenty of gentlemen and ladies about," she added, gesturing vaguely about. "There is the Duke of Buckingham and his cousin, we are acquainted."

Lord Jonathan tipped his hat to the oblivious pair and hurried away to the lumbering grey mass. It hardly seemed a creature at all, so slowly did it walk, so much was it surrounded by gawping crowds. It was like a vast rock come to life, moving slowly across a frozen lake after some unfortunate avalanche. She looked about herself for somewhere to leave the cup, she did not want to drink the chocolate just now, her mind was elsewhere. She saw a barrel with other abandoned cups on it and put it down. The swings were eliciting merry shrieks from children and grown women, some of whom were accompanied by officers, who were having a great deal of fun in pushing the swings ever higher to half-frighten their companions.

"Celia."

She turned at once and inhaled sharply at the sight of him. With the intake of breath came the scent of him, warm spices beneath the starch and leather of his clothing. She gazed up at him, her lips trembling from the cold – or from the desire to be kissed, she was not sure which. He looked into her eyes, then down at her lips, then further down, to her hands, clad in the red gloves he had sent her, the swansdown trim fluttering in the cold air.

He reached for her right hand, slowly removed the glove, then lifted her bare hand to his lips, kissed it. It shook in his grasp, and he held it to his chest, pressed against the thick wool of his greatcoat, protected within his warm hands.

"Oh, I say, found each other, then? Capital, capital." Lord Jonathan had returned. "Elephant's a mighty beast, I must say. Marvellous. How do you do, Comerford? Good to see you again."

Lord Comerford's voice held steady. "It is good to see you again. May I take Lady Celia on a sleigh ride?"

"Oh absolutely," agreed Lord Jonathan cheerfully. "Perfect weather for it, by Jove. Is the sleigh your own or one of these here ones they're trotting about on the ice?"

"My own."

"Capital!"

"I shall return her to the Duke and Duchess myself."

"Oh, good show, Comerford. Enjoy yourself, Cousin Celia."

"I will," she managed to murmur before Lord Comerford pulled her away, her arm tucked tightly against him, his other hand still holding her right hand. She felt the cold rush of air against the skin of her hand and there was something giddy in the sensation, that hand had never been uncovered outside since she was a very little child, and a rush of gratitude came up in her – he had already kept his word to her, she might show her hand anywhere she wished when he was with her, he did not care about what other people thought of it, was not ashamed of it – of her.

They walked in silence through the crowds, but without hurrying, as though they were alone, their only focus the sensation of their two bodies pressed close together. When they came to one of the planks, Lord Comerford dropped two pennies in the hand of the attendant boy and lightly held onto her shoulders as she walked up it and onto the riverbank, where the bay horses awaited with the red sleigh and one of the grooms.

"Charlie," said Lord Comerford, nodding his head.

"My lord. My lady."

She dipped her head to Charlie as he left and climbed into the sleigh, sat down carefully amidst the furs and blankets, then leant towards Lord Comerford as he tucked her in, her face close to his, her eyes searching his, waiting for his lips to touch hers. But instead he spoke.

"Don't do the season."

"What?"

"I cannot wait that long," he said, and his deep voice shook. "Do not make me wait, Celia. I love you. If you wish to attend balls and parties, I will take you to as many as you wish to attend but let me take you as my wife. I cannot bear to be apart from you, nor uncertain as to my fate – our fate. Tell me you will marry me, that you are not still determined to seek another suitor."

She nodded, words suddenly gone.

His eyebrows came together in a deep frown, his eyes anxious. "Yes, you *are* still seeking another suitor?"

She let out a gasp of laughter. "Yes, I will marry you. If you still wish us to marry, I am yours." She leant forwards and was suddenly wrapped tightly in his arms, the relief of the certainty between them rushing over her. "I was a fool to look elsewhere when I had you before me."

He lowered his face to speak against her ear, his voice low. "We shall be married on Valentine's Day. I cannot and will not wait longer." He pulled back from her and took a piece of paper from his pocket. "A special licence. One week and you will be the Countess of Comerford."

She nodded and leant closer, waiting for him to kiss her, but instead he put the paper away and took up the reins and shook them, spurring the horses into a fast trot. Disappointed, she sat back, gazing at him as they drove along. His face was not open and smiling, it was set, serious. Despite herself, she began to question her choice. She had understood that he was not a man to whom pretty phrases came naturally but she had expected that they would talk together, that he would kiss her, perhaps hold her to him or at least clasp her hands. And he had done so – and then stopped, as though that were enough, when she wanted more and more of him, of his words, his kisses, his closeness to her.

❅

At last he stopped, the sleigh still in the whiteness all around them. There was no-one in sight, they were all alone

"You are very quiet," he said.

"I – hoped you would – kiss me," she confessed.

He looked at her and his eyes were very dark. His voice, when he replied, was hoarse. "If I kiss you now, I will not be able to restrain myself."

"From what?"

"From – actions that are – more – appropriate to our wedding night," he managed.

They sat in silence.

"Alexander."

"Yes?"

"I would still like you to kiss me."

His hand brushed her cheek, then tightened around her nape, pulling her towards him, her mouth willingly seeking out his.

"That is – enough," he said, suddenly pulling away from her.

She shook her head and moved closer, pressing her body against his. "More," she whispered.

"You do not know what you are asking," he said, and his breathing had grown ragged.

"I have been promised to you my whole life," she whispered back, "I will be your wife within a week. I want more."

He looked into her eyes. Slowly, he unbuttoned her pelisse, showing the delicate silk dress beneath. He traced the outline of her bodice with one finger while she gazed at him, wondering and yet wanting.

"This is more," he whispered to her. "Is it what you want?"

She stared at him, finding herself trembling. "Yes," she said, so low she could hardly hear herself. "I want... more."

❄

Afterwards he held her to him, his hands now soft on her body, his kisses gentle and when she opened her eyes, she saw, in the snow beside the carriage, a miracle – a tiny snowdrop, its dark green stem strong against the snow, its white petals almost lost in it. She gazed at it, her body loose against him, before he touched her cheek, turning her face to him and smiled. He pulled up the furs about them, and she felt their silken touch brush over her bare skin.

"Will you marry me?"

She leant against him, helpless with laughter. "It is too late to ask that now."

"But I have never asked you at all."

She kissed him softly. "I will marry you." She gave a tiny gasp of laughter. "Whatever will Mama say? You are leaving no time at all for her to arrange clothes."

"Then I will marry you wrapped in furs and nothing else."

"Nothing at all?"

"I may allow a veil."

She giggled. "Oh, very well. If you insist."

"I do."

12

TO LOVE FOREVER

Celia woke on her wedding morning with a smile on her face, from a dream in which Alexander had kissed her as they stood amidst falling snowflakes.

"Lord Comerford's carriage arrived just now with packages for you," said an excited Aveline, coming into the room with her arms full. "Look, my lady."

There was a round jewellery box in red leather, which Celia opened to a gasp from Aveline. The tiara inside was made up of snowflake shapes, each with a diamond at its centre, so that it glittered as it moved.

"You can wear it this morning," said Aveline.

Celia nodded, touching the delicate shapes gently with one finger, thinking of her dream. It was as though Alexander had dreamt it alongside her and, waking, sent her this.

"And this," said Aveline, lifting a large cardboard box up onto the bed. It was beautifully decorated with pink floral paper and the name Harding, Howell & Co in swirling writing.

Celia lifted off the lid and let out a gasp of laughter at the white furs that spilled out of it, barely contained by the large container. Aveline helped her pull out a large white mink muff, as well as a scarlet hooded cloak in silk, lined with thick white fur. At the bottom was a lace veil.

"So beautiful!" exclaimed Aveline. "His Lordship is very generous, my lady."

Celia stroked the fur, her cheeks grown rosy at the memory of Lord Comerford's hands touching her in the sleigh, his mouth... "He is," she murmured, remembering his promise to marry her wrapped in furs with a veil and no more.

"And this, my lady," said Aveline.

Thick cream paper was elaborately folded into a square, addressed "To my Valentine," the whole decorated with hand-painted roses and hearts, their stems intertwining. Carefully, Celia opened it up, to find within a poem, written in Alexander's hand.

Join hands, join hearts
I shall endeavour
Be mine today
To love forever

SHE TOUCHED THE WORDS, TRACED THE ROSE STEMS with one finger and marvelled at the delicacy of the open petals. How had this man, who only a few weeks ago seemed so dour and duty-bound, opened his heart to her like this, so that now she was the recipient of a Valentine made by his hands? How had she ever thought she might find someone else more suited to her? She shivered. She could so easily have lost him, so eager had she been to seek out a suitor who would be more obvious in his wooing.

"You are cold," said Aveline at once. "It is time to dress. Come, your bath is ready."

A bath scented with rose perfume and soap was followed by a rapid drying and then Aveline began her work, dressing Celia in white silk stockings with pale blue silk ribbons to hold them up, then adding a longline corset over her shift. The dress itself was beautiful. Celia would have chosen red, but her mother would not countenance it and so instead it was white silk, worked with tiny red holly berries and green leaves around the hem. For warmth she had a white velvet pelisse trimmed in swansdown, topped with the white fur cloak and muff Alexander had sent. Her hair was carefully pinned into place and her curls arranged so that she might wear the snowflake tiara and veil.

"It is perfect," said Aveline with satisfaction. "Your flowers."

Celia took the little bouquet of snowdrops. Her mother had wanted something larger, grander, more showy, but Celia wanted this reminder of the moment in the sledge when she had seen the tiny flower emerging from the snow and known at last that she loved Alexander, one miracle echoing the other.

❋

THE FOUNDLING HOSPITAL WAS UNUSED TO WEDDINGS being held in their chapel. It had been decorated with simple greenery everywhere, tied with white ribbons, while hundreds of candles shimmered, bringing a soft warm light to the otherwise cold space. The children, arranged in rows and ready to sing, gazed open mouthed as Celia walked down the aisle, the diamond snowflakes of her tiara joined by real ones glinting as they melted in her veil. Those children who would shortly join the Comerford estate had been given new suits of clothes and carried little baskets of white rose petals to scatter before the bride. They walked stiffly, glowing with pride as they took their places as guests of the wedding party, sitting down as the choir began the hymn which would precede the vows being spoken.

> *"Be thou my vision, O Lord of my heart;*
> *Naught be all else to me save that thou art.*
> *Thou my best thought by day and by night;*
> *Waking or sleeping, thy presence my light."*

Try as she might, Celia could not hear the words of the service. She watched the vicar's mouth open and close, saw him open different pages of the Bible and read from them, knew he had asked for the ring when Alexander handed it over to be blessed. She heard none of it, only her beating heart and Alexander's breathing, soft as it was, but it was all she could make out, all she wanted to hear. Her senses were full, from the warmth of Alexander's fingers holding her hand in his, to the cold air of the chapel touching her exposed neck, the delicate tremor of the swansdown touching her skin. She smelled the honey-scent of the wax tapers burning all around them, but above all she looked up into Alexander's eyes, who met her gaze and returned it full of love. Sometimes she looked at his lips, when he spoke his vows, but they were too great a memory of being kissed by him, they made her shiver inside and a great swelling of desire rise up inside her, so that she had to look away lest she grow overcome and reach for him, shocking everyone present.

Her lips moved to say her vows, though Alexander bowed his head to hear her, a small smile on his lips, which made her think she must have spoken almost in a whisper, such was the emotion of promising to be his wife.

She knew the service was coming to a close when Alexander slipped the gold ring onto her left hand and looked to the vicar for their final blessing, then took her hand in his and turned her to face the congregation, heard suddenly a burst of noise as everyone made haste to congratulate them and a wave of light as the doors were flung open so that they might walk out into the world together as husband and wife.

Now the children opened large chests at the back of the chapel in which lay, carefully placed on sheets of paper, large and beautifully iced hearts of gingerbread, a piece given to every child and every guest as a wedding token as they left the chapel. Mrs Poole and her kitchen staff had worked hard to ensure there should be plenty for all, then going on to create the wedding breakfast which awaited the entire party back at Comerford House, with hot sweet rolls, tea, coffee and chocolate, French bread, plum cake, ham and eggs, saffron cake and little cups of gooseberry cream. The white-iced bride cake was prettily decorated with tiny strands of green icing as stems and more white icing to stand as the snowdrops which matched Celia's bouquet and was exclaimed over as a very pretty thing. Everyone ate abundantly and then began the toasts, with many blessings and good wishes called out over the bride and groom. But at last, all was done and, amidst many more well wishes and embraces, Celia and Alexander found themselves alone.

She came to him and rested her face against his chest, his arms closing about her.

"Are you happy?" he asked.

"It was everything beautiful."

"It is you who are everything beautiful." He looked into her warm brown eyes and lowered his face to kiss her rosy lips. "I do not want to tire you, but I am anxious to take you home to Castle Comerford. If we leave now, it will be growing dark for the last mile or so, but we can still manage." He looked at her and stroked her hair with one hand, holding her close with the other. "Unless you are too tired?"

She shook her head. "Let us set off," she said gaily. "I wish to see my new home. Although," she added, looking about her, "I will miss Comerford House. It feels so familiar to me now, it is as though I have always lived here."

"That is the benefit of being snowed in for many days with no escape," he teased. "You must either love it or hate it by the end, just as you found with its master."

She giggled and lifted her face for another kiss. "I will tell Aveline to fetch my pelisse. I know she has filled the carriage with footwarmers and blankets."

"And furs, I hope," he said, hoping to make her rosy cheeks blush more deeply.

"And furs," she murmured, moving closer to him, nestling into his body.

Soon enough they were in the carriage and travelling, the servants following close behind in the second carriage. Alexander looked down at Celia, almost in disbelief that he should be able to hold her close to him, that she was truly his wife and now about to enter Castle Comerford, her rightful home, as its Countess.

"You will take me everywhere, all over the estate? So that I will come to know it as my new home?"

"Absolutely not."

She stared at him, confused. "Why?"

"We shall not be leaving the bedchamber for days. Perhaps weeks," he said firmly.

She buried her face in his arm, laughing. "Will you not even take me out on sleigh rides?" she asked, lifting her face to him with a look of wide-eyed innocence.

"Why, are you fond of sleigh rides?" he asked, matching her innocent expression.

"Very," she said, moving close to him again. "I am very, very fond of sleigh rides. I would go so far as to say that they are my favourite pastime."

He tightened his arm about her. "Then we will leave the bedchamber only for sleigh rides and end the sleigh rides only when we may return immediately to the bedchamber."

"It sounds wonderful," she said, her voice dreamy.

He gazed down at her closed dark lashes and her curls, slowly feeling her weight against him grow greater as she fell asleep, tired from all the excitement and now safely bound to him after all their misunderstandings, the carriage's rocking lulling her to sleep. He rested his head against the thick cushions of the carriage and slept beside her, overwhelmed with happiness.

❄

"Celia."

She stirred sleepily on Alexander's shoulder, then managed to open her eyes. The interior of the carriage was dim despite the hanging lamp, outside all was darkness.

From somewhere in the night bells began ringing, a loud and joyful pealing, the sound of church on Christmas day. "What is it? What are the bells?"

"They are for us," he said, smiling down at her confusion. "To welcome you home."

"Home?" she asked, still dazed.

"Home to Castle Comerford," he said. "It is the bride blessing. I've heard of it but never seen it."

She sat up, still holding his arm, peering out of the carriage window. Ahead, she saw bobbing lights, many hundreds of them, as though the stars had fallen from the sky into water. "What are the lights?"

"People."

"People?"

"All the staff and villagers of Comerford Castle," he said, his voice full of emotion as they drew closer to the lights and sound. "They have come to bless you."

And now Celia could hear a chant, which grew clearer as the carriage slowed, the voices of the crowd she now saw dimly ahead, more than four hundred she guessed, men women and children all holding candles or lamps, all calling together, louder even than the church bells still pealing.

"Bless the bride, bless the bride!"

She looked up at Alexander in delight. "It is so kind. Have they always done it?"

He nodded, his eyes filling. "My mother said she never forgot it, that she was welcomed here like this. It has gone back generations, that the new bride at Comerford Castle should be welcomed by everyone. Be careful as you approach, they will all throw grain at you."

"Grain?"

"Wheat, oats and barley. To wish us many children and bountiful harvests for the estate."

The carriage stopped, and the door was opened. Alexander got out to a great shout of welcome and then offered her his hand. She hesitated.

"Do not be shy. They are happy to see you."

She took his hand and climbed out. Above her, a vast oak tree's branches stretched up to the starry sky, ahead of her the walls of Comerford Castle rose into turrets. At their centre, a vast wooden door surrounded by lamps showed that it had been decorated with many green boughs and red apples, giving it a festive air, while the chant of the hundreds of people rose louder still.

"Bless the bride, bless the bride!"

An older woman stepped forward from the crowd, dressed in neat dark clothes and a white cap. She came forward, curtseyed to Alexander and then, smiling, held out something to Celia. A heavy bunch of keys.

"The keys of the castle, Lady Comerford."

Celia took them as Alexander spoke close to her ear that she might hear him above the crowd.

"Mrs Bevdan, the housekeeper."

Celia nodded and smiled again as the woman returned to her place in the crowd.

The bells stopped their ringing, so that the people could be heard more clearly.

"Bless the bride, bless the bride!"

"It is time to go in," said Alexander. "But before we do, look up." He pointed above their heads.

Celia tipped back her head. Above them, in the oak's branches, she could just make out a shape that seemed familiar.

"Mistletoe," said Alexander, and he bent his head to kiss her, cupping her face in his hands as he did so, then without warning scooped her up in his arms, carrying her towards the door of the castle, as a shower of grain rained down upon them from all sides and they crossed the threshold of Comerford Castle to the joyful shouts of the crowd. Celia, nestled in Alexander's arms, heard the crowd call out as she entered her new home, but felt only his beating heart pressed close to her skin. He had promised they would not leave the bedchamber for days and she wanted nothing more than for that promise to be honoured, while below them the crowd continued to wish them the joy they had finally found together.

"Bless the bride!"

TO WIN HER HAND

I hope you have enjoyed *To Win Her Hand*. If you have, I would really appreciate it if you would leave a rating or brief review, so that new readers can find Alexander and Celia's story. I read all reviews and am always grateful for your time in writing them and touched by your kind words. There are more Regency Outsiders still to come, look out for their stories...

FREE NOVELLA

Have you read the Forbidden City series? Pick up the first in the series FREE from my website www.Melissa Addey.com

Lonely. Used as a pawn. One last bid for love.

18th century China. Imperial concubine Qing is neglected by the Emperor, passed over for more ambitious women. But when a new concubine comes to court, friendship blooms. But when the Empress' throne suddenly becomes available, Qing finds herself being used as a piece in power games. Can an insignificant pawn snatch victory from the jaws of defeat?

AUTHOR'S NOTE ON HISTORY

In Jane Austen's Pride and Prejudice, there is a scene between Elizabeth Bennet and Lady Catherine de Bourgh, who accuses Elizabeth of getting between Mr Darcy and her daughter, Miss Anne de Bourgh, who are supposedly engaged. When Elizabeth queries this, Lady Catherine de Bourgh "hesitates" and then says: *"The engagement between them is of a peculiar kind. From their infancy, they have been intended for each other. It was the favourite wish of his mother, as well as of hers. While in their cradles, we planned the union…"* No doubt there were many such arranged 'engagements' in grand families and I wondered what it would feel like to know, from childhood, that such a union was already promised and expected, whether you would go along with it out of a sense of duty or try to find a way out of it.

Second and younger sons were often dispatched to the church, navy, army or other such places to earn a living since everything would be left to the eldest son. Rory Muir's *Gentlemen of Uncertain Fortune* and Brian Southam's *Jane*

AUTHOR'S NOTE ON HISTORY

Austen and the Navy were both very helpful books in my research.

I wanted to write a Christmas-themed Regency romance, and the winter of 1813/14 was extraordinarily cold, temperatures were below freezing every night from the 27th of December right through to the 7th of February. There was such a heavy fog as to make travel impossible from the 26th December (I cheated by two days to have Celia and Alexander trapped in London!) all the way through to the 3rd of January. The whole of southern England experienced a very heavy snowfall and constant cold winds, while in London the last ever Frost Fair was held on the frozen-over Thames, from the 2nd February to the 7th February. It seemed like the perfect year for a snowy Christmas-focused story!

Part of the poem Alexander includes in his Valentine is from a real handmade 1816 Valentine card, which is beautifully painted with hearts and roses, you can see a photo of it on the Pinterest page for this book: https://uk.pinterest.com/melissaaddey/to-win-her-hand. All my books have a Pinterest page you can explore, with images that inspire me while writing and that I think readers would like, including a lot of clothes and bonnets that I have fun choosing for my heroines!

The charade for 'banknote' was written by Jane Austen herself, listed in Maria Hubert's *Jane Austen's Christmas: the festive season in Georgian England*.

Celia's hand is based on a condition from birth called Symbrachydactyly and was inspired by an early Victorian

AUTHOR'S NOTE ON HISTORY

tintype photograph showing a child with a hand missing some of the fingers. It is not genetic but comes from a lack of blood supply to the limb during pregnancy.

My great-grandmother Elizabeth Poole was a cook in grand households, and I always wanted her to be in one of these novels, so I thought Comerford House might be a nice home for her. The kitten Holly was named after a reader who asked to be in a novel... I hope you like your Christmassy feline twin!

Lord Comerford's London house is loosely based on the exterior of Clarendon House (the illustration at the start of the book) which no longer exists and the interiors of beautiful Spencer House (the home of Princess Diana's ancestors) and its garden set on the edge of London's Green Park, which you can still visit today, including the amazing Palm Room.

CURRENT AND FORTHCOMING BOOKS

18th century China: The Forbidden City series

The Consorts. A lonely and forgotten imperial concubine is faced with one last chance for love... if she is brave enough to seize it. Set in China's Forbidden City in the 18th century. (Novella)

The Fragrant Concubine. A new imperial concubine is keeping a dangerous secret. Is the Emperor right to fall in love with her, or is his life at risk? Based on the legends that grew up around a real concubine.

CURRENT AND FORTHCOMING BOOKS

The Garden of Perfect Brightness. Italian Jesuit painter Giuseppe Castiglione is tasked with creating a garden fit for an imperial concubine, but as flowers bloom, so do feelings. Based on one man's extraordinary life.

The Cold Palace. Chosen an a concubine against her will. Elevated to Empress. Accused of madness. Based on a real Empress of China's life, an award-winning novel.

❄

Medieval Morocco: The Moroccan Empire series

A String of Silver Beads. Seeking freedom, a young Berber woman marries an ambitious Muslim warrior but finds herself enmeshed in bitter rivalry with his powerful queen.

None Such as She. A false prophecy leads to the rise of a great empire across North Africa and Spain... and a dangerous queen who will stop at nothing to achieve her ambitions.

Do Not Awaken Love. A Spanish nun. A Muslim warlord. The destiny of an empire held between them. A woman must hold true to her faith, which is tested by great dangers... and by love.

The Cup. A gifted healer makes an impossible vow whose consequences ripple unstoppably outwards as an empire rises across North Africa and a future queen reaches for power.

❋

Ancient Rome: The Colosseum series

From the Ashes. Follow the quick-witted and fiercely loyal backstage team of the Colosseum as they inaugurate the gladiatorial games through the devastation of Pompeii, plague and fire.

Beneath the Waves. Flooding the Colosseum for epic sea battles brings both hidden dangers and emotions to the surface for the backstage team of the Colosseum.

On Bloodied Ground. Below the Colosseum's arena lies a dark labyrinth and a darker secret. As gladiators die before they even reach the arena, the backstage team grow fearful of what is still to come.

The Flight of Birds. Emperor Domitian has three final tasks for the backstage team to complete, and his erratic behaviour is beginning to frighten them. Is he just strange, or is he dangerous?

❋

Regency England: The Regency Outsiders series

Lady for a Season. A young duke declared mad. His nurse masquerading as a lady. One social season in which to marry him off. What could possibly go wrong?

The Viscount's Pearl. He's a carefree rake who wants a marriage of convenience. She's an awkward spinster who doesn't want to marry at all. Fate has other plans in store for them both.

To Win Her Hand. They've been promised since birth, so he sees no reason to woo her. She plans to find true love. Trapped in snowy London, Christmas might just bring them together.

MELISSA ADDEY

Melissa Addey writes richly researched historical fiction inspired by what she calls "the footnotes of history" – forgotten stories and intriguing lives from the past. Her novels span Ancient Rome, medieval Morocco, 18th-century China, and Regency England.

She has a PhD in Creative Writing, for which she explored the balancing act between fact and fiction that comes with writing historical fiction. She also spent a year as the Leverhulme Trust Writer in Residence at the British Library, where she continues to run workshops for writers.

Melissa grew up on a smallholding in Umbria, Italy and was home schooled. She now lives in London with her husband, two children, and two cats who love all the scrap paper that a writer produces. You can explore her books and download a free novella at www.melissaaddey.com

THANKS

Thank you to photographer Kathy at Servian Stock images and model Sophia for the front cover image.

Thank you to my beta readers for this book: Bernie, Etain, Helen, Martin and Susanne. Your comments and ideas are always insightful.

Enormous thanks to the community and teachers at Regency Fiction Writers, who generously share their knowledge and made my research so much easier.

All errors and fictional choices are of course mine.